Orient BlackSwan Abridged Texts

EMMA

Jane Austen

Abridged by
Manju Sambhunath Sen

Edited by
Seetha Srinivasan

Orient BlackSwan

Acknowledgements

The publishers and the editors would like to thank *Philological Quarterly* for permission to use the article, '*Emma* as Charade and the Education of the Reader' from Issue No. 65 (1986) of this journal. The publisher and the editors have applied for permission for 'Comic Symmetry in Jane Austen's *Emma*' by Bruce Stovel and are awaiting permission. No response was received at the time of going to press. Due acknowledgement will be made in all future editions of this book.

ORIENT BLACKSWAN PRIVATE LIMITED

Registered Office
3-6-752 Himayatnagar, Hyderabad 500 029 (A.P.), India
E-mail: centraloffice@orientblackswan.com

Other Offices
Bangalore, Bhopal, Bhubaneshwar, Chandigarh, Chennai,
Ernakulam, Guwahati, Hyderabad, Jaipur, Kolkata,
Lucknow, Mumbai, New Delhi, Noida, Patna

First Published 2010

ISBN 978 81 250 3955 6

Typeset in Warnock Pro 10.5/12.5 by
OSDATA, Hyderabad 500 029

Printed at
Graphica Printers
Hyderabad 500 013

Published by
Orient Blackswan Private Limited
3-6-752 Himayatnagar, Hyderabad 500 029 (A.P.), India
E-mail: hyderabad@orientblackswan.com

Contents

Introduction

Life of Jane Austen

Jane Austen was born in Steventon in Hampshire in 1775 into the family of landowning gentry, the hereditary ruling class. Her father was the rector of Steventon. She was the seventh of eight children in a family which had six boys and two girls. The eighteenth century in England was the age of taste and elegance, be it art, home decoration or women's clothes. Class distinctions were pronounced during this period. Manners and decorum were of utmost importance as they were indicators of the class one belonged to. This was the class Jane Austen was born into, the genteel, upper middle class, and this was the class she wrote about in her novels. Therefore the emphasis in her fiction is on how one conducted oneself, one's taste and manners and also social etiquette and behaviour patterns. At the same time, Jane Austen's society had sections that faced dire poverty and deprivation. The rich and the poor lived in two different worlds as it were. Her fiction is a record of the two worlds of contrast; however, the emphasis is more on the landed gentry rather than the socially deprived, unlike say the fiction of Dickens for example.

Jane Austen had a liberal education which included drawing, music, and languages, accomplishments that were seen as being important to women of the upper classes. She and her sister Cassandra attended boarding schools in Oxford, Southampton and Reading, but for the most part were educated at home. Jane Austen never married but lived with her parents till her father died and with her sister Cassandra and mother thereafter. Letter writing was a favourite pastime in her day, besides being a vital mode of communication. Jane Austen wrote to her sister Cassandra and nieces frequently. Many events in her life have been pieced together from the letters preserved by Cassandra. She died of Addison's disease (tuberculosis of the adrenal glands) on 17 July 1817. Jane Austen's novels include *Sense and Sensibility* (1811), *Pride and Prejudice* (1813), *Mansfield Park (*1814), *Emma (*1815), *Northanger Abbey* and *Persuasion* (published after her death in 1817).

Jane Austen's England was made up of rural communities, which in turn was composed of a network of families. Her novels reflect the cultural mores of the landed gentry particularly in matters concerning marriage and family life. It was important in her day to marry 'well', that is, to marry a man with money, if a woman was educated but lacked the means. The only other option for a young woman was to be a teacher or governess, and this was not considered favourably.

Jane Austen's works are gently satirical, as she observes, as if from a distance, the amusing behaviour of idiosyncratic fellow humans. They show an understanding of human weaknesses and an awareness that it is not always possible to change people from being who they essentially are. She presents a vast array of characters, male and female, young and old, with their oddities and excesses.

The 1740s marked the rise of the novel as a literary form but it was not until the nineteenth century that it came to be an established art form. The previous centuries and periods had affinities with other art forms such as drama, epic poetry and the folk ballad. The novel is a distinctly social form which was a product of the rise of the middle classes in England. Early and successful attempts at novel writing included Samuel Richardson's *Pamela: Or Virtue Rewarded*, Henry Fielding's *Joseph Andrews*, Daniel Defoe's *Robinson Crusoe* and *Moll Flanders*, and Richard Sterne's *Tristram Shandy*. Realism is fundamental to the novel which reflected the values and outlook of this class. It was a means by which the writer communicated social mores, religious and moral instruction, satire and amusement. The rise of a leisured class, particularly among the women, contributed to the growth of the English novel during this period. Women from the upper and middle classes were avid readers and frequently, were writers as well. However, it was still a nascent period for the developing woman writer. Appearing in print was not considered entirely respectable for a woman. Women wrote using male pseudonyms and did not openly display their talents as those of female writers. The increase in circulating libraries was also a factor in the growth of the novel.

Structure of *Emma*

The novel *Emma* is named after the heroine who dominates the plot. It is her fancy or imagination that the story is centred upon. Emma is intelligent, rich and unattached. Having been successful in matchmaking once (in the case of Mr and Mrs Weston), she imagines herself adept at it and commits a series of blunders in the process of her match-making ventures. This however leads to self-knowledge on her part and contributes to our understanding of the characters and society.

Emma Woodhouse and her father live in Hartfield, one of the more elaborate homes in the village of Highbury. Their neighbour is Mr Weston (who is married to Emma's former governess, Miss Taylor) who has a son, Frank Churchill, by an earlier marriage. Frank stays with his mother's relatives, Mr and Mrs Churchill, at Enscombe, the Scottish home of the Churchill family. They later move to Richmond, an area of south-west London on account of his aunt's illness. Mr George Knightley lives at the mansion Donwell Abbey, about a mile away from Hartfield. George Knightley's younger brother John Knightley is married to Emma's elder sister Isabella. They live in London with their son. Emma busies herself organising card games and parties in their home and balls for the neighbourhood gentry. With the departure of Miss Taylor from the home, Emma is at a loose end. Mrs Goddard who runs the local school, introduces a former pupil of hers, Harriet Smith, to Emma, at one of the card parties. Harriet is young and impressionable, little known in social circles, and ready to be moulded and shaped by the more capable and worldly-wise Emma.

Emma's unsuccessful attempts at matchmaking begins with a forced alliance between Harriet and Mr Elton, the local vicar. Harriet is a young girl of seventeen just out of Mrs Goddard's boarding school. Nothing much is known about her background but Emma takes an interest in her welfare. Harriet had spent some time at Abbey Mill Farm and seemed favourably disposed towards Robert Martin, the young farmer who owned the place. Emma cautions Harriet that not only was Mr Martin 'plain' in her estimation of him but that he lacked 'gentility'. Mr Elton the vicar on the other hand seemed drawn to Harriet; he was 'obliging and gentle', had an income and some property and had more to recommend him in Harriet's situation. Emma begins to channel Harriet's thoughts in that direction. Mr Elton is assigned the task of taking Harriet's portrait to London to be framed. Meanwhile, Harriet receives a marriage proposal from Mr Martin in the form of a letter. Harriet is confused and seeks the counsel of her mentor, Emma. While appearing to be objective, Emma directs Harriet to reject Mr Martin's proposal. Her argument is that if a woman does not feel strongly about a man, she ought to decline his offer. Mr Knightley, who knows Robert Martin, thinks that Emma has made a mistake in this case and is quite

displeased with Emma for manipulating the lives of others. Having convinced herself of an impending courtship between Mr Elton and Harriet, Emma tries to bring them together with the hope that Mr Elton would propose to Harriet.

Even as she pushes Harriet in Mr Elton's way, Emma is irritated with Mr Elton's deferential attitude towards herself but chooses to dismiss it. It is only when Mr Elton declares his love for her that Emma realises she has made a terrible mistake. Mr Elton had misunderstood Emma's friendliness for 'encouragement'. He claims that he had never been attracted to Harriet, and that he had paid his respects to her only as Emma's friend. Mr Elton then hastily leaves Highbury for Bath. Four weeks after Mr Elton's departure news reaches Highbury that Mr Elton is engaged to be married to Miss Augusta Hawkins.

At this stage in the novel a few more characters are introduced. Jane Fairfax comes to Highbury to spend three months with her aunt and grandmother, Miss and Mrs Bates, before embarking on her vocation as a governess. She is the daughter of Miss Bates's sister. Jane lost both her parents early in life. Emma has ambivalent feelings towards Jane Fairfax. It is expected that they would be friends because they are comparable in age and share many interests. Emma acknowledges that Jane is elegant and talented but she dislikes her detachment and cautious reserve. Jane seems to be the exact opposite of Emma who is readily judgmental, and unreserved in her remarks and social behaviour.

The arrival of Frank Churchill is eagerly awaited in Highbury. Frank is Mr Weston's son by a previous marriage. When his mother died, his uncle and aunt, the wealthy Mrs and Mr Churchill who had no children of their own stepped in and offered to raise him. Frank Churchill met his father, Mr Weston, periodically in London. As for his new stepmother, he communicated with her through letters and looked forward to meeting her. Emma is curious to meet Frank particularly because the Westons think so highly of him. 'If she were to marry he was the very person to suit her age, character, and condition,' says the author reading Emma's thoughts. On his arrival, Emma finds him very lively and companionable. They share interests and seek out each other in social gatherings. On Frank's prompting, they organise a ball at the Crown Inn but Frank is summoned to the Churchills' and the ball is called off much to everyone's disappointment. Jane Fairfax, however, looks unmoved. Emma resents the fact that Jane Fairfax looks composed and indifferent even at this juncture. Jane had been acquainted with Frank Churchill in Weymouth but is reluctant to offer any further information.

After Frank's departure, Emma deludes herself into thinking that she is in love with Frank Churchill but is not convinced that he is entirely necessary for her happiness. The Churchills move to Richmond for health reasons and Frank moves with them. This pleases the Westons immensely as Frank would now be only an hour away from Highbury. They secretly hope for a match between Frank and Emma. The arrangements are resumed for the ball at the Crown Inn. Everyone has a good time at the ball. The occasion brings out Mrs Weston's kindness and concern for others, Mr Elton's small-mindedness in avoiding Harriet totally, and Mr Knightley's large-heartedness in offering to dance with Harriet thereby rescuing her from neglect on the occasion. Emma deeply appreciates Mr Knightley's warmth and kindness; she later willingly agrees to dance with him.

Harriet goes out for a walk one day and is besieged by a group of gipsies; she is in a panic. Frank Churchill 'rescues' her: Emma then suspects an attachment between Harriet and Frank Churchill, and encourages Harriet in that direction. Frank's own attention to Emma and their friendship by now borders on courtship. At this point in the story it is discovered that Frank Churchill is secretly engaged to Jane Fairfax and that the engagement had taken place at Weymouth. The Westons who break the news to Emma are shocked at the turn of events. Emma is not shattered by the news but is shocked to learn that Frank who had been parading as a happy bachelor in their midst had actually deceived them all. She also begins to understand Jane's coldness towards her.

Emma's concern now is for Harriet whom she had encouraged to consider Frank as a future partner, after mistakenly supposing that there was a mutual attraction. Emma is shocked for the second time when Harriet confesses that she had never been attracted to Frank Churchill: her admiration and love were for someone far superior, for Mr. Knightley! It is at this point that Emma realises her folly in manipulating Harriet and trying to make her what she was not, and driving her on to presumptions above her status in life in outrageous ways. She makes arrangements for Harriet to spend some time away from Highbury in London at Isabella's invitation. Emma is convinced that if Mr Knightley is to marry at all, it must be she, Emma, whom he should marry. She had always been in love with Mr Knightley but had not acknowledged it.

Mr Knightley is concerned that Emma might be shattered on hearing the news of Frank Churchill's engagement. When he is assured of the contrary, he declares his love for Emma. She was 'his sweetest and best of all creatures, faultless in spite of all her faults.' Mr Knightley had always been protective of Emma, guided her as she grew, matured and got herself in and out of difficult situations. He had so loved her that he had been jealous of Frank Churchill's flirtations with Emma. She on her part had taken Mr Knightley for granted. The threat of losing him to someone else had jolted Emma into acknowledging and accepting her love of and dependence on Mr Knightley.

News is brought that Harriet had met her former acquaintance, Robert Martin in London and that they had agreed to marry. The marriage takes place in September that year followed by the wedding of Emma and Mr Knightley. Frank Churchill and Jane Fairfax are to be married in November. All the misunderstandings are cleared up and there is great happiness in the end for everyone.

Important themes and Motifs

1. *Emma* as a novel of self-knowledge

Self-knowledge through realising one's own faults is an important theme in *Emma*. Emma, the central character, starts off as a naïve and self-willed person given to having her own way in all things. She is superior in social status and is the object of regard and admiration by one and all in Highbury. She is much loved by her father, Mr Woodhouse, and indulged by her governess Miss Taylor (Mrs Weston). Harriet Smith looks up to her as a mentor and is in a way, her protege. Mr Knightley loves her and is accepting of her despite her numerous faults. In the social circle into which she is born, Emma has very little to do as a young woman. Being highly imaginative and popular and in constant touch with people of her class she takes on the task of directing the fate and fortunes of Harriet. She tries to wean Harriet away from her affection for Robert Martin, a neighbouring farmer, and persuades her to concentrate on Mr Elton the parish clergyman, and an eligible bachelor instead. Overawed by Emma's patronage, Harriet obliges by falling in love with the pompous Mr Elton. Mr Elton who is very conscious of his social position misinterprets Emma's attentions on Harriet's behalf as showing her own interest in him. He has the higher ambition of marrying Emma herself rather than Harriet, whom he would disdain to marry. Emma is jolted into realising her mistake and is left with the task of setting things right with Mr Elton and with Harriet. Emma fails again when she suspects that Frank Churchill might be in love with Harriet. Frank rescues Harriet from the gipsies through a chance encounter. This feeds Emma's imagination with fantasies of a courtship. Emma is proved wrong once again. Through her social interaction with people under Mr Knightley's watchful eye she gains maturity and is made aware of her inadequacies. Emma also comes to the realisation that she was responsible for what Harriet had become in the end: vain and presumptuous. Emma initially dismissed Robert Martin because he was a mere farmer and not genteel enough for Harriet. Ironically Harriet reconnects with Robert Martin in the end and marries him. Emma is deluded into thinking that Frank Churchill is in love with her. She emphatically denies any involvement between Frank Churchill and Jane Fairfax even though Mr Knightley suspects a private understanding between them. The revelation that they are engaged comes as a shock to Emma. 'I seem to have been doomed to blindness!' she remarks to Mr Knightley.

Self-knowledge requires taking the character through a series of events in the course of which she makes many blunders and emerges a more mature person who can look back and see the folly of her ways. Emma's self-knowledge is echoed in the following authorial statement: 'With insufferable vanity had she believed herself in the secret of everybody's feelings; with unpardonable arrogance proposed to arrange everybody's destiny.' Jane Stevenson, a critic, points out that this 'moral process' from 'revelation through shame to repentance' is central to all the novels of Jane Austen.

2. Marriage and women's independence in *Emma*

It is interesting to note that even though the novel centres round the experiences and exploits of its main character, Emma, the novelist cannot be termed feminist in the contemporary sense of the word. Emma, the central character is independent in more senses than one. She has wealth, social status, wit and intelligence but she is confined to Highbury. She makes social visits and charity visits, she participates in musical and other artistic activities. She declares that she will never marry, and might have kept her word if she had not woken up to the fact that she had been in love with Mr Knightley right from the start. Even in marriage she retains her independence. Mr Knightley offers to move to Hartfield rather than take Emma away from her father to Donwell. As for the women in the novel less endowed and less privileged than Emma, marriage is the only 'job' and passage to happiness. Women could not improve their social status through hard work or personal achievement. Few occupations were open to women as an alternative to marriage, the main one being that of a governess. Jane Fairfax in the novel is rescued by her marriage to Frank Churchill at the crucial juncture when she is to go off to Mrs Smallridge's as a governess. Miss Taylor (before she becomes Mrs Weston) worked as a governess at Hartfield. Even though she is sorely missed, her marriage is seen as a passport to her independence. In fact, Mrs Elton says patronisingly that she is astonished Emma's former governess is 'so very lady-like'.

Harriet who is only seventeen, not very clever but sweet and docile is without a definite occupation. Emma is convinced that 'marrying well' would make up for Harriet's deficiencies of birth and learning. She nudges Harriet in the direction of the clergyman Mr Elton who is a bachelor with an income and some independent property. We also gather from the novel that being a spinster or an 'old maid' is not an attractive proposition. An unmarried woman was dependent. She could not live on her own, but had to live with her family. Miss Bates who is a spinster lives with her mother and is a constant and talkative presence at all the social gatherings at Highbury. She is grateful for the charity extended to her by Mr Knightley, and by Mr Woodhouse and Emma.

It is evident that in Jane Austen's society, marriage was often a strategy to gain wealth or social standing. Love and romance were secondary considerations made to fit into practical schemes.

3. *EMMA* AS A NOVEL OF MANNERS AND CLASS CONSCIOUSNESS

Reading Jane Austen is being aware of the importance of 'class' in the late eighteenth and early nineteenth-century English society. This is particularly pronounced in a small town where people are well aware of each other's birth and lineage. There was enormous significance attached to the way people conducted themselves in personal relationships. Their social manners and morals, their sense of decorum and propriety, are all recorded carefully by the author in the course of the card-games, balls, and parties. The characters in the novel are also defined by their speech. Emma belongs to the class of landed gentry. She associates socially with people of her class and rank except when she is out on a charity visit. She does not approve of Robert Martin the farmer, since he is socially inferior to her and is surprised that he is capable of writing a well-phrased letter to Harriet. She comments that if Harriet were to marry him, she, Emma, would not be in a position to maintain a social connection with her.

When Mr Elton marries, the residents of Highbury are curious to know who he has married. We are told that he had not 'thrown himself away' in marrying Augusta Hawkins, meaning he had not married beneath his social standing. However, Miss Hawkins brought 'no name, no blood, no alliance.' Her social importance came from her older sister who is married to a gentleman and owned two carriages. It is evident that class consciousness is particularly pronounced when it comes to marriage. Marrying above one's status is frowned upon; marrying beneath is strongly discouraged. Both lead to strife in families. Mr Weston's first marriage to Miss Churchill was an unequal one because the Churchills were a wealthy family and he was a 'mere' tradesman. When Mrs Weston suggests the possibility of a connection between Mr Knightley and Jane Fairfax, Emma dismisses it as a 'shameful and degrading connection' were it to come about. It meant that Miss Bates (Jane's aunt), who was definitely not their social equal would become part of Donwell Abbey. Emma even goes on to mimic Miss Bates, the way she would ingratiate herself with Mr Knightley.

When the news of the marriage between Frank Churchill and Jane Fairfax is made public, there is general consternation. Mr Knightley feels that the marriage is acceptable because Frank would be able to raise Jane's station in life. She in turn might influence him for the good and might elevate his character.

Emma is extremely conscious of class and social position and does not withhold her opinions even when they seem harsh and unkind. Frank Churchill is compelled to keep his engagement to the orphan Jane Fairfax a secret because of the fear that his wealthy aunt (Mrs Churchill) would disapprove. To Emma, the narrator says 'the contrast between Mrs Churchill's importance in the world and Jane Fairfax's struck her; one was everything, the other nothing.' Of yet another family in Highbury the Coles, Austen says they were 'of low origin, in trade, and only moderately genteel.' Emma condescends to go to the dinner party at the Coles'. The ball at the Crown Inn is one of the occasions when class awareness rises to the surface. Class awareness also becomes the source of humour in the novel *Emma*.

Important Characters

Emma

Emma is the protagonist of the novel and considered to be an unusual heroine. Jane Austen in creating Emma has said that she is a heroine whom 'no one but myself will much like.' All the events in the novel are seen through Emma's eyes. Even though the novel is not a first-person narrative, Austen skilfully positions herself in such a way that we are inherently sympathetic to Emma's viewpoint even though she is only one of the characters. Emma is twenty-one years old, the daughter of Mr Woodhouse, a highly respected gentleman of means. She is rich, clever, witty and beautiful; she is also full of faults, vulnerable to folly and blunder. Emma is used to having her own way with most people and being the daughter of a leading citizen of the district, is looked up to by everyone. This importance has resulted in her being self-willed and over-confident. Mr Knightley is the only one close to Emma who is not blindly fond of her or overawed by her. He does not spare his criticism when her behaviour warrants it.

Terry Eagleton comments that Emma 'cuts reality to the shape of her own fancies' but 'reality strikes back stealthily to thwart her plotting.' Emma's faults spring from the fact that she is too imaginative and sprightly for the narrow social sphere in which she is placed. This leads to wanton interference in other people's lives. Christopher Gillie observes that unlike Jane Austen's heroines in the other novels, Emma has every 'worldly advantage.' This gives her the freedom to play with Harriet, daydream about Frank Churchill and make marriage plans for everyone. .Matchmaking is not just her favourite diversion, Tony Tanner says; rather, it becomes her occupation. She herself vows never to marry partly because of her concern for her father who depends on her emotionally. Her advice to Harriet on the question of marriage is, 'If a woman doubts as to whether she should accept a man or not, she certainly ought to refuse him. It is not a state to be safely entered into with doubtful feelings, with half a heart.' Of course, this is not an objective comment. Emma is, at the same time trying to dissuade Harriet from accepting Mr Martin's proposal and prompts her to consider Mr Elton as a possible suitor.

The two important turning points in Emma's life are her rudeness to Miss Bates, and the shock she receives on hearing of Harriet 'aspiring to' Mr Knightley. The former episode shows that she is capable of sensitivity and that she can apologise when she needs to. The latter makes her realise that she has always been in love with Mr Knightley and that her problems are of her own making! Emma's behaviour towards Miss Bates arises partly from snobbery and class consciousness on Emma's part. She mimics Miss Bates on another occasion and seems almost cruel and insensitive. Emma is not tolerant of other people's weaknesses. She dislikes Mrs Elton from the start for her presumption to social status, and says insultingly of her marriage to Mr Elton, 'Miss Hawkins perhaps wanted a home and thought this the best offer she was likely to have.'

Emma is honest and straightforward and declares that she likes an 'open temperament'. That is why she is deeply affected by Frank Churchill's duplicity, when the news of his engagement to Jane Fairfax is made public. Even though her own infatuation with Frank Churchill was a passing affair, she found the secrecy of the entire episode with Jane difficult to take.

In spite of Emma's errors of judgment, the reader is sympathetic towards the character of Emma. It is to Jane Austen's credit that she skilfully keeps us from disliking her 'blundering heroine'.

Mr George Knightley

George Knightley is about thirty-seven years old and lives at Donwell Abbey. He is far more mature and 'sensible' than any of the other characters in the novel. Darryl Jones calls him the 'true-born Englishman'. Mr Knightley has Emma's welfare at heart from the very beginning and is concerned about her impulsive behaviour. 'There is an anxiety in what one feels for Emma. I wonder what will become of her!' he remarks in Chapter 5. About her misguided attempts at matchmaking he says: 'If you were as much guided by nature in your estimate of men and women, and as little under the power of fancy and whim in your dealings with them … we might always think alike.' Jane Stevenson, a critic of Jane Austen remarks, 'Knightley is the nearest thing Austen ever produced to an unqualified hero.' Other critics have observed that Knightley's speeches sound like sermons and that he is a character for whom we have greater admiration than affection. He is gallant, kind, large-hearted and has an intuitive understanding of people and their character. Being sixteen years older than Emma, he is the only one in the novel who has the courage to point out Emma's faults to her face. She values his opinion even though she does not always agree with him. He expresses his displeasure at her unkind treatment of Miss Bates. Emma is truly ashamed of herself on the occasion, and weeps.

Knightley is very modest. Even when he extends an act of kindness or friendship he does not make a public show of it. For instance, he sends his carriage to Jane Fairfax to attend the party at the Coles,' and sends a sack of apples from Donwell Abbey to Mrs and Miss Bates. He also likes an open temper and finds Frank Churchill's double-dealing particularly hard to forgive. He approves of the marriage between Frank and Jane on second thoughts. It would be beneficial to both, he concludes. He would raise her station in life and she would make him a better person by her influence.

Frank Churchill

Frank is the son of Mr Weston by a former marriage to Miss Churchill. After his mother's death, he is taken over by his maternal uncle and aunt, Mr and Mrs Churchill, and grows up in their Scottish home, Enscombe. As a young man he is eagerly awaited at Highbury and fulfils the expectations of all when he finally arrives there. He had been exchanging letters with Mrs Weston and is anxious to meet his new step-mother in Highbury. Being extremely sociable and outgoing, he has little trouble making contact with the young ladies in Highbury particularly Emma. Frank is lively, cheerful, and gallant, and knows how to please women. He tells them what they want to hear. He makes sure there are umbrellas for the women when they are all out together on one occasion and there is talk of rain. He fastens the rivet on Mrs Bates' spectacles. He shows a great deal of respect and concern for his aunt Mrs Churchill who is his benefactor. She is very possessive and keeps him at her beck and call. It is after her death that he makes public the news of his engagement to Jane Fairfax.

Emma mistakenly believes that Frank is close to being in love with her and that it is her own indifference that stopped him from declaring it. When Frank comes to say goodbye to Emma on being called away to Enscombe, Emma misunderstands his hesitation and his sighs. She suspects a proposal is in the way. Ironically, it is his relationship with Jane that is on Frank's mind. Mr and Mrs Weston secretly hope for a connection between Frank Churchill and Emma. Frank participates fully in the social life at Highbury – the ball at the Crown Inn, card games, picnics, and parties.

The openness and honesty of Mr Knightley are contrasted with the deceit of Frank Churchill. Knightley, who is extremely observant and perceptive, suspects a 'private understanding' between Jane Fairfax and Frank Churchill but is unable to convince Emma of this fact. Churchill leads Emma to believe he is extremely attentive to her and repeatedly flirts with her in public; when news of his secret engagement to Jane becomes known, everyone is very disappointed in him. Frank Churchill stands for the corrupting influence of city life and the power that money has in manipulating people. He is seen as a 'less villainous version' of Wickham in *Pride and Prejudice* and Willoughby in *Sense and Sensibility.*

Minor Characters

The relationship between the minor and the major characters is intricate. Barbara Hardy points out that the heroines in Jane Austen's novels 'do not stand apart from the group in morally impressive positions, passive or commanding, but partake of its deficiencies.' The minor characters are integral parts of the social circle. They bring out the best or the worst in the major characters, as the case may be.

Miss Taylor, who is 'less a governess than a friend' to Emma, becomes Mrs Weston at the start of the novel. She has lived with the Woodhouses for sixteen years and continues to be concerned for Emma's welfare even after she moves away after marriage. She is affectionate towards Emma to the point that she is almost blind to her faults. 'Where Emma errs once, she is in the right a hundred times,' she declares. Emma, we are told, was instrumental in 'arranging' the Westons' marriage. She and her husband Mr Weston secretly hope that Emma and Frank Churchill would be attracted to each other.

Mr Weston, a native of Highbury, was born into a respectable family. He received a good education, worked hard and acquired some property. He joined the militia of his county and later married a Miss Churchill who hailed from a good Yorkshire family. The marriage did not receive the support of her family and she was disowned by her parents. The couple it was thought, lived beyond their means. After three years of marriage Mr Weston or Captain Weston as he was then called, lost his wife and was left with a son, Frank. At this point (the first) Mrs Weston's brother Mr Churchill offers to take care and raise little Frank. Mr Weston gave up the militia and began a life of trade. After about twenty years when he had made enough money to buy some property adjoining Highbury, he married Miss Taylor. He was very proud of his son Frank Churchill who had grown up in London.

Jane Fairfax is an orphan who initially grew up in Colonel Campbell's household. Her mother was the youngest daughter of Mrs Bates. Her father was Lt Fairfax who died in the war. Colonel Campbell who acknowledged her father's qualities as a soldier and felt personally indebted to him, took the child Jane to live in his home along with his own daughter. Here Jane Fairfax was groomed to become a governess at a future date. When Col. Campbell's daughter got married, Jane Fairfax decided to spend some time in Highbury with her aunt Miss Bates and grandmother Mrs Bates. Jane comes forth as a reserved and introverted person, quite a contrast to Emma. She is presented as an accomplished young woman, particularly talented on the piano, and of very striking appearance. She is tall, elegant, and has a 'pleasing beauty' about her. Her musical talents are highly appreciated in Highbury. Emma dislikes her at first (even envies her), because she is cold and reserved, but later has charitable feelings towards her that there is no young man in Highbury 'worthy of giving her independence'. Jane had met Frank Churchill at Weymouth but she does not divulge any information concerning him. They had sung together at Weymouth. It seems as if Jane is destined to become a governess. The relationship between Emma and Jane becomes more complex as Frank Churchill appears to woo Emma while being secretly engaged to Jane. The secrecy involved in her relationship with Frank Churchill makes Jane appear cold and reserved and even ill most of the time. While Emma, unknown to herself, is in love with Mr Knightley, she is relieved to hear Mr Knightley comment that Jane does not have the 'open temper which a man would wish for in a wife.'

Harriet Smith is seventeen years old when she comes into Emma's social orbit. Nothing much is known of her parentage but Emma is convinced that she is of respectable birth and lineage, unfortunate though her circumstances might be. She is in Mrs Goddard's school before she comes to Highbury, just when Emma needs someone to fill the vacuum left by Miss Taylor's departure. Harriet is docile and pliant and looks up to Emma with great regard and admiration. When Harriet spends a lot of time at the Abbey Mill Farm, Emma becomes suspicious that Harriet might be infatuated with the farmer Robert

Martin. She weans her away from Mr Martin, who in her estimation lacks 'gentility', and steers her in the direction of the vicar Mr Elton. He had a comfortable home and income and some independent property which Emma thought would suit Harriet very well. Emma is mortified when the pompous Mr Elton rejects Harriet and woos her (Emma) instead.

Harriet recovers from the episode that is not of her own making. Emma makes a second error in judgment concerning Harriet. When Frank Churchill 'rescues' Harriet from the gypsies, she jumps to conclusions about a possible romance that might bring the two of them together. Harriet however confesses to Emma that she has no feelings for Frank Churchill but that she looks up to Mr Knightley. The confession pushes Emma into acknowledging her own love for Mr Knightley. It also dawns on her that she had all along manipulated Harriet and made her what she was not. She wakes up to the class disparity between Mr Knightley and Harriet – 'Such an elevation on her side! Such a debasement on his!' It also shows a certain amount of presumption on Harriet's part, and Jane Austen is quick to indicate that a crossing of the social barrier is not always acceptable. An invitation is arranged and Harriet is conveniently sent off to London. Harriet marries Mr Robert Martin in the end.

In **Mr Woodhouse**, Jane Austen presents a convincing picture of the father-figure, self-absorbed and spoilt by his daughters. He is a 'nervous man', 'easily depressed', hates change of any kind and cannot be convinced that other people may think differently from himself. On the departure of Miss Taylor from the home he is well taken care of by Emma who arranges card-games and other social occasions for him, and Isabella who visits him with her family. During the snowstorm he looks to Emma for comfort and assurance. Mr Woodhouse is gallant and obliging when it comes to the women and they are greatly flattered by his kindness and his chivalry. One of the reasons Emma declares she will never marry is that she could not bear to part with her father and leave him without a caretaker.

There is actually another side to the character of Mr Woodhouse. Though very caring of Emma, there is an element of selfishness in his fatherhood and this, added to his obsession about his own health, makes him a rather weak and dependent person. When the question of Emma's marriage to Mr Knightley comes up Mr Woodhouse is more concerned about the impending change in his own living situation than about Emma. Fortunately for him, Mr Knightley offers to move in to Hartfield on marrying Emma and thereby alter things as little as possible for Mr Woodhouse.

Miss Bates is the aunt of Jane Fairfax. She stands out as the most talkative of all the characters – 'a great talker upon little matters.' Her small talk helps to further the plot and provides additional information about the characters. She is full of gratitude to Emma 'for the hind-quarters of pork' and to Mr Knightley for the apples. She is a kind and good-natured spinster totally devoted to caring for her mother, Mrs Bates. She makes her garrulous appearance at all the social gatherings in Highbury. Emma behaves in an unfeeling manner towards her on a visit to Box Hill. Mr Knightley rebukes Emma for her insensitivity and rudeness towards a woman of her 'character, age and situation.' The fate of the single unmarried woman in Jane Austen's society is evident from the character-portrayal of Miss Bates. She is past the age of marriage. She is dependent on the goodwill of others and is the butt of jokes on account of her idiosyncratic behaviour.

Mr Elton is the vicar of Highbury. Emma states quite early on in the novel that she has intentions of arranging a match for him as he looked lonely and in need of a wife. Mr Elton, however, is an opportunist who it appears would rather marry a woman of standing like Emma than a woman of uncertain parentage and circumstances such as Harriet. He openly insults Harriet at the ball in the Crown Inn by refusing to dance with her. He is also a shallow and pompous individual. When it becomes clear to him that Emma will not deign to consider him as a suitor, Mr Elton goes away angry and returns to Highbury with a wife. As the novelist puts it 'Mr Elton returned a very happy man. He had gone away rejected and mortified, he came back engaged to another, self-satisfied, eager and busy, caring nothing for Miss Woodhouse, and defying Miss Smith.' From that point on, Mr and Mrs Elton are always seen together and seem quite inseparable. Emma is particularly offended at their sneering attitude towards Harriet.

Mrs Elton is formerly Miss Augusta Hawkins. Mr Elton had barely gone from Highbury when in a matter of weeks he returns a happy man engaged to Miss Augusta Hawkins. She is the younger daughter of a Bristol merchant. She was in possession of an independent fortune. That her elder sister was married to a gentleman and had two carriages was something she boasted of continually. Mrs Elton is a vain, presumptuous and arrogant woman who constantly draws attention to herself. Emma feels that even though she is pretty, she is vulgar and without taste or elegance. She speaks too freely and without constraint and decorum. She comments too easily about the people of Highbury who were very dear to Emma. At the dinner party given by the Woodhouses for the newly married couple, Mrs Elton talks about her gown and her love of simplicity, her pearls and the fact that all eyes were on her. She thinks too highly of her social connections and acquaintances. 'Insufferable woman!' is Emma's remark on their first meeting. Mrs Elton takes a liking to Jane Fairfax and goes out of her way to offer her assistance and support.

The Coles were of low origin, settled in Highbury and living a 'moderately genteel' life from trade. They are a friendly family. When their situation improves they begin to have dinner parties in Highbury. Even though Emma feels superior to them, she attends the party at the Coles' because all her friends in society are invited to it.

Isabella is Emma's older sister and the wife of John Knightley (the younger brother of George Knightley). Isabella lives with her husband and five children in London. The novel tells us she is a pretty, gentle and affectionate woman of 'amiable disposition'. She is very attached to her father and sister. She is a devoted wife and a doting mother. During the visit of Isabella and her family to Hartfield, she is very concerned about her father's comfort and is worried that the children should not disturb him unduly. She also sympathises with her father on the departure of Miss Taylor.

Significant techniques and aspects of style

Barbara Hardy, the critic, sees Jane Austen as one of the pioneers of the modern novel who has quite significantly transformed the art of fiction. Jane Austen is generally commended for her incisive criticism of a small and narrow sphere of society. But Hardy recognises in her the dexterity of skill and intuition which brings the individual and society together unobtrusively, yet with a great deal of dynamism. 'She has the capacity', Barbara Hardy writes, 'to glide easily from sympathy to detachment, from one mind to many minds, from solitary scenes to social gatherings. The flexible medium is the dominant gift of her genius.'

Humour, irony and understatement are distinguishing characteristics of Jane Austen's style. She confines herself to the small world—'three or four families in a country village is the very thing to work on'—she says. As Charlotte Bronte commented, she worked on a miniature piece of ivory, carving and chiselling a miniature with care and detail. This has earned her the reputation of being 'parochial' but critics have also pointed out that in psychological depth and insight, and in her satirical wit and understatement, she goes far beyond the limited artistic frame within which she has been placed. Jane Austen's wit and irony are most often gentle, not harsh. She describes her art as 'a little bit (two inches wide) of ivory on which I work with so fine a brush as produces little effect after much labour'. She does not come down with a sledge-hammer on the foibles of this world. Her gentle exposure of the pretentiousness of her characters, the manners and morals of the society of her time is done without malice or ill-will. Each character unfolds through what he/she says and through his/her mannerisms. The vulgar affectations of the middle classes are gently prodded and frowned at. Mrs Elton is held up for ridicule in the novel. So also is Miss Bates who ingratiates herself with her constant chatter no matter what the occasion.

The novel is replete with ironical situations and statements: 'Do not think I want to influence you' says Emma to Harriet when the question of Mr Martin's marriage proposal comes up. It is ironical that Emma should say this when in fact she influences her friend strongly to reject Mr Martin. In yet another instance, Emma and Jane Fairfax are expected to be friends because they are of the same age with similar interests. But it is ironical that Jane sees Emma as a rival and Emma finds Jane too closed and reserved.

Sometimes the irony in a statement or situation which occurs earlier becomes evident later in the novel. Mr Knightley's carriage is made available to Jane Fairfax to attend the dinner party at the Coles'. This arouses Mrs Weston's suspicion that there may be a friendship developing between Mr Knightley and Jane. Emma is emphatic in rejecting the probability. She says, 'But Mr Knightley does not want to marry. I am sure he has not the least idea of it . . . He is as happy as possible by himself . . . He has no occasion to marry, either to fill up his time or his heart.' Emma's assessment of Mr Knightley's thoughts and feelings are so ironical in the context because a little later Mr Knightley and Emma declare their love for each other and are to be married. The scene where Frank says goodbye to Emma before going away to London is also loaded with irony. Frank's awkward behaviour suggests he is about to make a confession, Emma supposes it is a declaration of love for her. But the reality is that Frank wishes to tell Emma about his being engaged to Jane Fairfax. Circumstances prevent him from doing so.

Jane Austen's humour lies both in the authorial comments, the narrative, and in the way the characters reveal themselves through their speech and manners. She presents the delicate nuances of speech and the quirks and follies of her characters in their social setting. She is master of the art of presenting character through situation and dialogue and this indeed is the hallmark of her contribution to fiction.

The novel *Emma* has been adapted and modernised by Amy Heckerling in the film *Clueless* (1995). Juliet Archer has published a modern version of *Emma* called *The Importance of Being Emma* (2008).

Orient BlackSwan Drama Classics

Orient BlackSwan Drama Classics, with Professor S. Viswanathan as General Editor, is a series from Orient BlackSwan that fulfils the long-felt need of Indian students and teachers for a comprehensive Indian edition of drama classics in English. Edited and annotated with scholarly expertise and meticulous care by eminent professors and specialists in the field, each edition provides a rich understanding and appreciation of the play in easily comprehensible language.

Highlights of this series:

- A ***General Introduction*** which provides the cultural and historical background for the drama of the period and a brief biography of the playwright.
- An ***Introduction to the Play*** which discusses the theme, the structure and the plot. It also includes a comprehensive critical study and a brief stage history of the play.
- ***Detailed annotations*** which are provided at the bottom of each page to facilitate referencing.
- ***Suggestions for Further Reading*** which helps students acquire a wide understanding of the play.
- ***Topics for Discussion*** which initiates classroom analysis and study.

Titles in this series

1. The Tempest: *William Shakespeare*
2. The Tragedy of Julius Caesar: *William Shakespeare*
3. The First Part of Henry the Fourth: *William Shakespeare*
4. As You Like It: *William Shakespeare*
5. The Duchess of Malfi: *John Webster*
6. Othello, Moor of Venice: *William Shakespeare*
7. Measure for Measure: *William Shakespeare*
8. Hamlet, Prince of Denmark: *William Shakespeare*

CHAPTER ONE

Emma Woodhouse, handsome, clever and rich, with a comfortable home and happy disposition, seemed to unite some of the best blessings of existence; and had lived nearly twenty-one years in the world with very little to distress or vex her.

She was the youngest of the two daughters of a most affectionate indulgent father and had, in consequence of her sister's marriage, been mistress of his house from a very early period. Her mother had died too long ago for her to have more than an indistinct remembrance of her caresses, and her place had been supplied by an excellent woman as governess, who had fallen little short of a mother in affection.

Sixteen years had Miss Taylor been in Mr Woodhouse's family, less as a governess than a friend, very fond particularly of Emma. Between *them* it was more the intimacy of sisters. The mildness of Miss Taylor's temper had hardly allowed her to impose any restraint; and the shadow of authority had long passed away, Emma doing just what she liked; highly esteeming Miss Taylor's judgement, but directed chiefly by her own. The real evils indeed of Emma's situation were the power of having rather too much her own way, and a disposition to think a little too well of herself.

A gentle sorrow came—Miss Taylor married. The wedding over, her father and herself were left to dine together with no prospect of a third to cheer a long evening.

The event had every promise of happiness for her friend. Mr Weston was a man of unexceptionable character, easy fortune, suitable age and pleasant manners.

Emma recalled Miss Taylor's past kindness—the affection of sixteen years. A large debt of gratitude was owing here, but the intercourse of the last seven years was yet a clearer, tenderer recollection. She had been a friend and companion such as few possessed—intelligent, well informed, useful, gentle—one to whom she could speak every thought as it arose and one who had such an affection for her as could never find fault. Yet great must be the difference between a Mrs Weston only half a mile from them and a Miss Taylor in the house. She dearly loved her father, but he was no companion for her. Her sister Isabella, settled in London, only sixteen miles off,—was beyond her daily reach. Highbury, the large and populous village, almost a town, to which Hartfield did really belong, afforded her no equals. The Woodhouses were first in consequence there. All looked up to them. She had many acquaintances in the place, for her father was universally civil. But it was a melancholy change; and Emma could not but sigh over it, till her father woke and made it necessary to be cheerful. His spirits required support.

Her father was a nervous man, easily depressed, fond of everybody that he was used to, hating to part with them; hating change of every kind; and from his habits of gentle selfishness and of being never able to suppose that other people could feel differently from himself, he was disposed to think Miss Taylor had done as sad a thing for herself as for them.

Emma smiled and chatted as cheerfully as she could, to keep him from such thoughts, but when tea came he said "Poor Miss Taylor—I wish she were here again."

"I cannot agree with you, papa;" Emma replied, "and you would not have had Miss Taylor live with us for ever and bear all my odd humours, when she might have a house of her own?"

"A house of her own!—but where is the advantage of a house of her own? This is three times as large—And you have never any odd humours,·my dear."

Emma spared no exertions to get her father tolerably through the evening, and be attacked by no regrets but her own, but a visitor walked in and made it unnecessary.

Mr Knightley, a sensible man about seven or of eight—and—thirty, was not only a very old and intimate friend of the family, but particularly connected with it as the older brother of Isabella's husband. He lived about a mile from Highbury, was a frequent visitor, and at this time more welcome than usual as coming directly from their mutual connections in London. He had now walked up to say that all were well in Brunswick—square, and animated Mr Woodhouse for some time. Mr Knightley had a cheerful manner which always did him good; and his many inquiries after "poor Isabella" and her children were answered most satisfactorily.

"I have not wished you joy. Being pretty well aware of what sort of joy you must both be feeling," Mr Knightley said.

"Ah! poor Miss Taylor! 'tis a sad business."

"Poor Mr and Miss Woodhouse, if you please; but I cannot possibly say 'poor Miss Taylor.' I have a great regard for you and Emma, but when it comes to the question of dependence or independence! At any rate it must be better to have only one to please than two."

"Especially when *one* of those two is such a fanciful, troublesome creature!" said Emma playfully. "That is what you have in your head, I know—and what you would certainly say if my father were not by."

"I believe it is very true, my dear, indeed," said Mr Woodhouse with a sigh. "I am afraid I am sometimes very fanciful and troublesome."

"My dearest papa! You do not think I could mean you or suppose Mr Knightley to mean *you*: What a horrible idea. Oh, no! I meant only myself. Mr Knightley loves to find fault with me—it is all a joke. We always say what we like to one another."

Mr Knightley, in fact, was one of the few people who could see faults in Emma Woodhouse, and the only one who ever told her of them: and though this was not particularly agreeable to Emma herself, she knew it would be so much less so to her father.

"Emma knows I never flatter her," said Mr Knightley; "Miss Taylor has been used to have two persons to please; she will now have but one. The chances are that she must be a gainer."

"Dear Emma bears everything so well," said her father. "But she is really very sorry to lose poor Miss Taylor."

"It is impossible that Emma should not miss such a companion," said Mr Knightley. "We should not like her so well as we do, sir, if we could suppose it. But she knows how much the marriage is to Miss Taylor's advantage; she knows how very acceptable it must be at Miss Taylor's time of life to be settled in a home of her own, and how important to her to be secure of a comfortable provision, and therefore cannot allow herself to feel so much pain as pleasure. Every friend of Miss Taylor must be glad to have her so happily married."

"You have forgotten one matter of joy to me," said Emma, "—that I made the match myself."

Mr Knightley shook his head at her. Her father fondly replied, "Pray do not make any more matches."

"I promise you to make none for myself, papa; but I must indeed, for other people. Only one more, papa; only for Mr Elton. I thought when he was joining their hands today, he looked as if he would like the same done for him. I think very well of Mr Elton and this is the only way I have of doing him a service."

CHAPTER TWO

Mr Weston was a native of Highbury, and born of a respectable family. He had received a good education, on succeeding early in life to a small independence, had satisfied an active cheerful mind and social temper by entering into the militia of his county.

Captain Weston was a general favourite; and when Miss Churchill of a great Yorkshire family fell in love with him, nobody was surprised except her brother and his wife, who were full of pride and importance.

Miss Churchill, however, being of age and with the full command of her fortune, was not to be dissuaded from the marriage, and it took place. Mr and Mrs Churchill threw her off with due decorum. It was an unsuitable connection, and did not produce much happiness. They lived beyond their income.

Captain Weston, who had been considered, especially by the Churchills, as making such an amazing match, was proved to have much the worst of the bargain, for when his wife died after a three years' marriage, he was a poorer man than at first, and with a child to maintain. Mr and Mrs Churchill, having no children of their own, offered to take the whole charge of the little Frank soon after her decease. The child was given up to the care and wealth of the Churchills and Mr Weston had only his own comfort to seek, and his own situation to improve as he could.

A complete change of life became desirable. He quitted the militia and engaged in trade, and the next eighteen or twenty years of his life passed cheerfully away. He had, by that time, enough to purchase a little estate adjoining Highbury, marry a woman as portionless even as Miss Taylor, and to live according to the wishes of his own family.

He saw his son every year in London, and was proud of him; and his fond report of him as a very fine young man had made Highbury feel a sort of pride in him too. His coming to visit his father had been often talked of but never achieved.

Now, upon his father's marriage, it was very generally proposed, as a most proper attention, that the visit should take place. The hope strengthened when it was understood that he had written to his new mother on the occasion. Mrs Weston had, of course, formed a very favourable idea of the young man; and such a pleasing attention was an irresistible proof of his great good sense.

CHAPTER THREE

Mr Woodhouse was fond of society in his own way. From his long residence at Hartfield, and his good nature; from his fortune, his house, and his daughter, he could command the visits of his own little circle in a great measure as he liked. His horror of late hours and large dinner-parties made him unfit for any acquaintance, but such as would visit him on his own terms. Evening parties were what he preferred. There was scarcely an evening in which Emma could not make up a card-table for him.

Real long-standing regard brought the Westons and Mrs Knightley, and Mr Elton, a young man living alone without liking it. After these came a second set, among whom were Mrs and Miss Bates and Mrs Goddard. Mrs Bates, the widow of a former vicar of Highbury, was a very old lady. Her daughter enjoyed a most uncommon degree of popularity for a woman neither young, handsome, rich nor married. She had never boasted either beauty or cleverness. Her youth had passed without distinction, and her middle of life was devoted to the care of a failing mother, and the endeavour to make a small income go as far as possible. And yet she was a happy woman, and a woman whom no one named without good-will. She loved everybody, was interested in everybody's happiness, quicksighted to everybody's merits. She was a great talker upon little matters. Mrs Goddard was the mistress of a real, honest, old-fashioned boarding school.

One morning a note was brought from Mrs Goddard requesting to be allowed to bring Miss Smith with her. Harriet Smith, a girl of seventeen, was the natural daughter of somebody, who had placed her, several years back, at Mrs Goddard's school. She had no visible friends, and was now just returned from a long visit in the country to some young ladies who had been at school with her.

She was a very pretty girl and her beauty happened to be of a sort which Emma particularly admired. She was short, plump and fair, with a fine bloom, blue eyes, light hair, regular features and a look of great sweetness. Emma was as much pleased with her manners as her person, and quite determined to continue the acquaintance. She found her altogether very engaging—not inconveniently shy, unwilling to talk, yet seemingly so pleasantly grateful for being admitted to Hartfield and so artlessly impressed by the appearance of every thing in so superior a style to what she had been used to, that she must have good sense and deserve encouragement.

CHAPTER FOUR

Quick and decided in her ways, Emma lost no time in inviting and encouraging Harriet Smith to visit Hartfield. As their acquaintance increased, so did their satisfaction in each other.

Harriet certainly was not clever, but she had a sweet, docile, grateful disposition; was totally free from conceit and only desired to be guided by anyone she looked up to. She seemed to be exactly the young friend Emma wanted. Her friendship with Mrs Weston was based on gratitude and esteem. Harriet would be loved as one to whom she could be useful. For Mrs Weston there was nothing to be done; for Harriet everything. But Harriet could not tell who her parents were. She had been satisfied to hear and believe just what Mrs Goddard chose to tell her; and asked no further questions.

The Martins of Abbey Mill Farm occupied Harriet's thoughts a good deal; she had spent two very happy months with them and now loved to talk of the pleasures of her visit, and describe the many comforts and wonders of the place. For some time this talk amused Emma. But when it appeared that the Mr Martin, who was always mentioned with approbation for his great good nature, was a single man, and that there was no wife in the case, she did suspect danger to her poor little friend from all this hospitality and kindness.

Hence she led Harriet to talk more of Mr Martin. Harriet was very ready to speak of his share in their moonlight walks and merry evening games and dwelt a good deal upon his being so very good-humoured and obliging. She believed he was very clever and understood everything. His mother and sisters were very fond of him. "I believe he has read a good deal but not what you would think any thing of," she said.

The next question was: "What sort of looking man is Mr Martin?"

"Oh! not handsome. I thought him very plain at first, but I do not think him so plain now. One does not, after a time. He is in Highbury every now and then. He has passed you very often."

"That may be. A young farmer, whether on horseback or on foot, is the very last sort of person to raise my curiosity. I have no doubt of his being a very respectable young man and as such wish him well. What do you imagine his age to be"

"He was four-and-twenty last June."

"Only four-and-twenty. That is too young to settle. I wish you may not get into a scrape, Harriet. The misfortune of your birth ought to make you particularly careful as to your associates. There can be no doubt of your being a gentleman's daughter, and you must support your claim by everything in your own power, or there will be plenty of people who would take pleasure in degrading you."

"Yes—to be sure. But while you are so kind to me, Miss Woodhouse, I am not afraid of what anybody can do!" replied Harriet.

They met Mr Martin the very next day as they were walking down the Donwell Road. His appearance was very neat, and he looked sensible. Harriet and he remained a few minutes together, then she came running with a smiling face and in a flutter of spirits, "What do you think of him? Do you think him so very plain?" she asked.

"He is undoubtedly remarkably plain; but that is nothing, compared with his entire want of gentility. I had no idea that he could be so very clownish. I had imagined him a degree or two nearer gentility."

"To be sure," said Harriet in a mortified voice, "he is not so genteel as real gentlemen." "Compare Mr Martin with either Mr Weston or Mr Elton."

"Compare their manner of carrying themselves, of walking, of speaking, of being silent. You must see the difference. I think a young man might be very safely recommended to take Mr Elton as a model. Mr Elton is good humoured, cheerful, obliging and gentle. He seems to be grown particularly gentle of late. I, do not know whether he has any design of ingratiating himself with either of us by additional softness, but it strikes me that his manners are softer than they used to be. It must be to please you."

She then repeated some warm personal praise which she had drawn from Mr Elton, and Harriet blushed and smiled, and said she had always thought Mr Elton very agreeable.

Mr Elton was the very person fixed on by Emma for driving the young farmer out of Harriet's head. She thought it would be an excellent match. Mr Elton's situation was most suitable, quite the gentleman himself and without low connections, at the same time not of any family that could object to the doubtful birth of Harriet. He had a comfortable home, for her, and Emma imagined a very sufficient income; for though the vicarage of Highbury was not large, he was known to have some independent property. She had already satisfied herself that he thought Harriet a beautiful girl, which she trusted was foundation enough on his side; and on Harriet's, there could be little doubt that the idea of being preferred by him would have all the usual weight and efficacy.

CHAPTER FIVE

"I do not know what your opinion may be, Mrs Weston," said Mr Knightley," of this great intimacy between Emma and Harriet Smith, but I think it a bad thing."

"You surprise me! Emma must do Harriet good and by supplying her with a new object of interest, Harriet may be said to do Emma good. I have been seeing their intimacy with great pleasure. How well she looked last night."

"I shall not attempt to deny Emma's being pretty."

"Pretty! say beautiful rather. Can you imagine anything nearer perfect beauty than—Emma altogether—face and figure?"

"I confess that I have seldom seen a face or figure more pleasing to me than hers. But I am a partial old friend."

"Such an eye!—the true hazel eye—and so brilliant—! regular features, open countenance, oh! what a bloom of full health, and such a pretty height and size; such a firm and upright figure.

"She is loveliness itself, Mr Knightley, is not she?"

"I have not a fault to find with her person," he replied. "I love to look at her; and I will add this praise, that I do not think her personally vain. Her vanity lies another way. Mrs Weston, I am not to be talked out of my dislike of her intimacy with Harriet Smith, or my dread of its doing them both harm."

"And I, Mr Knightley, am equally stout in my confidence of its not doing them any harm. With all dear Emma's little faults, she is an excellent creature. Where shall we see a better daughter, or a kinder sister, or a truer friend? She has qualities which may be trusted; she will never lead anyone really wrong; she will make no lasting blunder; where Emma errs once, she is in the right a hundred times."

"Be satisfied," said he, "I will not raise any outcry. There is an anxiety in what one feels for Emma. I wonder what will become of her!"

"She always declares she will never marry, which, of course, means just nothing at all. But I have no idea that she has yet ever seen a man she cared for. I should like to see Emma in love, and in some doubt of a return; it would do her good. But there is nobody hereabouts to attach her; and she "goes so seldom from home."

"While she is so happy at Hartfield, I cannot wish her to be forming any attachment which would be creating such difficulties on poor Mr Woodhouse's account. I do not recommend matrimony at present to Emma."

Part of her meaning was to conceal some favorite thoughts of her own and Mr Weston's on the subject. There were wishes at Randalls respecting Emma's destiny, but it was not desirable to have them suspected.

CHAPTER SIX

Emma could not feel a doubt of having given Harriet's fancy a proper direction, for she found her decidedly more sensible than before of Mr Elton's being a remarkably handsome man, with most agreeable manners. She was quite convinced of Mr Elton's falling in love, if not in love already. He talked of Harriet, and praised her so warmly.

"She was a beautiful creature when she came to you, but in my opinion, the attractions you have added are infinitely superior to what she received from nature."

She was not less pleased another day with the manner in which he seconded a sudden wish of hers to have Harriet's picture.

"Let me entreat you," cried Mr Elton, "to exercise so charming a talent in favour of your friend."

Emma had soon fixed on the size and sort of portrait Harriet, smiling and blushing and afraid of not keeping her attitude and countenance, presented a very sweet mixture of youthful expression. But there was no doing anything with Mr Elton fidgeting behind Emma and watching every touch. He was ready at the smallest intermission of the pencil, to jump up and see the progress and be charmed. The setting was altogether very satisfactory. The whole progress of the picture was rapid and happy. Every body who saw it was pleased, but Mr Elton was in continual raptures and defended it through every criticism.

The next thing wanted was to get the picture framed. Mr Elton's gallantry was always on the alert. It was impossible to say how much he should be gratified by being employed on such an errand.

Mr Elton was to take the drawing to London, choose the frame and give directions.

"What a precious deposit!" said he with a tender sigh, as he received it.

"This man is almost too gallant to be in love," thought Emma, "but I suppose there may be a hundred different ways of being in love. He is an excellent young man and will suit Harriet exactly. But he does sigh and languish and study for compliments rather more than I could endure as a principle."

CHAPTER SEVEN

Mr Martin, finding that Harriet was not at home, had left a little parcel for her from one of his sisters, and gone away. On opening this parcel she had found, besides the two songs which she had lent Elizabeth, a letter to herself from Mr Martin, and it contained a direct proposal of marriage. She was so surprised she did not know what to do—and so, she was come as fast as she could to ask Miss Woodhouse what she should do.

"Will you read the letter?" cried Harriet, "Pray do." Emma was not sorry to be pressed. The style of the letter was much above her expectation. As a composition it would not have disgraced a gentleman; the language though plain, was strong and unaffected. It was short, but expressed good sense, warm attachment, liberality, propriety, even delicacy of feeling.

"Yes, so good a letter, Harriet, that I think one of his sisters must have helped him. I can hardly imagine the young man could express himself so well, if left quite to his own powers. No doubt he is a sensible man, and when he takes a pen his hand, his thoughts naturally find proper words. Yes, I understand the sort of mind.

Vigorous, decided, with sentiments to a certain point, not coarse. A better written letter, Harriet, than I had expected."

"Well," said Harriet; "and what shall I do?"

"You must answer it of course—and speedily."

"What shall I say? Dear Miss Woodhouse, do advise me."

"You will express yourself very properly, your meaning must be unequivocal: no doubts and demurs; and such expressions of gratitude and concern for the pain you are inflicting as propriety requires, will present themselves unbidden to your mind. You need not be prompted to write with the appearance of sorrow for his disappointment."

"You think I ought to refuse him then," said Harriet, looking down.

"My dear Harriet. Are you in any doubt as to that? Perhaps I have been under a mistake. I certainly have been misunderstanding you, if you feel in doubt as to the purport of your answer. I had imagined you were consulting me only as to the wording of it. You mean to return a favourable answer, I collect."

"No. I do not; that is, I do not mean—Pray, dear Miss Woodhouse, tell me what I ought to do."

"Harriet, I will have nothing to do with it. This is a point which you must settle with your own feelings. If woman *doubts* as to whether she should accept a man or not, she certainly ought to refuse him. It is not a state to be safely entered into with doubtful feelings, with half a heart. I thought it my duty as a friend, and older than yourself; to say thus much to you. But do not imagine that I want to influence you."

"As you say, one's mind ought to be quite made up—It is a very serious thing—Do you think l had better, say 'No'?"

"Not for the world," said Emma, smiling graciously, "would I advise you either way. You must be the best judge of your own happiness. If you prefer Mr Martin to every other person, why should you hesitate? You blush, Harriet. Does any body else occur to you at this moment under such a definition? Harriet, do not deceive yourself. At this moment whom are you thinking of?"

The symptoms were favourable. Instead of answering, Harriet turned away confused, and stood thoughtfully by the fire. At last with some hesitation, Harriet said—

"Miss Woodhouse, as you will not give me your opinion, I must do as well as I can by myself, and really I have almost made up my mind—to refuse Mr Martin. Do you think I am right?"

"Perfectly right, my dearest Harriet, you are doing just what you ought. I have no hesitation in approving. It would have grieved me to lose your acquaintance, which must have been the consequence of your marrying Mr Martin. I could not have visited Mrs Robert Martin of Abbey Mill Farm."

"You could not have visited me!" she cried, looking aghast. "Dear Miss Woodhouse, I would not give up the pleasure and honour of being intimate with you for any thing in the world. He is very good-natured, and I shall always feel much obliged to him and have a great opinion of him, and his being so much attached to me. But I am quite determined to refuse him. What shall I say?"

Emma assured her there would be no difficulty in the answer, and though Emma continued to protest against any assistance being wanted, it was in fact given in the formation of every sentence.

The letter was written, and sealed and sent. The business was finished, and Harriet safe.

CHAPTER EIGHT

Mr Knightley called. He began speaking of Harriet, with more voluntary praise than Emma had ever heard before.

"I cannot rate her beauty as you do," said he, but she is a pretty little creature. In good hands she will turn out a valuable woman. You have improved her.

He presently added with a smile, "I have good reason to believe your little friend will soon hear of something to her advantage."

Emma was more than half in hopes of Mr Elton having dropped a hint. Mr Knightley was a sort of general friend and adviser, and she knew Mr Elton looked up to him.

"I have reason to think," he stated, "that Harriet Smith will soon have an offer of marriage, and from a most unexceptionable quarter. Robert Martin is desperately in love and means to marry her. He came to the Abbey to consult me about it. He knows I have a thorough regard for him and all his family and I believe considers me as one of his best friends. He came to ask me whether I approved his choice altogether. He told me his circumstances and plans. He is an excellent young man both as son and brother. I had no hesitation in advising him to marry."

"Come" said she. "I will tell you something. He wrote, and was refused."

"Mr Knightley actually looked red with surprise and displeasure as he stood up, in tall indignation.

"Emma, this is your doing. You persuaded her to refuse him."

"And if I did, I should not feel that I had done wrong. I cannot admit him to be Harriet's equal."

"Not Harriet's equal! he is as much her superior in sense as in situation. What are Harriet Smith's claims, either of birth, nature or education, higher than Robert Martin? She is the daughter of nobody knows whom, with probably no settled provision at all and certainly no respectable relations. She is not a sensible girl, nor a girl of any information. Your views for Harriet are best known to yourself; but as you make no secret of your love of match making and as a friend I shall just hint to you that if Elton is the man, I think it will be all labour in vain."

Emma laughed and disclaimed. He continued. "Elton is not at all likely to make an imprudent match. He knows the value of a good income as well as anybody. Elton may talk sentimentally but he will act rationally. He knows that he is a very handsome young man and a great favourite wherever he goes. I am convinced that he does not mean to throw himself away."

"If I had set my heart on Mr Elton's marrying Harriet, it would have been very kind to open my eyes, but at present I only want to keep Harriet myself. I have done with match making indeed."

"Good morning to you," said he, rising and walking off abruptly. He felt the disappointment of the young man, and was mortified to have been the means of promoting it by the sanction he had given.

CHAPTER NINE

Mr Knightley was much displeased. Emma was sorry but could not repent. On the contrary, his plans were more and more justified and endeared to her by the general appearances of the next few days.

The picture, elegantly framed, came safely to hand soon after Mr Elton's return. He got up to look at it and sighed out his half sentences of admiration just as he ought and Harriet's feelings were visibly forming themselves into as strong and steady an attachment as her youth and sort of mind admitted.

Emma's views of improving her little friend's mind by a great deal of useful reading and conversation had never yet led to more than a few first chapters. The only mental provision she was making for the evening of her life, was collecting and transcribing all the riddles of every sort that she could meet with.

Mr Woodhouse tried very often to recollect something worth their putting in. Mr Elton was the only one whose assistance she asked for. He was invited to contribute any really good enigmas, charades or conundrums that he might recollect.

"Why will not you write one yourself for us, Mr Elton?" said she. "Nothing could be easier for you." The very next day produced some proof of inspiration. He called just to leave a charade. Emma cast her eye over it and caught the meaning.

"Very well, Mr Elton, *Courtship* – a very good hint. This is saying very plainly—Pray Miss Smith, give me leave to pay my addresses to you. An excellent charade indeed! and very much to the purpose."

She was obliged to break off from these very pleasant observations by Harriet's wondering questions, "What can it be, Miss Woodhouse? I cannot guess it in the least, do you think we shall ever find out?"

"Give me the paper and listen.

My first displays the wealth of pomp and kings,
Lords of the earth! their luxury and ease.
This is *court*.
Another view of man, my second brings;

Behold him there, the monarch of the seas!
That is *ship*, plain as can be—Now for the cream.
But ah! united (*courtship*, you know,) what reverse we have!
Man's boasted power and freedom, all are flown.
Lord of the earth and sea, he bends a slave,
And woman, lovely woman, reigns alone.
A very proper compliment!—and then follows the application.
Thy ready wit the word will soon supply.
May its approval beam in that soft eye!

You cannot find much difficulty in comprehending it. There is so pointed a meaning in this compliment, that I cannot have a moment's doubt as to Mr Elton's intentions. You are his object. I am very happy, I congratulate you, my dear Harriet. This is a connection which offers nothing but good. It will give you every thing that you want—consideration, independence, a proper home."

"That Mr Elton should really be in love with me—me of all people: the very handsomest man that ever was and a man that everybody looks up to. And so excellent in the church!"

"It is one thing," said she presently—"to sit down and write a letter, and say just what you must in a short way; and another, to write verses and charades like this." Emma could not have desired a more spirited rejection of Mr Martin's prose.

CHAPTER TEN

On the morrow, Emma had a charitable visit to pay, to a poor sick family. Their road was down Vicarage lane. The lane made a slight bend; and when that bend was passed Mr Elton was immediately in sight. Mr Elton then turned back to accompany them.

Anxious to separate herself from them, she soon afterwards took possession of a narrow footpath, leaving them together. But she found that Harriet's habits of dependence and imitation were bringing her up too. She immediately stopped, under pretence of having some alteration to make in the lacing of her half-boot; and begged them to walk on; and she would follow. She had the comfort of further delay, being overtaken by a child. To walk by the side of this child, and talk to, and question her, was most natural, and by this means the others were still able to keep ahead. However, the child's pace was quick, and theirs rather slow, and she was obliged to join them.

They now walked on together; when a sudden resolution, of at least getting Harriet into the house, made her again find something amiss about her boot, and fall behind to arrange it once more. She then broke the lace off short, and dexterously throwing it into a ditch, was obliged to entreat them to stop.

"Part of my lace is gone," said she. "Mr Elton, I must beg leave to stop at your house, and ask your house-keeper for a bit of string, or any thing just to keep my boot on."

By engaging the housekeeper in incessant conversation, she hoped to make it practicable for him to chase his own subject in the adjoining room. For ten minutes she could hear nothing but herself. She was then obliged to be finished and make her appearance.

The lovers were standing together at one of the windows. Emma felt the glory of having schemed successfully. But he had not come to the point. He had been most agreeable, most delightful, but nothing serious.

Still, however, though everything had not been accomplished by her ingenious device, it must be leading them forward to the great event.

CHAPTER ELEVEN

The coming of Emma's sister's family was so very near at hand, that it become henceforth her prime object of interest; and during the ten days of their stay at Harfield she did not herself expect that any thing beyond occasional assistance could be afforded by her to the lovers.

Mr Woodhouse, who could not be induced to get so far as London, even for poor Isabella's sake, was now most nervously and apprehensively happy in forestalling this visit.

Mr and Mrs John Knightley, their five children, and a competent number of nursery maids all reached Hartfield in safety. The bustle and joy of such an arrival produced a noise and confusion, but the feelings of her father were so respected by Mrs Knightley that the children were never allowed to be long a disturbance to him.

Mrs John Knightley was a pretty, elegant little woman, of gentle quiet manners, and a disposition remarkably amiable and affectionate; wrapt up in her family; a devoted wife, a doting mother, and tenderly attached to her father and sister. She could never see a fault in any of them.

Mr John Knightley was a tall, gentleman-like, and very clever man; rising in his profession, domestic and respectable in his private character. He was not an ill-tempered man; but his temper was not his great perfection. He had all the clearness and quickness of mind which his wife wanted, and he could sometimes act ungracious, or say a severe thing. He was not a great favourite with his fair sister-in-law. Nothing wrong in him escaped her. She was quick in feeling the little injuries to Isabella, which Isabella never felt herself. He had a really great regard for his father-in-law, and generally a strong sense of what was due to him.

They had not been long seated when Mr Woodhouse, with a melancholy shake of the head and sigh said, "Ah! my dear, poor Miss Taylor—it is a grievous business."

"Oh! yes, sir," cried Isabella with ready sympathy. "I could not imagine how you could possibly do without her. Do you see her, sir, tolerably often ?"

"Not near so often, my dear, as I could wish."

"Papa, if you speak in that melancholy way—you will be giving Isabella a false idea of us all. Everybody must be aware that Miss Taylor must be missed, but everybody ought also to be assured that Mr and Mrs Weston do really prevent our missing her by any means to the extent we ourselves anticipated."

"Where is the young man?" said John Knightley. "Has he been here on this occasion—or has he not?"

"There was a strong expectation of his coming soon after the marriage, but it ended in nothing," said Emma.

"He wrote a letter to poor Mrs Weston, to congratulate her, and a very proper, handsome letter it was," said her father.

"How very pleasing and proper of him!" cried the good-hearted Mrs John Knightley. I have no doubt of his being a most amiable young man. But how sad it is that he should not live at home with his father."

CHAPTER TWELVE

Mr Knightley was to dine with them—rather against the inclination of Mr Woodhouse, who did not like that anyone should share with him in Isabella's first day. Emma's sense of right however had decided it; and besides, she had particular pleasure, from the circumstance of the late disagreement between Mr Knightley and herself, in procuring him the proper invitation.

She hoped they might now become friends again. Making up indeed would not do. *She* certainly had not been in the wrong, and *he* would never own that he had, but it was time to appear to forget that they had ever quarrelled. When he came into the room she had one of the children with her. Though he began with grave looks and short questions, he was soon led on to talk of them all in the usual way and to take the child out of her arms with all the unceremoniousness of perfect amity. Emma felt they were friends again.

She could not help saying,

"What a comfort it is that we think alike about our nephews and nieces. As to men and women, our opinions are sometimes very different."

"If you were as much guided by nature in your estimate of men and women, and as little under the power of fancy and whim in your dealings with them, as you are where these children are concerned, we might always think alike."

"To be sure—our discordancies must always arise from my being in the wrong."

"Yes," said he smiling, "and reason good. I was sixteen years old when you were born. Come, my dear Emma, let us be friends and say no more about it."

"Now, Mr Knightley, as far as good intentions went, we were *both* right, and I must say that no effects on my side of the argument have yet proved wrong. I only want to know that Mr Martin is not very, very bitterly disappointed."

"A man cannot be more so," was his short, full answer.

"Ah!—Indeed I am very sorry–come, shake hands with me."

The evening was quiet and conversible. The brothers talked of their own concerns and pursuits, but principally of those of the elder, whose temper was by much the most communicative. As a magistrate, he had generally some point of law to consult John about or at least some curious anecdote to give; and as a farmer as keeping in hand the home farm at Donwell, he had to tell what every field was to bear next year and to give all such local information as could not fail of being interesting to a brother whose home it had equally been the longest part of his life.

While they were thus comfortably occupied Mr Woodhouse was enjoying a full flow of happy regrets and fearful affection with his daughter.

CHAPTER THIRTEEN

There could hardly be a happier creature in the world than Mrs John Knightley in this short visit to Hartfield. It was a delightful visit. In general their evenings were less engaged with friends than their mornings: but one complete dinner engagement there was no avoiding. Mr Weston would take no denial. Even Mr Woodhouse was persuaded to think it a possible thing. Harriet, Mr Elton and Mr Knightley, their own especial set, were the only persons invited to meet them.

The evening before this great event Harriet had gone home indisposed with a cold. Emma called on her the next day and found that she was very feverish and had a bad sore throat.

Emma sat with her to attend her, and raise her spirits by representing how much Mr Elton would be depressed when he knew her state; then left her. She had not advanced many yards when she was met by Mr Elton himself. He had been going to inquire about Harriet that he might carry some report of her to Hartfield. They were overtaken by Mr John Knightley returning from the daily visit to Donwell. Emma was describing the nature of her friend's complaint—"A throat very much inflamed, Harriet was liabIe to very bad sore throats."

Mr Elton looked all alarm as he exclaimed,

"A sore throat! I hope not infectious. Indeed you should take care of yourself as well as your friend. Let me entreat you to run no risks."

Soon afterwards Mr Elton quitted them, and she could not but do him the justice of feeling that there was a great deal of sentiment in the tone of his voice while assuring her that he should call at Mrs Goddard's for news of her friend.

After a few minutes of silence between them, Mr John Knightley began.

"I never in my life saw a man more intent on being agreeable than Mr Elton. He seems to have a great deal of good-will towards you.

"Mr Elton in love with me! what an idea!"

"I do not say it is so; but you will do well to consider whether it is so or not, and to regulate your behaviour accordingly. I think your manners to him encouraging. I speak as a friend, Emma."

"I thank you; but I assure you you are quite mistaken. Mr Elton and I are very good friends, and nothing more," and she walked on, amusing herself in the consideration of the blunders which often arise from a partial knowledge of circumstances, and not very well pleased with her brother for imagining her blind and ignorant and in want of counsel. He said no more.

CHAPTER FOURTEEN

To Emma, it was real enjoyment to be with the Westons. Mr Weston was a great favourite and there was not a creature in the world to whom she spoke with such unreserve, as to his wife.

Emma's project of forgetting Mr Elton for a while, made her rather sorry to find, when they had all taken their places, that he was close to her. His behaviour was such that she could not avoid the internal suggestion of, "Can it really be as my brother imagined?—Absurd and insufferable"—yet he would be so anxious for her being perfectly warm, would be so interested about her father and so delighted with Mrs Weston, and at last would begin admiring her drawings with so much zeal and so little knowledge as seemed terribly like a would-be lover, and made it some effort with her to preserve her good manners. For her own sake she could not be rude; and for Harriet's, in the hope that all would yet turn out right, she was even positively civil, but it was an effort.

Now it so happened that in spite of Emma's resolution of never marrying, there was something in the name, in the idea of Mr Frank Churchill, which always interested her. If she were to marry, he was the very person to suit her in age, character and condition. That Mr and Mrs Weston did think of it, she was very strongly persuaded. She had a great curiosity to see him, a decided intention of finding him pleasant, of being liked by him to a certain degree, and a sort of pleasure in the idea of their being coupled in their friends' imaginations. With such sensations, Mr Elton's civilities were dreadfully ill-timed.

Mr Weston made use of the very first interval in the cares of hospitality to say to her,

"I believe you did not hear me telling the others that we are expecting Frank? I had a letter from him this morning. He will be with us within a fortnight. He has been wanting to come, but he cannot command his own time. He has those to please who must be pleased. But now I have no doubt of seeing him here about the second week in January. Mrs Churchill is an odd woman! But I never allow myself to speak ill of her, on Frank's account; for I do believe her to be very fond of him. I used to think she was not capable of being fond of any body, except herself: but she has always been kind to him. And it is no small credit, to him that he should excite such an affection; for she has no more heart than a stone to people in general; and the devil of a temper."

Emma liked the subject so well, that she began upon it, to Mrs Weston, very soon after, wishing her joy. Mrs Weston agreed, but added, "I cannot depend on his coming. It depends entirely upon his aunt's spirits and pleasure; I cannot bear to imagine any reluctance on his side; but I am sure there is a great wish on the Churchills' side to keep him to themselves. There is jealousy. They are jealous even of his regard for his father. She is so very unreasonable, and everything gives way to her."

Emma listened, and then coolly said, "I shall not be satisfied, unless he comes."

CHAPTER FIFTEEN

Emma, in good spirits from the amusement afforded her mind by the expectation of Mr Frank Churchill, was willing to forget Mr Elton's late improprieties. He began with great earnestness to entreat her to refrain from visiting the sick chamber again for the present to entreat her to *promise him.* She was vexed. It did appear exactly like the pretence of being in love with her, instead of Harriet. She had difficulty in behaving with temper. He turned to Mrs Weston to implore her assistance, "Would not she give him her support? Have not I some right to complain?"

Emma saw Mrs Weston's surprise and felt it must be great. She was too much provoked and offended. She could only give him a look; but it was such a look as she thought must restore him to his senses.

Mr John Knightley now came into the room from examining the weather. He gave them all the information of the ground being covered with snow, and of its still snowing fast, concluding with these words to Mr Woodhouse:

"This will prove a spirited beginning of your winter engagements, sir. Something new for your coachman and horses to be making their way through a storm of snowing."

Poor Mr Woodhouse was silent from consternation. Mrs Weston and Emma tried earnestly to cheer him, and turn his attention from his son-in-law, who was pursuing his triumph rather unfeelingly.

"I admired your resolution very much, sir," said he, "in venturing out in such weather, for of course you saw there would be snow very soon. I admired your spirit; and I dare say we shall get home very well. Another hour or two's snow can hardly make the road impassable; and we have two carriages; if one is blown over in the bleak part of the common field there will be the other at hand. I dare say we shall be all safe at Hartfield before midnight."

"What is to be done, my dear Emma?" was Mr Woodhouse's first exclamation, and all that he could say for some time. To her he looked for comfort, and her assurances of safety, her representation of the excellence of the horses, and of James, and of their having so many friends about them, revived him a little.

Mr Knightley, who had left the room immediately after his brother's first report of the snow , came back again and told them that he could answer for there not being the smallest difficulty in their getting home.

The carriages came, Mr Woodhouse was carefully attended to his own by Mr Knightley and Mr Weston. Isabella stepped in after her father; John Knightley stepped in after his wife. So Emma found, on being escorted and followed into the second carriage by Mr Elton, that the door was to be lawfully shut on them. It would have been a pleasure previous to this day; she could have talked to him of Harriet. But now she would rather it had not happened. He would want to be talking nonsense.

Scarcely had they passed the sweep-gate than she found—her hand seized—and Mr Elton actually making violent love to her, hoping—fearing—adoring—ready to die if she refused him. It really was so. Mr Elton, the lover of Harriet, was professing himself *her* lover. She tried to stop him, but vainly; he would go on and say it all. She felt that half this folly must be drunkenness. Accordingly, with a mixture of the serious and the playful, she replied,

"I am very much astonished, Mr Elton. This to *me*! you forget yourself—you take me for your friend—any message to Miss Smith I shall be happy to deliver, but no more of this to *me* if you please.

"Message to Miss Smith! What could she possibly mean"—And he repeated her words, with such boastful pretence of amazement, that she could not help replying with quickness.

"Mr Elton, this is the most extraordinary conduct! and I can account for it only in one way; you are not yourself, or you could not speak either to me, or of Harriet, in such a manner. Command yourself enough to say no more and I will endeavour to forget it."

But Mr Elton had only drunk wine enough to elevate his spirits, not at all to confuse his intellect. He perfectly knew his own meaning; he resumed the subject of his own passion, and was very urgent for a favourable answer.

She thought more of his inconsistency and presumption, and with fewer struggles for politeness, replied.

"It is impossible for me to doubt any longer. You have made yourself too clear. Mr Elton, my astonishment is much beyond anything I can express. After such behaviour, as I have witnessed during the last month, to Miss Smith—such attentions as I have been in the daily habit of observing—to be addressing me in this manner—this is an unsteadiness of character, indeed, which I had not supposed possible! Believe me, sir, I am far, very far, from gratified in being the object of such professions."

"Good heaven"! cried Mr Elton, "I never thought of Miss Smith in the whole course of my existence—never cared whether she was dead or alive, but as your friend. If she fancied otherwise, her own wishes have misled her—who can think of Miss Smith, when Miss Woodhouse is near! No, upon my honour, there is no unsteadiness of character. I have thought only of you. Everything that I have said or done, for many weeks past, has been with the sole view of marking my adoration of yourself—I am sure you have seen and understood me."

It would be impossible to say what Emma felt, on hearing this. She was too completely overpowered to be immediately able to reply: and two moments of silence being ample encouragement for Mr Elton, he tried to take her hand again, as he joyously exclaimed—

"Charming Miss Woodhouse! allow me to interpret this interesting silence. It confesses that you have long understood me". "No, sir," cried Emma, "it confesses no such thing. So far from having long understood you, I have been in a most complete error with respect to your views, till this moment. Nothing could be further from my wishes. But had I supposed that she was not your attraction to Hartfield, I should certainly have thought you judged ill in making your visits so frequent."

"Miss Smith is a very good sort of a girl. I wish her extremely well: and, no doubt, there are men who might not object to—everybody has their level; but as for myself I am not, I think, quite so much at a loss, as to be addressing myself to Miss Smith. No, madam, my visits to Hartfield have been for yourself only, and the encouragement l received—"

"Encouragement!—I give you encouragement!—sir, you have been entirely mistaken in supposing it. I have seen you only as the admirer of my friend, but it is well that the mistake ends where it does. Had the same behaviour continued, Miss Smith might have been led into a misconception of your views; not being aware of the very great inequality which you are so sensible of. I have no thoughts of matrimony at present."

He was too angry to say another word; her manner too decided to invite supplication. Without knowing when the carriage turned, they found themselves at the door of his house. Emma then felt it indispensable to wish him a good night. The compliment was just returned coldly and proudly, and she was then conveyed to Hartfield.

CHAPTER SIXTEEN

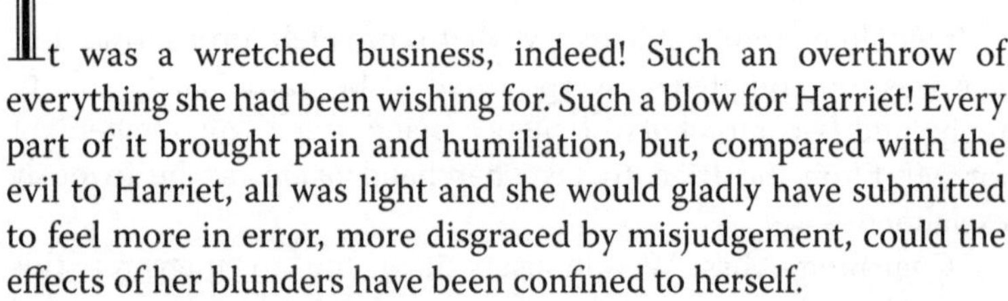

It was a wretched business, indeed! Such an overthrow of everything she had been wishing for. Such a blow for Harriet! Every part of it brought pain and humiliation, but, compared with the evil to Harriet, all was light and she would gladly have submitted to feel more in error, more disgraced by misjudgement, could the effects of her blunders have been confined to herself.

How she could have been so deceived! She had taken up the idea, she supposed, and made every thing bend to it. She had, of late, thought his manners to herself unnecessarily gallant, but it had passed as a mere error of judgement, of knowledge, of taste, as one proof among others that he had not always lived in the best society, that with all the gentleness of his address true elegance was sometimes wanting. She had never, for an instant, suspected it to mean any thing but grateful respect to her as Harriet's friend.

To Mr John Knightley she was indebted for her first idea on the subject. Mr Elton was proving himself, in many respects, the reverse of what she had meant and believed him: proud, assuming, conceited, and little concerned about the feelings of others.

Mr Elton's wanting to pay his addresses to her had sunk him in her opinion. His professions and his proposals did him no service. She thought nothing of his attachment and was insulted by his hopes. He wanted to marry well, and, having the arrrogance to raise his eyes to her, pretended to be in love. She was perfectly easy as to his not suffering any disappointment that need be cared for. There had been no real affection either in his language or manners. Sighs and fine words had been given in abundance, but she could hardly devise any set of expressions, or fancy any tone of voice, less allied with real love. She need not trouble herself to pity him. He only wanted to enrich himself, and if Miss Woodhouse, the heiress of thirty thousand pounds, were not quite so easily obtained, he would soon try for Miss somebody else with twenty, or with ten.

Perhaps it was not fair to expect him to feel how very much he was her inferior in talent, and all the elegancies of mind; the very want of such equality might prevent his perception of it. He must know that in fortune she was greatly his superior. He must know that the Woodhouses had been settled for several generations at Hartfield and that the Eltons were nobody. The landed property of Hartfield was inconsiderable, being but a sort of notch in Donwell Abbey estate, to which all the rest of Highbury belonged. But their fortune from other sources was such as to make them scarcely secondary to Donwell Abbey itself, and the Woodhouses had long held a high place in the consideration of the neighbourhood which Mr Elton had first entered not two years ago, to make his way as he could without any alliance but in trade, or any thing to recommend him to notice but his situation and his civility.

The first error and the worst lay at her door. It was foolish, it was wrong to take so active a part in bringing any two people together. She was ashamed, and resolved to do such things no more.

It was a great consolation that Mr Elton should not be really in love with her, or so particularly amiable as to make it shocking to disappoint him—that Harriet's nature should not be of that superior sort in which the feelings are most acute and retentive, and that there could be no necessity, especially, for her father's being given a moment's uneasiness about it.

The sight of a great deal of snow on the ground did her further service, for any thing was welcome that might justify all three (Harriet, Mr Elton and herself) being quite asunder at present. She was for many days a most honourable prisoner. No intercourse with Harriet possible but by note; no church for her on Sunday; and no need to find excuses for Mr Elton's absenting himself.

Her brother, whose feelings must always be of great importance to his companions, had so thoroughly cleared off his ill-humour at Randalls, that his amiableness never failed him, during the rest of his stay at Hartfield. He was always agreeable and obliging, and speaking pleasantly of everybody.

CHAPTER SEVENTEEN

Mr and Mrs John Knightley were not detained long at Hartfield. The weather soon improved enough for those to move who must move. Mr Woodhouse was obliged to see the whole party set off.

The evening of the very day brought a note from Mr Elton to Mr Woodhouse, to say "that he was proposing to leave the following morning on his way to Bath, where, with some friends, he had engaged to spend a few weeks, and very much regretted the impossibility of taking personal leave of Mr Woodhouse and had Mr Woodhouse any commands, he should be happy to attend to them."

Emma was most agreeably surprised. Mr Elton's absence just at this time was the very thing to be desired. She admired him for contriving it.

She went to Mrs Goddard's the very next day. She had to destroy all the hopes which she had been so industriously feeding—to appear in the ungracious character of the one preferred—and acknowledge herself grossly mistaken in all her ideas.

Harriet bore the intelligence very well—blaming nobody. Harriet did not consider herself at having any thing to complain of. The affection of such a man as Mr Elton would have been too great a distinction. Her tears fell abundantly—but her grief was so truly artless, that no dignity would have made it more respectable in Emma's eyes. She got her to Hartfield, and showed her the most unvarying kindness, striving to occupy and amuse her, and by book and conversation, to drive Mr Elton from her thoughts.

CHAPTER EIGHTEEN

Mr Frank Churchill did not come. He could not be spared, but still "he looked forward with hope of coming to Randalls at no distant period."

Mrs Weston was exceedingly disappointed. For half an hour Mr Weston was surprised and sorry; but then he began to perceive that Frank's coming two or three months later would be a much better plan; better time of the year; better weather; and that he would be able to stay considerably longer than if he had come sooner.

Emma was not in a state to care really about Mr Frank Churchill's not coming. She wanted to be quiet, and out of temptation. But as it was desirable that she should appear like her usual self, she took care to express much interest in the circumstances, and enter warmly into Mr and Mrs Weston's disappointment.

She was the first to announce it to Mr Knightley and exclaimed quite as much as was necessary at the conduct of the Churchills in keeping him away. She then found herself directly involved in a disagreement with Mr Knightley; and to her great amusement, perceived that she was taking the other side of the question from her real opinion, and making use of Mr Weston's arguments against herself.

CHAPTER NINETEEN

Jane Fairfax was an orphan, the only child of Mrs Bates's youngest daughter.

The marriage of Lieut. Fairfax and Miss Jane Bates had had its day of fame and pleasure, hope and interest; but nothing now remained of it, save the melancholy remembrance of him dying in action abroad—of his widow sinking under consumption and grief soon afterwards—and this girl.

Colonel Campbell, who had very highly regarded Fairfax as an excellent officer and most deserving young man; and further, had been indebted to him for such attentions during a severe camp fever, as he believed had saved his life, sought out the child and took notice of her. He was a married man, with only one living child, a girl, about Jane's age. Jane became their guest, paying them long visits and growing a favourite with all; and before she was nine years old, his daughter's great fondness for her and his own wish of being a real friend, united to produce an offer. It was accepted, and from that period Jane had belonged to Colonel Campbell's family, and had lived with them entirely, only visiting her grandmother from time to time.

The plan was that she should be brought up for educating others; the very few hundred pounds which she inherited from her father making independence impossible. By giving her an education he hoped, to be supplying the means of respectable subsistence hereafter. Living constantly with right-minded and well-informed people, her heart and understanding had received every advantage of discipline and culture, every lighter talent had been done full justice to by the attendance of first-rate masters. Her disposition and abilities were equally worthy of all that friendship could do; and at eighteen or nineteen she was, as far as such an early age can be qualified for the care of children, fully competent to the office of instruction herself. But she was too much loved to be parted with. The evil day was put off, and Jane remained with them, sharing, as another daughter, in all the rational pleasures of an elegant society, and a judicious mixture of home and amusements, with only her own good understanding to remind her that all this might soon be over.

They continued together till the marriage of Miss Campbell to Mr Dixon, a young man, rich and agreeable. This event had lately taken place; too lately for anything to be yet attempted by her less fortunate friend towards entering on her path of duty. With regard to her not accompanying them to Ireland, it was her own choice to give the time of their absence to Highbury; to spend her last months of perfect liberty with those kind relations to whom she was so dear, and Highbury, instead of welcoming that perfect novelty—Mr Frank Churchill—must put up for the present with Jane Fairfax.

Emma was sorry;—to have to pay civilities to a person she did not like through three long months!—to be always doing more than she wished, and less than she ought! why she did not like Jane Fairfax might be a difficult question to answer; Mr Knightley had once told her it was because she saw in her the really accomplished young woman which she wanted to be thought herself; and though the accusation had been eagerly refuted, there were moments of self-examination in which her conscience could not quite acquit her. But she could never get acquainted with her. She did not know how it was, but there was such coldness and reserve—such apparent indifference whether she pleased or not—and then her aunt was such an eternal talker! and she was made such a fuss with by everybody!—because their ages were the same, everybody had supposed they must be so fond of each other.

It was a dislike so little just—every imputed fault was so magnified by fancy, that she never saw Jane Fairfax the first time after any considerable absence without feeling that she had injured her; and now, when the due visit was paid, on her arrival; after a two years' interval, she was particularly struck with the very appearance and manners which for those two whole years she had been depreciating. Jane Fairfax was very elegant, remarkably elegant; and she had herself the highest value for elegance. Her height was pretty, just such as almost everybody would think tall, and nobody could think very tall; her figure particularly graceful; her size a most becoming medium, between fat and thin; her face her features—there was more beauty in them all together than she had remembered; it was not regular, but it was very pleasing beauty. Her eyes, a deep grey, with dark eyelashes and eyebrows; but the skin had a clearness and delicacy which really needed no fuller bloom. It was a style of beauty, of which elegance was the reigning character. Elegance, which, whether of person or of mind, she saw so little in Highbury. There, not to be vulgar, was distinction and merit.

In short, she sat, during the first visit, looking at Jane Fairfax with twofold complacency; the sense of pleasure and the sense of rendering justice; and was determined that she would dislike her no longer. When she considered what all this elegance was destined to, what she was going to sink from, it seemed impossible to feel anything but compassion.

Upon the whole, Emma left her with such softened, charitable feelings as made her look around in walking home, and lament that Highbury afforded no young man worthy of giving her independence; nobody that she could wish to scheme about for her.

These were charming feelings—but not lasting. Former provocations reappeared. The aunt was as tiresome as ever; more tiresome because anxiety for her health was now added to admiration of her powers; and they had to listen to the description of exactly how little bread and butter she ate for breakfast, and how small a slice of mutton for dinner, and Jane's offences rose again. They had music; Emma was obliged to play, and the thanks and praise which necessarily followed appeared to her an affection of candour, an air of greatness meaning only to show off in higher style her own very superior performance. She was, besides, which was the worst of all, so cold, so cautious! There was no getting at her real opinion. Wrapt up in a cloak of politeness, she seemed determined to hazard nothing. She was disgustingly, was suspiciously reserved. She and Mr Frank Churchill had been at Weymouth at the same time. But not a syllable of real information could Emma procure as to what he truly was. "Was he handsome?"—"She believed he was reckoned a very fine young man." "Was he agreeable?" "He was generally thought so". Emma could not forgive her.

CHAPTER TWENTY

As neither provocation nor resentment were discerned by Mr Knightley, who had been of their party, and had seen only proper attention and pleasing behaviour on each side, he was expressing the next morning his approbation of the whole. He had been used to think her unjust to Jane.

"I am happy you approved," said Emma, smiling.

"My dear," said her father instantly, "there is nobody half so attentive and civil as you are. If anything you are too attentive. The muffin last night—if it had been handed round once I think it would have been enough."

"Miss Fairfax is reserved."

"A little: but you will soon overcome all that part of her reserve which ought to be overcome, all that has its foundation in diffidence."

"You think her diffident. I do not see it. I was pleased with my own perseverance in asking questions, and amused to think how little information I obtained."

"She must have found the evening agreeable, Mr Knightley, because she had Emma."

Emma saw his anxiety, and wishing to appease it, said with a sincerity which no one could question.

"She is a sort of elegant creature that one cannot keep one's eyes from. I am always watching her to admire and I do pity her from my heart."

Mr Woodhouse said, "It is a great pity that their circumstances should be so confined. It is so little one can venture to do. Now we have killed a porker, and Emma thinks of sending them a loin or a leg. I think we had better send the leg."

"My dear papa, I sent the whole hind quarter. I knew. You would wish it."

"Emma," said Mr Knightley presently, "I have a piece of news for you, that I think will interest you."

"News! oh! I always like news. Where did you hear it? At Randalls?"

He had time only to say, “No, not at Randalls,” when the door was thrown open, and Miss Bates and Miss Fairfax walked into the room. Full of thanks and full of news, Miss Bates knew not which to give quickest.

“My dear Miss Woodhouse—I come quite overpowered. Such a beautiful hind quarter of pork! You are too bountiful! Have you heard the news? Mr Elton is going to be married.”

Emma had not had time even to think of Mr Elton, and she was so completely surprised that she could not avoid a little start, and a blush at the sound.

“There is my news. I thought it might interest you,” said Mr Knightley, with a smile.

“But where could you hear it?” cried Miss Bates. “For it is not five minutes since I received Mrs Cole’s note. I was only gone down to speak to Patty again about the pork—Jane was standing in the passage—were not you, Jane ?—for my mother was so afraid that we had not any salting pan large enough. So I said I would go down and see, and Jane said, ‘Shall I go down instead? for I think you have a little cold, and Patty had been washing the kitchen.’ ‘Oh! my dear, said I’—well and just then came the note. A Miss Hawkins—that’s all I know.”

“I was with Mr Cole on business an hour and half ago. He had just read Elton’s letter as I was shown in, and handed it to me directly.” “I suppose that never was a piece of news more generally interesting. My dear sir, you really are too bountiful. My mother desires her very best compliments and regards and a thousand thanks, and says you really quite oppress her.”

“We consider our Hartfield pork,” replied Mr Woodhouse—“so very superior to all other pork that Emma and I cannot have a greater pleasure than—”

“Oh! my dear sir, as my mother says our friends are only too good to us. If ever there were people, who, without having great wealth themselves, had every thing they could wish for, I am sure it is us. Well Mr Knightley, and you actually saw the letter; well—”

“It was short,—but cheerful, of course. The information was, as you state, that he was going to be married to a Miss Hawkins. I should imagine it just settled.”

"Mr Elton going to be married!" said Emma, as soon as she could speak. "He will have everybody's wishes for his happiness."

"He is very young to settle," was Mr Woodhouse's observation.

"One feels that it cannot be a very long acquaintance," said Emma, "He has been gone only four weeks."

"Well, my dear Jane, I believe we must be running away. The weather does not look well: and Jane, you had better go home directly—I would not have you in a shower. Oh! Mr Knightley is coming too."

Emma, alone with her father, had half her attention wanted by him—and the other half she could give to her own view of the subject. It was to herself an amusing and a very welcome piece of news, as proving that Mr Elton could not have suffered long; but she was sorry for Harriet: Harriet must feel it.

The shower was heavy, but short. In came Harriet, with just the heated, agitated look which hurrying thither with a full heart was likely to give. Harriet ran eagerly through what she had to tell. She had set out from Mrs Goddard's—she had been afraid it would pour down, she had hurried on as fast as possible, it began to rain, she took shelter at Ford's—Fords' was the principal woollen-draper, linen-draper, and haberdasher's shop united.—And so, there she had sat, when all of a sudden—who should come in, but Elizabeth Martin and her brother. "Elizabeth saw me directly; but he did not; and they both went to the farther end of the shop. Oh! dear; I was so miserable! At last, I fancy he looked round and saw me. Presently she came forward and asked me how I did, she said she was sorry we never met now. I found he was coming up towards me too, he came and spoke, and I said I must go. I had not got three yards from the door, when he came after me, only to say, I had much better go round by Mr Cole's stables, for I should find the near way quite floated by this rain. Oh! Miss Woodhouse, do talk to me and make me comfortable again."

Emma exerted herself, and did try to make her comfortable, by considering all that had passed as a mere trifle, and quite unworthy to be dwelt on. In order to put the Martins out of her head, she was obliged to hurry on the news, which she had mean to give with so much tender caution. Emma learned to be rather glad that there had been such a meeting. It had been serviceable in deadening the first shock, without retaining any influence to alarm.

CHAPTER TWENTY-ONE

Mr Elton returned, a very happy man. He had gone away rejected and mortified, he came back engaged to another, self-satisfied, eager and busy, caring nothing for Miss Woodhouse, and defying Miss Smith.

The charming Augusta Hawkins was in possession of an independent fortune, of so many thousands as would always be called ten; a point of some dignity as well as some convenience; he had not thrown himself away—he had gained her with such delightful rapidity—the first hour of introduction had been so very soon followed by distinguishing notice; the steps so quick from the accidental *rencontre*—smiles and blushes rising in importance—the lady had been so easily impressed, so very ready to have him, that vanity and prudence were equally contented.

The wedding was no distant event. When he next entered Highbury he would bring his bride.

Of the lady, individually, Emma thought very little. *What* she was, must be uncertain, but *who* she was might be found out, and setting aside the £ 10,000, it did not appear that she was at all Harriet's superior. She brought no name, no blood, no alliance. Miss Hawkins was the youngest of the two daughters of a Bristol merchant. As the profits of his mercantile life appeared so moderate it was not unfair to guess the dignity of his line of trade had been very moderate also.

Bristol was her home. Though the father and mother had died some years ago, an uncle remained—in the law line—Emma guessed him to be drudge of some attorney, and too stupid to rise. All the grandeur of the connection seemed dependent on the elder sister who was *very well married*, to a gentlemen in a *great way* who kept two carriages! That was the glory of Miss Hawkins.

CHAPTER TWENTY-TWO

Mr Weston accosted Emma with: "Frank comes tomorrow, he comes for a whole fortnight."

There was no resisting such news, no possibility of avoiding the influence of such a happy face as Mr Weston's. She listened, and smiled, and congratulated.

"I shall soon bring him over to Hartfield," said he.

The morning of the interesting day arrived. She opened the parlour, and saw two gentlemen sitting with her father—Mr Weston and his son. The Frank Churchill so long talked of, so high in interest, was actually before her; he was a *very* good-looking young man; height, air, address, all were unexceptionable, and his countenance had a great deal of the spirit and liveliness of his father's; he looked quick and sensible. She felt immediately that she should like him; and there was a well-bred ease of manner and a readiness to talk, which convinced her that he came intending to be acquainted with her, and acquainted they soon must be.

He had reached Randalls the evening before. She was pleased with the eagerness to arrive which had made him alter his plan, and travel earlier and quicker, that he might gain half a day.

"It is a great pleasure where one can indulge in it," said the young man. "In *coming home* I felt I might do any thing."

The word *home* made his father look on him with fresh complacency. Emma was directly sure that he knew how to make himself agreeable; the conviction was strengthened by what followed. He was very much pleased with Randalls, thought it a most admirably arranged house, admired the situation, the walk to Highbury, Highbury itself, Hartfield still more. He contrived to find an opportunity, while their two fathers were engaged with each other, of introducing his mother-in-law, and speaking of her with so much handsome praise, so much warm admiration, so much gratitude for the happiness she secured to his father, and her very kind reception of himself, as was additional proof of his knowing how to please. She must see more of him to understand his ways, at present she only felt they were agreeable.

A reasonable visit paid, Mr Weston began to move. His son rose also, saying,

"I have the honour of being acquainted with a neighbour of yours, a lady residing in Highbury; a family of the name of Fairfax.

I shall have no difficulty, I suppose, in finding the house?"

"True, true; you are acquainted with Miss Fairfax," cried his father. "Call upon her, by all means." And with a cordial nod from one, and a graceful bow from the other, the two gentlemen took leave.

CHAPTER TWENTY-THREE

The next morning brought Mr Frank Churchill again. He came with Mrs Weston, to whom and to Highbury he seemed to take very cordially. Emma had hardly expected them, and it was an agreeable surprise to perceive them walking up to the house together, arm in arm, especially to see him in company with Mrs Weston, upon his behaviour to whom Emma's opinion of him was to depend. On seeing them together, she became perfectly satisfied. Nothing could be more proper or pleasing than his whole manner to Mrs Weston.

They were all three walking about for an hour or two, first round Hartfield, and afterwards in Highbury. He was delighted with everything. Some of the objects of his curiosity spoke very amiable feelings. He begged to be shown the house which his father had lived in so long, and on recollecting that an old woman who had nursed him was still living, walked in quest of her cottage.

Their first pause was at the Crown Inn. In passing it they gave the history of the large room visibly added; it had been built many years ago for a ball-room. He was immediately interested. They ought to have balls there at least every fortnight through the winter. Why had not Miss Woodhouse revived the former good old days of the room?

At last he was persuaded to move on, and being now almost facing the house where the Bateses lodged, Emma recollected his intended visit the day before.

"And how did you think Miss Fairfax looking?"

"Ill, very ill—Miss Fairfax is naturally so pale, as almost always to give the appearance of ill health."

Emma would not agree to this, and began a warm defence of Miss Fairfax's complexion. He listened with all due deference but he must confess, that to him nothing could make amends for the want of the fine glow of health.

"Did you see her often at Weymouth?" At this moment they were approaching Ford's, and he hastily exclaimed, "Pray let us go in, that I may prove myself to belong to the place. I must buy something at Ford's."

They went in; and while the well-tied parcels were bringing down on the counter he said,—"But I beg your pardon, Miss Woodhouse, you were speaking to me, I will speak the truth. I met her frequently at Weymouth."

"You know Miss Fairfax's situation in life, I conclude; what she is destined to be."

"Yes (rather hesitatingly)—I believe I do."

When they quitted the shop again, "Did you ever hear the young lady we were speaking of, play?" said Frank Churchill.

"I have heard her every year of our lives since we both began. She plays charmingly."

"You think so, do you?—I wanted the opinion of some one who could really judge."

After walking together so long, and thinking so much alike, Emma felt herself well acquainted with him. He was not exactly what she had expected; less of the man of the world in some of his notions, less of the spoiled child of fortune, therefore better than she had expected. His ideas seemed more moderate—his feelings warmer.

CHAPTER TWENTY-FOUR

Emma's very good opinion of Frank Churchill was a little shaken the following day, by hearing that he was gone off to London merely to have his hair cut. There was an air of foppery and nonsense in it which she could not approve.

With the exception of this little blot, he appeared to have a very open temper—certainly a very cheerful and lively one; she could observe nothing wrong in his notions, a great deal decidedly right; he spoke of his uncle with warm regard; and though there was no being attached to the aunt, he acknowledged her kindness with gratitude. This was all very promising; there was nothing to denote him unworthy of the distinguished honour which her imagination had given him; if not of being really in love with her, of being at least very near it, and saved only by her own indifference—(for still her resolution held of never marrying)—the honour, in short, of being marked out for her by all their joint acquaintance.

Mr and Mrs Weston's visit this morning was particularly opportune. She wanted exactly the advice they gave.

This was the occurrence:—The Coles had been settled some years in Highbury, and were friendly, liberal and unpretending, but they were of low origin, in trade, and only moderately genteel. They had lived in proportion to their income, quietly, keeping little company, and that little unexpensively; but the last year or two fortune in general had smiled on them. They added to their expenses of every sort; and by this time were, in fortune and style of living, second only to the family at Hartfield. Their love of society and their new dining-room, prepared everybody for their keeping dinner company; and a few parties, chiefly among the single men, had already taken place. The regular and best families Emma could hardly suppose they would presume to invite. Nothing should tempt *her* to go, if they did. The Coles were very respectable in their way, but they ought to be taught that it was not for them to arrange the terms on which the superior families would visit them. This lesson, she very much feared, they would receive only from herself.

But she had made up her mind so many weeks before that when the insult came at last, it found her very differently affected. Donwell and Randalls had received their invitation, and none had come for her father and herself. She felt that she should like to have the power of refusal; and afterwards, as the idea of the party to be assembled there consisted precisely of those whose society was dearest to her, she did not know that she might not have been tempted to accept.

It was the arrival of this very invitation while the Westons were at Hartfield, which made their presence so acceptable; their advice for her going was most prompt and successful.

The Coles expressed themselves so properly—there was so much real attention in the manner of it, so much consideration for her father.

Mr Woodhouse was to be talked into an acquiescence of his daughters going out to dinner on a day now near at hand, and spending the whole evening away from him. As for *his* going Emma did not wish him to think it possible; the hours would be too late and the party too numerous. He was soon pretty well resigned.

"I am not fond of dinner—visiting," said he. "I never was. No more is Emma. Late hours do not agree with us. The dews of a summer evening are what I would not expose any body to. However, as they are so very desirous to have dear Emma, I cannot wish to prevent it, provided the weather be what it ought, neither damp, nor cold, nor windy." Then turning to Mrs Weston, with a look of gentle reproach—"Ah! Miss Taylor, If you had not married you would have stayed at home with me."

But first of all there must be an answer written to Mrs Cole.

"You will make my excuses, my dear, as civilly as possible. You will say that I am quite an invalid, and go nowhere, and therefore must decline their obliging invitation, beginning with my compliments, of course. But you will do everything right. I need not tell you what is to be done. We must remember to let James know that the carriage will be wanted on Tuesday. I shall have no fears for you with him. And when you get there you must tell him at what time you would have him come for you again.

"Oh, yes papa, I have no fears at all for myself; and I should have no scruples of staying as late as Mrs Weston, but on your account. You must promise me not to sit up."

He did, on the condition of some promises on her side, such as that, if she came home cold she would be sure to warm herself; if hungry, that she would take something to eat; that her own maid should sit up for her.

CHAPTER TWENTY-FIVE

Emma meant to be very happy, in spite of the scene being laid at Mrs Cole's. She was received with a cordial respect which could not but please. The party was rather large. At dinner they were too numerous for any subject of conversation to be general.

Mrs Cole seemed to be relating something that was expected to be very interesting. She had been calling on Miss Bates, and as she entered the room had been struck by the sight of a large-sized square pianoforte. This pianoforte had arrived the day before, to the great astonishment of both aunt and niece—entirely unexpected. Jane herself was quite at a loss, to think who could possibly have ordered it—but now they were both perfectly satisfied that it must be from Col. Campbell.

"My dear Emma," said Mrs Weston, "I am longing to talk to you, I must tell you while the idea is fresh. A little while ago it occurred to me how very sad it would be to have Jane Fairfax walking home and cold as the nights are now. I made my way directly to Miss Bates to assure her that the carriage would be at her service. She was as grateful as possible, but Mr Knightley's carriage had been brought and was to take them home again."

"Very likely," said Emma, "and for an act of unostentatious kindness there is nobody whom I would fix on more than on Mr Knightley.

"Well," said Mrs Weston smiling, "you give him credit for more simple disinterested benevolence than I do. A suspicion darted into my head. I have made a match between Mr Knightley and Jane Fairfax. What do you say to it ?"

"Mr Knightley and Jane Fairfax!" exclaimed Emma, "Dear Mrs Weston, how could you think of such a thing. Mr Knightley must not marry—You would not have little Henry cut out from Donwell. I am amazed that you should think of such a thing."

"My dear Emma, I do not want to injure dear little Henry. If Mr Knightley really wished to marry you would not have him refrain on Henry's account, a boy six years old."

"Mr Knightley marry!—No, I have never had such an idea and I cannot adopt it now. And Jane Fairfax, too, of all women! The imprudence of such a match!"

"I am not speaking of its prudence: merely its probability."

"I see no probability in it. Jane Fairfax mistress of the Abbey! Oh! no, no;—every feeling revolts. I would not have him do so mad a thing."

"Imprudent if you please—but not mad. Except inequality of fortune, and perhaps a little disparity of age, I can see nothing unsuitable."

"But Mr Knightley does not want to marry. I am sure he has not the least idea of it. Do not put it into his head. He is as happy as possible by himself; with his farm, and his sheep, and his library; and he is extremely fond of his brother's children. He has no occasion to marry, either to fill up his time or his heart."

"My dear Emma, as long as he thinks so, it is so; but if he really loves Jane Fairfax—"

"Nonsense! He does not care about Jane Fairfax. In the way of love I am sure he does not. He would do any good to her, or her family; but . . ."

"Well," said Mrs Weston laughing, "perhaps the greatest good he could do them, would be to give Jane such a respectable home.

"If it would be good to her, I am sure it would be evil to himself: a very shameful and degrading connection. How would he bear to have Miss Bates belonging to him?—To have her haunting the Abbey, and thanking him all day long for his great kindness in marrying Jane?—So very kind and obliging!—But he always had been such a kind neighbour! And then fly off, through half a sentence, to her mother's old petticoat. Not that it was such a very old petticoat either—for still it would last a great while—and, indeed, she must thankfully say that their petticoats were all very strong.

"For shame, Emma! Do not mimic her. You divert me against my conscience. And, upon my word, I do not think Mr Knightley would be much disturbed by Miss Bates. Little things do not irritate him. She might talk on and if he wanted to say any thing himself, he would only talk louder, and drown her voice. But the question is not, whether it would be a bad connection for him but whether he wishes it; and I think he does. I have heard him speak so very highly of Jane Fairfax. The interest he takes in her—his anxiety about her health—his concern that she should have no happier prospect. Such an admirer of her performance on the pianoforte, and of her voice! Oh! and I had almost forgotten one idea that occurred to me—this pianoforte, may it not be from Mr Knightley? I think he is just the person to do it, even without being in love."

"Then it can be no argument to prove that he is in love. But I do not think it is at all a likely thing for him to do. Mr Knightley does nothing mysteriously. You take up one idea, Mrs Weston, and run away with it. I see no sign of attachment—believe nothing of the pianoforte—and proof only shall convince me that Mr Knightley has any thought of marrying Jane Fairfax."

They combated the point some time longer till a little bustle in the room showed them Mrs Cole's grand pianoforte in preparation;—and at the same moment Mr Cole approaching to entreat Miss Woodhouse to do them the honour of trying it. Frank Churchill followed Mr Cole, to add his very pressing entreaties, and as, in every respect it suited Emma best to lead, she gave a very proper compliance.

She knew the limitations of her own powers too well to attempt more than she could perform with credit. She wanted neither taste nor spirit in the little things which are generally acceptable. Emma would then resign her place to Miss Fairfax, whose performance, both vocal and instrumental, she never could attempt to conceal from herself, was infinitely superior to her own.

With mixed feelings, she seated herself at a little distance. Frank Churchill sang again. They had sung together once or twice, it appeared, at Weymouth. But the sight of Mr Knightley among the most attentive, soon drew away half Emma's mind. Her objection to Mr Knightley's marrying did not in the least subside. She could see nothing but evil in it. It would be a great disappointment to Mr John Knightley, a real injury to the children—a most mortifying change, and material loss to them all—a very great deduction from her father's daily comfort—and as to herself, she could not at all endure the idea of Jane Fairfax at Donwell Abbey. A Mrs Knightley for them all to give way to! No—Mr Knightley must never marry. Little Henry must remain the heir of Donwell.

Presently Mr Knightley came and sat down by her. As a sort of touchstone, she began to speak of his kindness in conveying the aunt and niece; and though his answer was in the spirit of cutting the matter short, she believed it to indicate only his disinclination to dwell on any kindness of his own.

"This present from the Campbells," said she—"This pianoforte is very kindly given."

"Yes," he replied, and without the smallest apparent embarrassment—"But they would have done better had they given her notice of it. Surprises are foolish things. The pleasure is not enhanced, and the inconvenience is often considerable. I should have expected better judgement in Colonel Campbell."

Soon the proposal of dancing was promoted by Mr and Mrs Cole; and Frank Churchill, coming up with most becoming gallantry to Emma had secured her hand, and led her up to the top.

Two dances, unfortunately, were all that could be allowed. It was growing late.

"Perhaps it is as well," said Frank Churchill, as he attended Emma to her carriage. "I must have asked Miss Fairfax, and her languid dancing would not have agreed with me, after yours."

CHAPTER TWENTY-SIX

Emma did not repent her condescension in going to the Coles. The visit afforded her many pleasant recollections the next day. She must have delighted the Coles—worthy people, who deserved to be made happy!—And left a name behind her that would not soon die away.

Harriet had business at Ford's—Emma thought it most prudent to go with her: another accidental meeting with the Martins would be dangerous. While Harriet was still hanging over muslins and changing her mind, Emma went to the door for amusement.

Mrs Weston and her son-in-law were walking into Highbury. They crossed the road and came forward to her. Mrs Weston informed her that she was going to call on the Bateses in order to hear the new instrument.

"And while Mrs Weston pays her visit, I may be allowed, I hope," said Frank Churchill, "to join your party and wait for her at Hartfield—if you are going home."

"But you had better go with Mr Weston and hear the instrument."

"Do come with me," said Mrs Weston.

Emma watched them in, and, then joined Harriet. Voices approached the shop—or rather one voice and two ladies. Mrs Weston and Miss Bates met them at the door.

"My dear Miss Woodhouse," said the latter. "Come and sit down with us a little while, and give us your opinion of our new instrument; you and Miss Smith—I begged Mrs Weston to come with me, that I might be sure of succeeding".

"I hope Mrs Bates and Miss Fairfax are—"

"Very well, I am much obliged to you. My mother is delightfully well; and Jane caught no cold last night. How is Mr Woodhouse?—I am so glad to hear such a good account. Mrs Weston told me you were here.—Oh! then, said I, I must run across, I am sure Miss Woodhouse will allow me just to run across and entreat her to come in; my mother will be so very happy to see her and now we are such a nice party, she cannot refuse, 'Aye, pray do,' said Mr Frank Churchill—'Miss Woodhouse's opinion of the instrument will be worth having.' But said I, I shall be more sure of succeeding if one of you will go with me—'Oh!' said he, 'wait half-a-minute till I have finished my job'—For, would you believe it, Miss Woodhouse, there he is, in the most obliging manner in the world, fastening in the rivet of my mother's spectacles. I meant to take them over to John Saunders the first thing, but something or other hindered me all the morning. Then the baked apples came home, Mrs Wallis sent them by her boy; they are extremely civil and obliging to us—I have heard some people say that Mrs Wallis can be uncivil and give a very rude answer, but we have never known anything but the greatest attention from them. And it cannot be for the value of our custom now, for what is our consumption of bread, you know. Only three of us—besides dear Jane at present—and she really eats nothing. I dare not let my mother know how little she eats. But about the middle of the day she gets hungry, and there is nothing she likes so well, as these baked apples, and they are extremely wholesome, for I took the opportunity the other day of asking Mr Perry. We have apple dumplings, however, very often. Patty makes an excellent apple-dumpling".

Emma would be very happy to wait on Mrs Bates etc., and they did at last move out of the shop.

"What was I talking of?" said she, beginning again when they were all in the street. "I declare I cannot recollect what I was talking of—When I brought out the baked apples from the closet, and hoped our friends would be so very obliging as to take some, 'Oh!' said, he directly, 'there is nothing in the way of fruit half so good and these are the finest looking home-baked apples I ever saw in my life.' The apples themselves are the very finest sort for baking, beyond a doubt; all from Donwell—some of Mr Knightley's most liberal supply. He sends us a sack every year. There never was such a keeping apple anywhere as one off his trees. My mother says the orchard was always famous in her younger days. Mr Knightley called one morning and Jane was eating these apples, and he asked whether we were not got to the end of our stock. I am sure you must be,' said he and I will send you another supply, I begged he would not—for really as to ours being gone, I could not absolutely say that we had a great many left, it was but half a dozen indeed but they should be all kept for Jane. And when he was gone she almost quarrelled with me—No, I should not say quarrelled, for we never had a quarrel in our lives, but she was quite distressed that I had owned the apples were so nearly gone; she wished I had made him believe we had a great many left. However, the very same evening William Harkins came over with a large basket of apples. I found afterwards that it was all the apples of *that* sort his master had, and now his master had not one left to bake or boil. Mrs Hodges, he said, was quite displeased at their all being sent away. She could not bear that her master should not be able to have another apple-tart this spring. I wanted to keep it from Jane's knowledge; but unluckily, I had mentioned it before I was aware."

Miss Bates had just done, as her visitors walked upstairs at her house, without having any regular narration to attend to, pursued only by the sounds of her good will.

CHAPTER TWENTY-SEVEN

The appearance of the little sitting room as they entered, was tranquillity itself; Mrs Bates slumbering on one side of the fire, Frank Churchill, at a table near her, occupied about her spectacles.

Busy as he was, the young man was yet able to show a most happy countenance on seeing Emma again.

"This is a pleasure," said he, in rather a low voice, "coming earlier than I had calculated."

He contrived that she should be seated by him and was employed in looking out the best baked apple for her, till Jane Fairfax was quite ready to sit down to the pianoforte.

At last Jane began. Mrs Weston had been delighted before and was delighted again, Emma joined her in all her praise, and the pianoforte was pronounced to be altogether of the highest promise.

Emma found the visit had already lasted long; and on examining watches, so much of the morning was perceived to be gone that Mrs Weston and her companion taking leave also, could allow themselves only to walk with the two young ladies to Hartfield gates before they set off for Randalls.

CHAPTER TWENTY-EIGHT

Frank Churchill had danced once at Highbury, and longed to dance again; and the last half hour of an evening which Mr Woodhouse was persuaded to spend with his daughter at Randalls was passed by the two young people in schemes on the subject. Frank's was the first idea, But she had inclination enough for showing people again how delightfully Mr Frank Churchill and Miss Woodhouse danced—for doing that in which she need not blush to compare herself with Jane Fairfax.

His first proposition and request, that the dance begun at Mr Cole's should be finished there—that the same party should be collected, and the same musician engaged, met with the readiest acquiescence. Before the middle of the next day, he was at Hartfield. It soon appeared that he came to announce an improvement.

"Well, Miss Woodhouse," he began. "I bring a new proposal on the subject, a thought of my father's, which wants only your approbation to be acted upon. May I hope for the honour of your hand for the two first dances of this little projected ball to be given, not at Randalls, but at the Crown Inn?—I hope you consent?"

"It appears to me a plan that nobody can object to, if Mr and Mrs Weston do not. I think it admirable and shall be most happy. Papa, do you not think it an excellent improvement ?"

"No, he thought it a very bad plan. A room at an inn was always damp and dangerous. He had never been in the room at the Crown in his life—did not know the people who kept it by sight. They would catch worse colds at the Crown than anywhere—but these sort of things require a good deal of consideration. One cannot resolve upon them in a hurry. If Mr and Mrs Weston will be so obliging as to call here one morning, we may talk it over, and see what can be done—if I could be sure of the rooms being thoroughly aired.

"I can answer for everything of that nature, Sir, because it will be under Mrs Weston's care."

"There, papa!—Now you must be satisfied—our own dear Mrs Weston, who is carefulness itself."

"My father and Mrs Weston are at the Crown at this moment," said Frank Churchill. "I left them there and came for your opinion, hoping you might be persuaded to join them and give your advice on the spot."

Emma was most happy to be called to such a council, and her father engaging to think it all over while she was gone, the two young people set off together without delay. There were Mr and Mrs Weston, delighted to see her and receive her approbation.

"I wish," said Mrs Weston, "one could know which arrangement our guests in general would like best."

'Yes, very true,' said Frank. "You want your neighbours' opinion. Suppose I go and invite Miss Bates to join us?"

"Well," said Mrs Weston, "if you think she will be of any use."

"You will get nothing from Miss Bates," said Emma, "She will be all delight and gratitude, but she will tell you nothing. She will not even listen to your questions."

Here Mr Weston joined them, "Aye, do, Frank. Fetch Miss Bates. Fetch them both. I shall think you a great blockhead, Frank, if you bring the aunt without the niece."

Long before he reappeared, Mrs Weston, like a sweet-tempered woman and a good wife, had found the evils much less than she had supposed before and here ended the difficulties of decision.

When Miss Bates arrived, as a counsellor she was not wanted, but as an approver, she was truly welcome. The party did not break up without Emma's being positively secured for the two first dances by the hero of the evening, nor without her overhearing Mr Weston whisper to his wife. "He has asked her, my dear. That's right. I knew he would."

CHAPTER TWENTY-NINE

One thing only was wanting to make the. prospect of the ball completely satisfactory to Emma—its being fixed for a day within the granted term of Frank Churchill's stay. Enscombe however was gracious, gracious in fact, if not in word. His wish of staying longer evidently did not please; but it was not opposed.

Mr Knightley, either because he did not dance himself, or because the plan had been formed without his being consulted, seemed resolved that it should not interest him. It was not in compliment to Jane Fairfax, however, that he was so indifferent, or so indignant, he was not guided by *her* feelings, for *she* enjoyed the thought of it to an extraordinary degree. She said:—

"Oh! Miss Woodhouse, I hope nothing may happen to prevent the ball. I do look forward to it, with *very* great pleasure."

It was not to oblige Jane Fairfax therefore. She was more and more convinced that Mrs Weston was quite mistaken in that surmise.

Alas! A letter arrived from Mr Churchill to urge his nephew's instant return. Mrs Churchill was far too unwell to do without him. The substance of this letter was forwarded to Emma, in a note from Mrs Weston, instantly. He must be gone within a few hours, though without feeling any real alarm for his aunt. He knew her illnesses; they never occurred but for her own convenience.

Mrs Weston added, that he might be expected at Hartfield very soon. There was no doing any thing, but lament and exclaim. The loss of the ball—the loss of the young man—It was too wretched!—Such a delightful evening as it would have been! Everybody so happy! And she and her partner the happiest!

Emma was ready for her visitor some time before he appeared. His dejection was most evident. He sat really lost in thought; and when rousing himself, it was only to say,

"Of all horrid things, leave-taking is the worst."

"Our poor ball must be given up."

"Ah! why did we wait for any thing? How often is happiness destroyed by foolish preparation—You told us it would be so.—Oh! Miss Woodhouse, why are you always so right? Such a fortnight as it has been! "he continued; "every day more precious and more delightful than the day before!"

"And you must be off this very morning?

"Yes, my father is to join me here, and I must be off immediately."

"Not five minutes to spare even for your friends Miss Fairfax and Miss Bates?"

"Yes—I *have* called there. It was a right thing to do. Miss Bates is a woman, that one *must* laugh at; but that one would not wish to slight. 'It was better to pay my visit, then—"

He hesitated, got up, walked to the window.

"In short," said he, "perhaps, Miss Woodhouse—I think you can hardly be quite without suspicion—"

He looked at her, as if wanting to read her thoughts. It seemed like the forerunner of something absolutely serious, which she did not wish. Forcing herself to speak, therefore, in the hope of putting it by, she calmly said,

"You were quite in the right: it was most natural to pay your visit, then—"

He was silent. She believed he was looking at her; probably reflecting on what she had said, and trying to understand the manner. She heard him sigh. It was natural for him to feel that he had *cause* to sigh. He could not believe her to be encouraging him. A few awkward moments passed, and he sat down again, and in a more determined manner said,

"It was something to feel that all the rest of my time might be given to Hartfield. My regard for Hartfield is most warm—"

He stopped again, rose again, and seemed quite embarrassed. He was more in love with her than Emma had supposed; and who can say how it might have ended, if his father had not made his appearance.

Mr Weston, always alert when business was to be done, said, "It was time to go," and the young man, though he might and did sigh, could not but agree, and rise to take leave.

"I shall hear about you all," said he, "I have engaged Mrs Weston to correspond with me. In her letters I shall be at dear Highbury again."

A very friendly shake of the hand, a very earnest "Goodbye," and the door had soon shut out Frank Churchill.

Emma felt so sorry to part and foresaw so great a loss to their little society from his absence as to begin to be afraid of being too sorry, and feeling it too much. The expectation of seeing him which every morning had brought, the assurance of his attention, his liveliness, his manners! To complete every other recommendation, he had *almost* told her that he loved her. At present she could not doubt his having, a decidedly warm admiration, a conscious preference of herself, and this persuasion, joined to all the rest, made her think that she *must* be a little in love with him, in spite of every previous determination against it.

"I certainly must," said she. "I must be in love; I should be the oddest creature in the world if I were not—for a few weeks at least. Well!—evil to some is always good to others. I shall have many fellow mourners for the ball, but Mr Knightley will be happy."

Mr Knightley however, showed no triumphant happiness. He said, and very steadily, that he was sorry for the disappointment of the others, and with considerable kindness added,

"You, Emma, who have so few opportunities of dancing, you are really out of luck; you are very much out of luck."

It was some days before she saw Jane Fairfax, to judge of her honest regret; but when they did meet, her composure was odious. It was charity to impute some of her unbecoming indifference to the languor of ill health.

CHAPTER THIRTY

Emma continued to entertain no doubt of her being in love. At first, she thought it was a good deal; and afterwards, but little. She had great pleasure in hearing Frank Churchill talked of; she was very often thinking of him, and quite impatient for a letter. But on the other hand, she was still busy and cheerful; and pleasing as he was, she could yet imagine him to have faults; and farther, though thinking of him so much, and forming a thousand amusing schemes for the progress and close of their attachment, the conclusion of every imaginary declaration on his side was that she *refused him.* When she became sensible of this, it struck her that she could not be very much in love. "I do suspect that he is not really necessary to my happiness. So much the better. I am quite enough in love. I should be sorry to be more."

Upon the whole, she was equally contented with her view of his feelings.

"*He* is undoubtedly very much in love—and when he comes again, if his affection continue, I must be on my guard not to encourage it, as my own mind is quite made up. If he had believed me at all to share his feelings, he would not have been so wretched. Could he have thought himself encouraged, his looks and language at parting would have been different. His feelings are warm, but I can imagine them rather changeable. I shall do very well again after a little while, it will be a good thing over; for they say everybody is in love once in their lives, and I shall have been let off easily."

When his letter to Mrs Weston arrived Emma read it with a degree of pleasure and admiration which made her at first shake her head over her own sensations and think she had undervalued their strength. *Miss Woodhouse* appeared more than once, and never without a something of pleasing connection. Compressed into the very lowest vacant corner were these words—"I had not a spare moment for Miss Woodhouse's beautiful little friend. Pray make my excuses and adieus to her."

She yet found, when it was folded up and returned to Mrs Weston, that it had not added any lasting warmth, that she could still do without the writer, and that he must learn to do without her. His recollection of Harriet suggested to her the idea of Harriet's succeeding her in his affections. For Harriet, it would be advantageous and delightful indeed.

Now upon Frank Churchill's disappearance Mr Elton's concerns were assuming the most irresistible form. His wedding day was named. "Mr Elton and his bride" was in everybody's mouth. Poor Harriet was in a flutter of spirits which required all the reasonings and soothings and attention of every kind that Emma could give. Harriet listened submissively, but no change of subject could avail, and the next half hour saw her as anxious and restless about the Eltons as before.

CHAPTER THIRTY-ONE

Mrs Elton was first seen at Church. It must be left for the visits which were then to be paid to settle whether she was very pretty indeed, or only rather pretty or not pretty at all.

Emma had feelings, less of curiosity than of pride or propriety, to make her resolve on not being the last to pay her respects, and she made a point of Harriet's going with her, that the worst of the business might be gone through as soon as possible.

She could not enter the house again without *recollecting*. It was not to be supposed that poor Harriet should not be recollecting too; but she behaved very well, and was only rather pale and silent.

Emma did not really like Mrs Elton. She would not be in a hurry to find fault, but she suspected that there was no elegance. She was almost sure that for a young woman, a stranger, and a bride, there was too much ease. Her person was rather good; her face not unpretty, but neither feature, nor air, nor voice, nor manner, were elegant.

As for Mr Elton, it was an awkward ceremony, to be receiving wedding visits, and when she considered how peculiarly unlucky poor Mr Elton was in being in the same room at once with the woman he had just married, the woman he had wanted to marry and the woman he had been expected to marry, she must allow him to have the right to look as little wise, and as really easy as could be.

"Well, Miss Woodhouse", said Harriet when they had quitted the house,

"I dare say she was very much attached to him."

"Perhaps she might; but it is not every man's fate to marry the woman who loves him best. Miss Hawkins perhaps wanted a home, and thought this the best offer she was likely to have."

"Yes," said Harriet, "nobody could ever have a better."

When the visit was returned Emma could see more and judge better, and the quarter of an hour convinced her that Mrs Elton was a vain woman, extremely well satisfied with herself and thinking much of her own importance; that she meant to shine and be very superior, but with manners which had been formed in a bad school, pert and familiar, that all her notions were drawn from one set of people and one style of living; that if not foolish she was ignorant, and that her society would certainly do Mr Elton no good.

Harriet would have been a better match. If not wise or refined herself, she would have connected him with those who were.

The very first subject after being seated was Maple Grove, "My brother Mr Suckling's seat"—a comparison of Hartfield to Maple Grove followed. "My brother and sister will be enchanted with this place. They have promised us a visit in the spring. They will have their barouche—landau, and therefore, without saying, anything of *our* carriage, we should be able to explore the different beauties extremely well. You have many parties of that kind here, Miss Woodhouse?"

"No; not immediately here, we are rather out of distance of the very striking beauties which attract the sort of parties you speak of."

"Your father's state of health must be a great drawback. Why does he not try Bath?"

"My father tried it more than once, but without receiving any benefit."

"It would be a charming introduction for you, who have lived so secluded a life. A line from me would bring you a host of acquaintance, and my particular friend, Mrs Partridge, would be the very person for you to go into public with."

It was as much as Emma could bear, without being impolite. The idea of her being indebted to Mrs Elton for what was called an *introduction*. The dignity of Miss Woodhouse, of Hartfield was sunk indeed! To prevent further outrage and indignation she changed the subject.

"I do not ask whether you are musical, Mrs Elton. Highbury has long known that you are a superior performer."

"Oh! no, indeed; I am passionately fond of music but my performance is mediocre. I absolutely cannot do without music, *the world* I could give up. Blessed with so many resources within myself, I could do very well without it. I had been accustomed to every luxury at Maple Grove but two carriages were not necessary to my happiness, nor were spacious apartments. But without music, life would be a blank to me. I think, Miss Woodhouse, you and I must establish a musical club." After a moment's pause, Mrs Elton chose another subject.

"We have been calling at Randalls. Mr Weston seems an excellent creature—quite a first-rate favourite with me already. And *she* appears so truly good. She was your governess, I think. I was rather astonished to find her so very lady-like."

"Mrs Weston's manners," said Emma, "were always particularly good. Their propriety, simplicity, and elegance would make them the safest model for any young woman."

"And who do you think came in while we were there? Knightley himself! I must do my husband the justice to say that he need not be ashamed of his friend. Knightley is quite the gentleman."

Happily they were off, and Emma could breathe. "Insufferable woman!" was her immediate exclamation. "Never seen him in her life before, and calls him Knightley! and discover that he is a gentleman. All this ran glibly through her thoughts. Her mind returned to Mrs Elton's offences, and long, very long, did they occupy her.

CHAPTER THIRTY-TWO

Such as Mrs Elton appeared to Emma on this second interview, such she appeared whenever they met again. In one respect Mrs Elton grew even worse than she had appeared at first. Her feelings altered towards Emma. Offended probably, by the little encouragement which her proposals of intimacy met with, she gradually became much more cold and distant. Her manners, too—and Mr Elton's—were unpleasant towards Harriet. They were sneering and negligent.

Mrs Elton took a great fancy to Jane Fairfax. She was not satisfied with expressing a natural and reasonable admiration, she must be wanting to assist and befriend her.

"Jane Fairfax is absolutely charming, Miss Woodhouse. A sweet, interesting creature. So mild and ladylike. I think she has extraordinary talents. Miss Woodhouse, we must exert ourselves and endeavour to do something for her. I shall certainly have her very often at my house, shall introduce her wherever I can, shall have musical parties to draw out her talents, and shall be constantly on the watch for an eligible situation. My acquaintance is so very extensive, that I have little doubt of hearing of something to suit her shortly."

"Poor Jane Fairfax!" thought Emma, "You have not deserved this. This is a punishment beyond what you can have merited. The kindness and protection of Mrs Elton!" She looked on with some amusement. She could not believe it possible that the taste or the pride of Miss Fairfax could endure such society and friendship as the Vicarage had to offer.

Jane had come to Highbury professedly for three months: but now the Campbells had promised their daughter to stay at least till mid-summer. Mrs Dixon had written most pressingly.

But still Jane had declined it!

"She must have some motive, more powerful than appears, for refusing this invitation," was Emma's conclusion. "There is great fear, great caution, great resolution somewhere. She is *not* to be with the *Dixons*. The decree is issued by somebody. But why must she consent to be with the Eltons? Here is quite a puzzle."

Upon her speaking her wonder aloud Mr Knightley said warmly, "Miss Fairfax would not have chosen her. But (with a reproachful smile at Emma) she receives attentions from Mrs Elton, which nobody else pays her."

With a faint blush, she presently replied,

"I know how highly you think of Jane Fairfax. And yet perhaps, you may hardly be aware yourself how highly it is."

"But you are miserably behind-hand. Mr Cole gave me a hint of it six weeks ago. . . . That will never be; however, I can assure you; Miss Fairfax, I dare say, would not have me if I were to ask her; and I am very sure I, shall never ask her."

Emma was pleased enough to exclaim, "You are not vain, Mr Knightley. I will say that for you."

"So you have been settling that I should marry Jane Fairfax."

"No, indeed I have not. You scolded me too much for matchmaking, for me to presume to take such a liberty with you.

I have not the smallest wish for your marrying Jane Fairfax or Jane anybody. You would not come in and sit with us in this comfortable way, if you were married."

"Jane Fairfax is a very charming young woman—but not even Jane Fairfax is perfect. She has a fault. She has not the open temper which a man would wish for in a wife. Her sensibilities, I suspect, are strong—and her temper excellent in its power of forbearance, patience, self-control. She is more reserved, I think, than she used to be—And I love an open temper. No—till Cole alluded to my supposed attachment, it had never entered my head. I saw Jane Fairfax and conversed with her, with admiration and pleasure always—but with no thought beyond."

"Well, Mrs Weston," said Emma triumphantly when he left them—"What do you say now to Mr Knightley's marrying Jane Fairfax?"

"Why really, dear Emma, I say that he is so very much occupied by the idea of *not* being in love with her, that I should not wonder if it were to end in his being so at last."

CHAPTER THIRTY-THREE

Emma could not be satisfied without a dinner at Hartfield for the Eltons. They must not do less than others, or she should be exposed to odious suspicion. After Emma had talked about it for ten minutes, Mr Woodhouse felt no unwillingness.

The persons to be invited, besides the Eltons, must be the Westons and Mr Knightley. Emma was particularly pleased by Harriet's begging to be allowed to decline it. She was delighted with the fortitude of her little friend. She could now invite the very person whom she really wanted to make the eighth, Jane Fairfax. Since her last conversation with Mr Knightley, she was more conscience-stricken about Jane Fairfax than she had often been.

"This is very true," said she, "and it is very shameful—of the same age—and always knowing her—I ought to have been more her friend—She will never like me now."

Every invitation was successful. A circumstance rather unlucky occurred. The two eldest little Knightleys were engaged to pay their grandpapa and aunt a visit of some weeks and their papa now proposed bringing them, which would be the very day of the party. Mr Woodhouse considered eight persons at dinner together as the utmost that his nerves could bear.

John Knightley came; but Mr Weston was unexpectedly summoned to town. He might be able to join them in the evening, but certainly not to dinner.

The day came, and Mr John Knightley, while they waited for dinner, was talking to Miss Fairfax.

"I hope you did not venture far, Miss Fairfax, this morning, or I am sure you must have been wet."

"I went only to the post office," said she. "I always fetch the letters when I am here."

"When you have lived to my age, you will begin to think letters are never worth going through the rain for."

"I can easily believe that letters are very little to you. You have everybody dearest to you always at hand. I, probably, never shall again, and therefore a post office, I think, must always have power to draw me out, in worse weather than today."

"As an old friend, you will allow me to hope, Miss Fairfax, that ten years hence you may have as many concentrated objects as I have."

It was kindly said, and very far from giving offence. A pleasant "thank you" seemed meant to laugh it off, but a blush, a quivering lip, a tear in the eye, showed that it was felt beyond a laugh.

Her attention was now claimed by Mr Woodhouse, who being—according to his custom on such occasions,—making the circle of his guests, and paying his particular compliments to the ladies, was ending with her—and with all his mildest urbanity, said,

"I am very sorry to hear, Miss Fairfax, of your being out this morning in the rain. Young ladies should take care of themselves—young ladies are delicate plants. They should take care of their health and their complexion. My dear, did you change your stockings?"

"Yes, sir, I did, indeed; and I am very much obliged by your kind solicitude about me."

"My dear Miss Fairfax, young ladies are very sure to be cared for—I hope your good grandmamma and aunt are well. They are some of my very old friends. I wish my health allowed me to be a better neighbour. You do us a great deal of honour today, I am sure. My daughter and I are both highly sensible of your goodness, and have the greatest satisfaction in seeing you at Hartfield."

The kind-hearted, polite old man might then sit down and feel that he had done his duty and made every fair lady welcome and easy.

By this time, the walk in the rain had reached Mrs Elton.

"My dear Jane. It is a sign I was not there to take care of you. The man who fetches our letters every morning (one of our men, I forget his name) shall inquire for yours too and bring them to you."

"Excuse me," said Jane earnestly, "I cannot by any means consent, to such an arrangement, so needlessly troublesome to your servants."

Jane looked as if she did not mean to be conquered. Jane's solicitude about fetching her own letters had not escaped Emma. She had heard and seen it all; and felt some curiosity to know whether the wet walk of this morning had produced any. She suspected that it had; that it would not have been so resolutely encountered but in full expectation of hearing from some one very dear, and that it had not been in vain. She thought there was an air of greater happiness than usual—a glow both of complexion and spirits.

She could have made an inquiry or two, but she abstained. She was determined not to utter a word that should hurt Jane Fairfax's feelings; and they followed the other ladies out of the room, arm in arm, with an appearance of goodwill highly becoming to the beauty and grace of each.

CHAPTER THIRTY-FOUR

When the ladies returned to the drawing room after dinner, Emma found it hardly possible to prevent their making two distinct parties. She and Mrs Weston were obliged to be almost always talking together or silent together. Mrs Elton left them no choice. If Jane repressed her for a little time, she soon began again. Much that passed between them was in a half whisper, especially on Mrs Elton's side. The post office—catching cold—fetching letters—and friendship, were long under discussion, Inquiries whether she had yet heard of any situation likely to suit her, and professions of Mrs Elton's meditated activity.

"Mrs Elton, I am quite serious in wishing nothing to be done till the summer."

"And I am quite serious too," replied Mrs Elton gaily, "in resolving to be always on the watch, that nothing really unexceptionable may pass us."

"In this style she ran on, till Mr Woodhouse came into the room.

Emma heard her saying in the same half-whisper to Jane,

"Here comes this dear old beau of mine. Only think of his gallantry in coming away before the other men! What a dear creature he is; I assure you I like him excessively. I admire all that quaint, old-fashioned politeness, it is much more to my taste than modern ease; modern ease often disgusts me. But this good old Mr Woodhouse, I wish you had heard his gallant speeches to me at dinner. Oh! I assure you I began to think my *caro sposo* would be absolutely jealous. I fancy I am rather a favourite; he took notice of my gown. How do you like it? Selina's choice—handsome; I think, but I do not know whether it is not over-trimmed; I have the greatest dislike to the idea of being over-trimmed—quite a horror of finery. I must put on a few ornaments now, because it is expected of me. A bride, you know, must appear like a bride, but my natural taste is all for simplicity. But I am quite in the minority. I have some notion of putting such a trimming as this to my white and silver poplin. Do you think it will look well?"

The whole party was just assembled in the drawing-room when Mr Weston made his appearance among them. Happy and cheerful as usual, he was making himself agreeable among the rest. He gave Mrs Weston a letter; it was from Frank.

"Read it," said he. "it will give you pleasure. Well, he is coming, you see; good news, I think." Mrs Weston was most comfortably pleased on the occasion.

Emma was a little occupied in weighing her own feelings and trying to understand the degree of her agitation, which she rather thought was considerable.

CHAPTER THIRTY-FIVE

A very little quiet reflection was enough to satisfy Emma as to the nature of her agitation on hearing this news of Frank Churchill. It was not for herself she was feeling at all apprehensive or embarrassed; it was for him. Her own attachment was not worth thinking of; but if he who had undoubtedly been always so much the most in love of the two, were to be returning with the same warmth of sentiment, it would be very distressing. She did not mean to have her own affections entangled again.

She wished she might be able to keep him from an absolute declaration. That would be so very painful a conclusion of their present acquaintance!

Frank Churchill was at Highbury very soon afterwards. He rode down for a couple of hours. They met with the utmost friendliness. There could be no doubt of his great pleasure in seeing her. She watched him well. It was a clear thing he was less in love than he had been.

This was the only visit from Frank Churchill in the course of ten days. His aunt could not bear to have him leave her. That she was really ill was very certain, he had declared himself convinced of it.

It soon appeared that London was not the place for her. They were going to remove immediately to Richmond. Mrs Churchill had been recommended to the medical skill of an eminent person there.

Mr Weston's own happiness was indisputable. It was the very circumstance he could have wished for. Now, it would be really having Frank in their neighbourhood—What were nine miles to a young man?—An hour's ride. He would be always coming over.

One good thing was immediately brought to a certainty by this removal—the ball at the Crown. Every preparation was resumed. A very few tomorrows stood between the young people of Highbury and happiness.

CHAPTER THIRTY-SIX

No misfortune occurred again to prevent the ball. The day arrived; Frank Churchill, in all the certainty of his own self, reached Randalls before dinner, and everything was safe.

No second meeting had there yet been between him and Emma. The room at the Crown was to witness it. Mr Weston had been so very earnest in his entreaties for, her arriving there as soon as possible after themselves, before any other persons came, that she could not refuse him. Frank Churchill seemed to have been on the watch, and though he did not say much, his eyes declared that he meant to have a delightful evening. They all walked about together to see that everything was as it should be.

Frank was standing by her but not steadily; there was a restlessness, which showed a mind not at ease—impatient to begin, or afraid of being always near her.

Mr and Mrs Elton appeared, all smiles. "But Miss Bates and Miss Fairfax!" said Mr Weston, looking about. "We thought you were to bring them."

The mistake had been slight. The carriage was sent for them. Emma longed to know what Frank's first opinion of Mrs Elton might be; how he was affected by the studied elegance of her dress and her smiles of graciousness. He was immediately qualifying himself to form an opinion, by giving her very proper attention, after the introduction had passed.

In a few minutes the carriages returned. Somebody talked of rain—"I will see that there are umbrellas, sir," said Frank to his father, and away he went. Mr Weston was following; but Mrs Elton detained him, to gratify him by her opinion of his son; and so briskly did she begin that the young man himself, though by no means moving slowly, could hardly be out of hearing.

"A very fine young man indeed, Mr Weston. You know I candidly told you I should form my own opinion; and I am happy to say that I am extremely pleased with him—You may believe me. I never compliment. I think him a very handsome young man and his manners are precisely what I like and approve—so truly the gentleman, without the least conceit or puppyism." Mrs Elton turned to Mrs Weston. "I have no doubt of its being our carriage with Miss Bates and Jane, I believe we drive faster than anybody—What a pleasure it is to send one's carriage for a friend—I understand you were so kind as to offer, but another time it will be quite unnecessary. You may be very sure I shall always take care of *them*."

Miss Bates came in talking,

"So very obliging of you!—No rain at all. I do not care for myself. Quite thick shoes. Well! This is brilliant indeed! Nothing waiting. Could not have imagined it. Oh! Mr Weston, you must really have had Aladdin's lamp. Ah! dear Mrs Elton, so obliged to you for the carriage! Oh! and I am sure our thanks are due to you, Mrs Weston, on that score. Mrs Elton had most kindly sent Jane a note. But two such offers in one day—Never were such neighbours. My dear Jane, are you sure you did not wet your feet? It was but a drop or two, but I am so afraid:—but Mr Frank Churchill was so extremely—and there was a mat to step upon—I shall never forget his extreme politeness Ah! here's Miss Woodhouse—Dear Miss Woodhouse, how do you do?—Very well I thank you, quite well. This is meeting quite in fairyland! Such transformation! Must not compliment. I know—(eyeing Emma most complacently)—that would be rude but upon my word, Miss Woodhouse, you do look—how do you like Jane's hair? You are a judge—She did it all herself. Quite wonderful how she does her hair!—No hairdresser from London I think could."—

Frank Churchill returned to his station by Emma. She found herself necessarily overhearing the discourse of Mrs Elton and Miss Fairfax. He was thoughtful. Whether he were overhearing too she could not determine. Mrs Elton was evidently wanting to be complimented herself. "How do you like my gown?—How do you like my trimming? Nobody can think less of dress in general than I do—but upon such an occasion as this, when everybody's eyes are so much upon me, and in compliment to the Westons—who I have no doubt are giving this ball chiefly to do me honour—I would not wish to be inferior to others. And I see very few pearls in the room except mine—So Frank Churchill is a capital dancer, I understand—We shall see if our styles suit—A fine young man certainly is Frank Churchill. I like him very well."

At this moment Frank began talking so vigorously that Emma could not but imagine he had overheard his own praise and did not want to hear more. Mr Elton joined the ladies and his wife was heard exclaiming. "I was this moment telling Jane I thought you would begin to be impatient for tidings of us."

"Jane!" repeated Frank Churchill, with a look of surprise and displeasure—"that is easy—but Miss Fairfax does not disapprove it. I suppose—Where is my father?—When are we to begin dancing?"

Emma could hardly understand him: he seemed in an odd humour. He walked off to find his father. It had just occurred to Mrs Weston that Mrs Elton must be asked to begin the ball; that she would expect it; which interfered with all their wishes of giving Emma that distinction—Emma heard the sad truth with fortitude.

"She will think Frank ought to ask her."

Frank turned instantly to Emma to claim her former promise, and boasted himself an engaged man. Then Mr Weston and Mrs Elton led the way, Mr Frank Churchill and Miss Woodhouse followed; though she had always considered the ball as peculiarly for her. In spite of this little rub, however, Emma was smiling with enjoyment; that she had so many hours of unusual festivity before her. She was more disturbed by Mr Knightley's not dancing, than by anything else. There he was among the standers-by. He ought to be dancing,—not classing himself with the husbands, and fathers. So young he looked! He could not have appeared to greater advantage perhaps anywhere, than where he had placed himself. His tall, firm, upright figure, among the bulky forms and stooping shoulders of the elderly men, was such as Emma felt must draw everybody's eyes. He moved a few steps nearer, and those few steps were enough to prove in how gentlemanlike a manner, with what natural grace, he must have danced, would he but take the trouble. She wished he could love a ballroom better and could like Frank

Churchill better. There was nothing like flirtation between her and her partner. They seemed more like cheerful, easy friends, than lovers.

The ball proceeded pleasantly. Everybody seemed happy. The two last dances before supper were begun. Harriet had no partner. Emma saw Mr Elton sauntering about. He would not ask Harriet to dance if it were possible to be avoided; she was sure he would not. The kind hearted, gentle Mrs Weston had left her seat to join him and say, "Do not you dance, Mr Elton?" to which his prompt reply was, "Most readily, Mrs Weston, if you will dance with me."

"Me!—oh! no—I would get you a better partner than myself. I am no dancer."

"If Mrs Gilbert wishes to dance," said he, "I shall have great pleasure at any time to stand up with an old friend like Mrs Gilbert."

"Mrs Gilbert does not mean to dance but there is a young lady whom I should be very glad to see dancing—Miss Smith."

"Miss Smith!—oh!—I had not observed. You are extremely obliging. But my dancing days are over, Mrs Weston. You will excuse me.

"Mrs Weston said no more; and Emma could imagine with what surprise and mortification she must be returning to her seat. This was Mr Elton! the amiable, obliging, gentle Mr Elton. He had joined Mr Knightley, and was arranging himself for settled conversation, while smiles of high glee passed between him and his wife.

In another moment a happier sight caught her. Mr Knightley leading Harriet to the set!—Never had she been more surprised, seldom more delighted. She was all pleasure and gratitude, both for Harriet and herself and longed to be thanking him.

His dancing proved to be extremely good. It was not thrown away on Harriet. She bounded higher than ever, flew farther down the middle, and was in a continual course of smiles.

Mr Elton had retreated into the cardroom, looking (Emma trusted) very foolish. She did not think he was quite so hardened as his wife, though growing very like her—she spoke some of her feelings, by observing audibly to her partner.

"Knightley has taken pity on poor little Miss Smith! Very good-natured, I declare—".

Supper was announced: and Miss Bates might be heard from that moment, without interruption.

"Jane, Jane where are you? Excellent dancing indeed! Yes, my dear, I ran home, as I said I should, to help grandmamma to bed, and got back again, and nobody missed me."

Emma had no opportunity of speaking to Mr Knightley till after supper; her eyes invited him irresistibly to come to her and be thanked. He was warm in his reprobation of Mr Elton's conduct; it had been unpardonable rudeness.

"They aimed at wounding more than Harriet," said he. "Emma, why is it that they are your enemies? But confess, Emma, that you did want him to marry Harriet."

"I did," replied Emma, "and they cannot forgive me. I do own myself to have been completely mistaken in Mr Elton. There is a littleness about him which you discovered, and which I did not."

"And, in return for your acknowledging so much, I will do you the justice to say, that you would have chosen for him better than he has chosen for himself. Harriet Smith has some first-rate qualities, which Mrs Elton is totally without. An unpretending, single-minded, artless girl—infinitely to be preferred by any man of sense and taste to such a woman as Mrs Elton. I found Harriet more, conversible than I expected . . . whom are you going to dance with ?" asked Mr Knightley.

She hesitated a moment, and then replied, "With you, if you will ask me."

"Will you?" said he, offering his hand.

"Indeed I will."

CHAPTER THIRTY-SEVEN

Emma walked about the lawn the next morning. She was just turning to the house with spirits freshened up, when the great iron sweepgate opened, and two persons entered whom she had never less expected to see together—Frank Churchill, with Harriet leaning on his arm—actually Harriet!—A moment sufficed to convince her that something extraordinary had happened. Harriet looked white and frightened, and he was trying to cheer her. They were all three soon in the hall, and Harriet immediately sinking into a chair, fainted away.

A few minutes made Emma acquainted with the whole. Miss Smith, and Miss Bickerton, another parlour boarder at Mrs Goddard's, had walked out together. About half a mile beyond Highbury, they had suddenly perceived a party of gipsies. A child came towards them to beg. Miss Bickerton, excessively frightened, gave a great scream, and calling on Harriet to follow her, ran and made the best of her way back to Highbury. But poor Harriet could not follow. She suffered from cramp and was soon assailed by half a dozen children, headed by a stout woman, and a great boy, all clamorous and impertinent in look. More and more frightened, taking out her purse, she gave them a shilling. But she was surrounded by the whole gang, demanding more.

In this state Frank Churchill had found her. By a most fortunate chance his leaving Highbury had been delayed so as to bring him to her assistance at this critical moment. Harriet eagerly clinging to him, had just strength enough to reach Hartfield, before her spirits were quite overcome.

Such an adventure as this—a fine young man and a lovely young woman thrown together in such a way, could hardly fail of suggesting certain ideas to the coldest heart and the steadiest brain. So Emma thought at least—especially with such a groundwork of anticipation as her mind had already made.

CHAPTER THIRTY-EIGHT

A very few days after this Harriet came to Emma with a small parcel in her hand. "Cannot you guess what this parcel holds?" said she, with a conscious look. "I am going to throw it in the fire, and I wish you to see me do it. It was very wrong of me, you know, to keep any remembrances, after he was married. I shall be happier to burn them. There it goes, and there is an end, thank Heaven! of Mr Elton."

"And when," thought Emma, "'will there be a beginning of Mr Churchill?" She had soon afterwards reason to believe that the beginning was already made.

About a fortnight after the alarm, they came to a sufficient explanation and quite undesignedly. She merely said, in the course of some trivial chat, "Well, Harriet, whenever you marry I should advise you to do so and so." She heard Harriet say, "I shall never marry."

"Never marry!—This is a new resolution."

"It is one that I shall never change, however."

"I hope it is not in compliment to Mr Elton."

"Mr Elton indeed!" cried Harriet indignantly, "Oh! no—" and Emma could just catch the words, "so superior to Mr Elton."

Emma believed it would be wiser for her to say and know at once, all that she meant to say and know. Plain dealing was always best. She was decided, and spoke.

"Harriet, I will not affect to be in doubt of your meaning. Your resolution, or rather your expectation of never marrying results from your idea that the person whom you might prefer, would be too greatly your superior in situation to think of you. Is not it so?"

"Oh! Miss Woodhouse, it is a pleasure to me to admire him at a distance—and to think—of his infinite superiority to all the rest of the world, with the gratitude, wonder and veneration, which are so proper, in me especially."

"Harriet, the service he rendered you was enough to warm your heart."

"Service! oh! it was such an inexpressible obligation!—The very, recollection of it—when I saw his coming—his noble look—and my wretchedness before. Such a change! From perfect misery to perfect happiness."

"It is very natural and it is honourable, I think, to choose so well and so gratefully. Perhaps it will be wisest in you to check your feelings while you can. Be observant of him. Let his behaviour be the guide of your sensations. I give you this caution now because I shall never speak to you on the subject. Let no name pass our lips. He is your superior, no doubt, but Harriet, more wonderful things have taken place, there have been matches of greater disparity. But I would not have you too sanguine, though, however it may end, be assured that your raising your thoughts to *him* is a mark of good taste which I still always know how to value."

Harriet kissed her hand in silent and submissive gratitude.

Emma was very decided in thinking such an attachment no bad thing for her friend. It must be saving her from the danger of degradation.

CHAPTER THIRTY-NINE

Mr Knightley, who had taken an early dislike to Frank Churchill, was only growing to dislike him more. He began to suspect him of some double dealing in his pursuit of Emma. That Emma was his object appeared indisputable. Everything declared it; his own, attentions, his father's hints, his mother-in-law's guarded silence: words, conduct, discretion and indiscretion told the same story. Mr Knightley began to suspect him of some inclination to trifle with Jane Fairfax. There were symptoms of intelligence between them—he thought so at least—symptoms of admiration on his side. He had seen a look, more than a single look, at Miss Fairfax, which, from the admirer of Miss Woodhouse, seemed somewhat out of place, nor could he avoid observations which brought him yet stronger suspicion of private understanding between Frank Churchill and Jane.

He had walked up one day after dinner, as he very often did, to spend his evening at Hartfield. Emma and Harriet were going to walk; he joined them, and on returning they fell in with a larger party, Mr and Mrs Weston, and their son, Miss Bates and her niece. Emma pressed them all to go in and drink tea.

Mr Perry passed by on horseback. "By the bye," said Frank Churchill to Mrs Weston, "what became of Mr Perry's plan of setting up his carriage?"

Mrs Weston looked surprised, and said, "I did not know that he ever had any such plan."

"Nay, I had it from you. You wrote me word of it three months ago."

"Me! impossible! I never heard of it till this moment."

"What is this," cried Mr Weston, "You had it from himself, had you?"

"No, sir", replied his son, laughing. "I seem to have had it from nobody—very odd!—I really was persuaded of Mrs Weston's having mentioned it in one of her letters to Enscombe, many weeks ago, with all these particulars—but as she declares she never heard a syllable of it before, of course it must have been a dream. I am a great dreamer."

"It is odd though," observed his father, "that you should have such a regular connected dream about people whom it was not very likely you should be thinking of at Enscombe."

"Why, to own the truth," cried Miss Bates, who had been trying in vain to be heard, "there is no denying that Mr Frank Churchill might have—I do not mean to say that he did not dream it. I am sure I have sometimes the oddest dreams in the world—but if I am questioned I must acknowledge that there was such an idea last spring; for Mrs Perry herself mentioned it to my mother, but it was quite a secret known to nobody else. Jane, don't you remember grandmama's telling us of it when we got home, she had no objection to telling us, of course, but it was not to go beyond—Extraordinary dream indeed!"

They were entering the hall. Mr Knightley's eyes had preceded Miss Bates in a glance at Jane. From Frank Churchill's face, where he thought he saw confusion suppressed or laughed away, he had involuntarily turned to her but she was too busy with her shawl. Mr Knightley suspected in Frank Churchill the determination of catching her eye—he seemed watching her intently in vain—Jane passed between them into the hall and looked at neither.

There was no time for further remark or explanation. The dream must be borne with, and Mr Knightley must take his seat with the rest. Tea passed pleasantly.

"Miss Woodhouse," said Frank Churchill, "have your nephews taken away their box of letters? I want to puzzle you again." Emma produced the box. They were rapidly forming words for each other or any body else who would be puzzled. Frank Churchill placed a word before Miss Fairfax. She gave a slight glance around the table and applied herself to it. Mr Knightley so placed, as to see them all and it was his object to see as much as he could with as little apparent observation. The word was discovered and with a faint smile pushed away. Harriet, eager after every fresh word, fell to work. The word was *blunder* and as, Harriet exultingly proclaimed it, there was a blush on Jane's cheek which gave it a meaning not otherwise ostensible.

Mr Knightley connected it with the dream; but how it could all be was beyond his comprehension. He feared there must be some decided involvement. Double-dealing seemed to meet him at every turn. These letters were but the vehicle for gallantry and trick. It was a child's play, chosen to conceal a deeper game on Frank Churchill's part.

With great indignation did he continue to observe him, with great alarm and distrust.

He remained at Hartfield after the rest. He certainly must, as a friend—an anxious friend—give Emma some hint, ask her some question. He could not see her in a situation of such danger, without trying to preserve her. It was his duty.

He owed it to her, to risk anything that might be involved in an unwelcome interference, rather than for welfare; to encounter any thing, rather than the remembrance of neglect in such a cause.

"My dear Emma," said he, with earnest kindness, "do you think you perfectly understand the degree of acquaintance between Mr Frank Churchill and Miss Fairfax?"

"Between Mr Frank Churchill and Miss Fairfax? Oh! Yes, perfectly—why do you make a doubt of it?"

"Have you never at any time had reason to think that he admired her, or that she admired him?"

"Never, never," she cried with an open eagerness—"Never, for the twentieth part of a moment did such an idea occur to me."

"I have lately imagined that I saw symptoms of attachment between them—certain expressive looks, which I did not believe meant to be in public."

"Oh! you amuse me excessively, There is no admiration, between them I do assure you. They are as far from any attachment or admiration for one another, as any two beings of the world can be. That is, I *presume* it to be so, on her side, and an *answer*, for its being so on his.

She spoke with a confidence which staggered, with a satisfaction which silenced Mr Knightley. He found he could not be useful, and soon afterwards he took a hasty leave, and walked home to the solitude of Donwell Abbey.

CHAPTER FORTY

Mr and Mrs Suckling could not possibly come till the autumn. Mrs Elton was very much disappointed. But everything need not be put off. Why should not they explore to Box Hill though the Sucklings did not come? That there was to be such a party had been long generally known. Emma had never been to Box Hill and she and Mr Weston had agreed to choose some fine morning and drive thither, in a quiet unpretending elegant way.

Emma could not but feel some surprise; and a little displeasure on hearing from Mr Weston that he had been proposing to Mrs Elton that the two parties should unite, and go together. She found herself therefore obliged to consent to an arrangement which she would have done a great deal to avoid. Every feeling was offended. A lame carriage horse threw everything into sad uncertainty. Mrs Elton's resources were inadequate to such an attack.

"Is not this most vexatious, Knightley?" she cried, "What are we to do?"

"You had better explore to Donwell," replied Mr Knightley.

"That may be done without horses. Come and eat my strawberries. They are ripening fast."

If Mr Knightley did not begin seriously, he was obliged to proceed so for his proposal was caught at with delight; and the "Oh! I should like it of all things," was not plainer in words than manner. Donwell was famous for its strawberry beds, which seemed a plea for the invitation, but no plea was necessary: cabbage beds would have been enough to tempt the lady, who only wanted to be going somewhere. She was extremely grateful for such a proof of intimacy, such a distinguishing compliment as she chose to consider it.

"You may depend upon me," said she, "I certainly will come. Name your day, and I will come. You will allow me to bring Jane Fairfax?"

"I cannot name a day," said he, "till I have spoken to some others whom I would wish to meet you."

"Oh! leave all that to me. Only give me a *carte blanche*—I am Lady Patroness, you know. It is my party. I will bring friends with me."

"I hope you will bring Elton," said he, "but I will not trouble you to give any other invitations."

"Oh! now you are looking sly. But consider;—you need not be afraid of delegating power to *me*. I am no young lady. Married women, you know, may be safely authorised. It is my party. Leave it all to me. I will invite your guests."

"No," he calmly replied,—"there is but one married woman in the world whom I can ever allow to invite what guests she pleases to Donwell, and that one is—"

"Mrs Weston, I suppose," interrupted Mrs Elton, rather mortified.

"No—Mrs Knightley;—and, till she is in being, I will manage such matters myself."

"Well, I shall bring Jane with me—Jane and her aunt. The rest I leave to you. I have no objections at all to meeting the Hartfield family. I know you are attached to them. I shall wear a large bonnet, and bring one of my little baskets hanging on my arm. And Jane will have such another. We are to walk about your gardens, and gather the strawberries ourselves, and sit under trees—a table spread in the shade, you know. Everything as natural and simple as possible. Is not that your idea?"

"Not quite. My idea of the simple and natural will be to have the table spread in the dining room. When you are tired of eating strawberries in the garden there shall be cold meat in the house."

Mr Knightley wished to persuade Mr Woodhouse, as well as Emma, to join the party; and he knew that to have any of them sitting down out of doors to eat would inevitably make him ill.

Mr Woodhouse did consent. He could sit still with Mrs Weston, while the dear girls walked about the gardens.

In the meantime the lame horse recovered so fast, that the party to Box Hill was again under happy consideration; and at last Donwell was settled for one day, and Box Hill for the next.

It was long since Emma had been at the Abbey. She was glad to look around her till it was necessary to do as the others did and collect around the strawberry beds.

The whole party were assembled, excepting Frank Churchill, who was expected every moment from Richmond. It was hot; and after walking some time over the gardens in a scattered, dispersed way, they followed one another to the delicious shade of a broad, avenue of limes. Emma perceived Mr Knightley and Harriet distinct from the rest, quietly, leading the way. Mr Knightley and Harriet!—But she was glad to see it. There had been a time when he could have scorned her as a companion. Now they seemed in pleasant conversation. She joined them. He was giving Harriet information as to modes of agriculture.

Emma walked into the hall—and was hardly there, when Jane Fairfax appeared, coming quickly in from the garden, and with a look of escape.

"Will you be so kind," said she, "when I am missed, as to say that I am gone home?"

"Certainly, if you wish it;—but you are not going to Highbury alone?"

"Yes, I shall be at home in twenty minutes."

"But it is too far, to be walking quite alone. Let my father's servant go with you—Let me order the carriage. It can be round—in five minutes."

"Thank you—I would rather walk—And for *me* to be afraid of walking alone! I, who may so soon have to guard others!"

She spoke with great agitation; and Emma very feelingly replied, "I must order the carriage. You are fatigued already."

"I am," she answered, "quick walking will refresh me. Miss Woodhouse, we all know at times what it is to be wearied in spirits. Mine, I confess, are exhausted. The greatest kindness you can show me will be to let me have my own way."

Emma had not another word to oppose, and watched her safely off with the zeal of a friend. Her parting look was grateful and her parting words, "Oh! Miss Woodhouse, the comfort of being sometimes alone!" seemed to burst from an overcharged heart, and to describe somewhat of the continual endurance to be practised even towards some of those who loved her best.

Jane had not been gone a quarter of an hour, when Frank Churchill entered the room. *They* were right who had named Mrs Churchill as the cause. He had been detained by a temporary increase of illness in her, and had quite given up every thought of coming, till very late. The heat was excessive—almost wished he had stayed at home. "You will all be going soon I suppose; the whole party breaking up. I met *one* as I came—Madness in such weather!—absolute madness!"

Emma perceived that Frank Churchill's state must be best defined by the expressive phrase of being out of humour, saying in secret—.

"I am glad I have done being in love with him. I should not like a man who is so soon discomposed by a hot morning. Harriet's sweet easy temper will not mind it."

He was not in his best spirits, but seemed trying to improve them. "Go and eat and drink a little more, and you will do very well," she said.

"No—I shall sit by you. You are my best cure."

"We are going to Box Hill tomorrow. You will stay, and go with us?"

"No, certainly not; I shall go home in the cool of the evening."

It was time for everybody to go. With a short final arrangement for the next day's scheme, they parted. Frank Churchill's little inclination to exclude himself increased so much, that his last words to Emma were:

"Well, if you wish me to stay and join the party, I will." She smiled her acceptance.

CHAPTER FORTY-ONE

They had a very fine day for Box Hill. Nothing was wanting but to be happy when they got there. But in the general amount of the day there was a want of spirits, which could not be got over.

At first it was downright dullness to Emma. She had never seen Frank Churchill so silent and stupid. When they all sat down it was a great deal better, for Frank Churchill grew talkative and gay. Every distinguished attention that could he paid was paid to her. To amuse her and to be agreeable in her eyes seemed all that he cared for, and Emma, glad to be enlivened, not sorry to be flattered, was gay and easy too, and, gave him all the friendly encouragement, which now in her own estimation, meant nothing, though in the judgement of most people looking on, it must have had such an appearance as no English word but flirtation could very well describe. Not that Emma was gay and thoughtless, it was rather because she felt less happy than she had expected. She laughed because she was disappointed, and though she liked him for his attentions, they were not winning back her heart. She still intended him for her friend.

"Ladies and gentlemen—I am ordered by Miss Woodhouse to say, that she only requires something very entertaining from each of you, in a general way. Either one thing very clever or two things moderately clever—or three things very dull indeed, and she engages to laugh heartily at them all."

"Oh! very well," exclaimed Miss Bates, "then I need not be uneasy. I shall be sure to say three dull things as soon as ever I open my mouth, shan't I?"

Emma could not resist.

"Ah! ma'am, but there may be a difficulty. Pardon me—but you will be limited as to number—only three at once."

Miss Bates, deceived by the mock ceremony of her manner, did not immediately catch her meaning; but, when it burst on her, it could not anger, though a slight blush showed that it could pain her.

"Ah! Yes, I see what she means (turning to Mr Knightley) and I will try to hold my tongue. I must make myself very disagreeable, or she would not have said such a thing to an old friend."

"Oh! for myself, I protest I must be excused," said Mrs Elton. "Yes, pray pass *me*," added her husband. "An old married man quite good for nothing. Shall we walk, Augusta?"

"With all my heart. Come, Jane, take my other arm."

Jane declined it, however, and the husband and wife walked off. "Happy couple!" said Frank Churchill, "How well they suit one another!—Very lucky—marrying as they did, upon an acquaintance formed only in a public place!—They only knew each other, I think, a few weeks in Bath! It is only by seeing women in their own homes, among their own set, just as they always are, that you can form any judgement. How many a man has committed himself on a short acquaintance, and rued it all the rest of his life."

Miss Fairfax, who had seldom spoken before, spoke now.

"Such things do occur, undoubtedly." She was stopped by a cough. Frank Churchill turned towards her to listen.

"You were speaking," said he gravely. She recovered her voice.

"Though such unfortunate circumstances do sometimes occur both to men and women, I cannot imagine them to be frequent. A hasty and imprudent attachment may arise—but there is generally time to recover from it afterwards. I would be understood to mean, that it can be only weak, irresolute characters (whose happiness must be always at the mercy of chance), who will suffer an infortunate acquaintance to be an inconvenience, an oppression for ever."

He made no answer; merely looked and bowed in submission; and soon afterwards said, in a lively tone,

"Well, I have so little confidence in my own judgement, that whenever I marry, I hope somebody will choose my wife for me. Will you? (turning to Emma) I am sure I should like any body fixed on by you. I am in no hurry. Adopt her, educate her."

"And make her like myself."

"By all means, if you can."

"Very well. I undertake the commission. You shall have a charming wife."

Emma was in no danger of forgetting. It was a commission to touch every favourite feeling. Would not Harriet be the very creature described?

"Now, ma'am," said Jane to her aunt. "Shall we join Mrs Elton?"

"If you please, my dear. With all my heart. I am quite ready." They walked off followed in half a minute by Mr Knightley. The young man's spirits now rose to a pitch almost unpleasant. Even Emma grew tired at last of flattery and merriment. The appearance of the carriages was a joyful sight. Such another scheme, composed of so many ill-assorted people. She hoped never to be betrayed into it again.

While waiting for the carriage, she found Mr Knightley by her side.

"Emma, I must once more speak to you as I have been used to do. I cannot see you acting wrong, without a remonstrance. How could you be so unfeeling to Miss Bates? How could you be so insolent in your wit to a woman of her character, age, and situation?

Emma recollected, blushed, was sorry, but tried to laugh it off.

"Nobody could have helped it. I dare say she did not understand me."

"I assure you she did. She talked of it. I wish you could have heard her honouring your forbearance, in being able to pay her such attention, as she was for ever receiving from yourself and your father, when her society must be so irksome. She is poor. You, whom she had seen grow up from a period when her notice was an honour, to have you now, in thoughtless spirits, and the pride of the moment, laugh at her, humble her—and before her niece too. This is not very pleasant to you, Emma—and it is very far from pleasant to me; but I must, I will tell you truths while I can, satisfied with proving myself your friend by very faithful counsel."

While they talked, they were advancing towards the carriage, and before she could speak again, he had handed her in. He had misinterpreted the feelings which had kept her face averted, and her tongue motionless. They were combined only of anger against herself, mortification, and deep concern. Reproaching herself for having taken no leave, parting in apparent sullenness, she looked out with voice and hand eager to show a difference, but it was just too late. He had turned away. Never had she felt so agitated, mortified, grieved at any circumstance in her life. How could she have been so brutal, so cruel to Miss Bates! And how suffer him to leave her without saying one word of gratitude, of common kindness.

Time did not compose her. She never had been so depressed. Emma felt the tears running down her cheeks, without any trouble to check them.

CHAPTER FORTY-TWO

The wretchedness of a scheme to Box Hill was in Emma's thoughts all the evening. In the warmth of true contrition she would call upon Miss Bates the very next morning, and it should be the beginning, on her side, of a regular, equal, kindly intercourse.

She went early. The ladies were all at home. There was a bustle on her approach. She heard Miss Bates' voice, the maid looked frightened and awkward, and then ushered her in too soon.

Jane she had a distinct glimpse of, looking extremely ill; she heard Miss Bates saying, "Well, my dear. I shall *say*, you are laid down upon the bed, and I am sure you are ill enough."

Miss Bates soon came—"Very happy and obliged"—but Emma's conscience told her there was less ease of look and manner. A very friendly inquiry after Miss Fairfax, she hoped might lead the way to a return of feelings. The touch seemed immediate. "Ah! Miss Woodhouse, how kind you are! I suppose you have heard—and are come to give us joy (twinkling away a tear or two). She has a dreadful headache just now, writing all the morning, to Colonnel Campbell, and Mrs Dixon: and though she is amazingly fortunate—such a situation—I suppose as no young woman before ever met with on first going out. Do not think us ungrateful, Miss Woodhouse. When one is in great pain, you know one cannot feel any blessing quite as it may deserve. Your kindness will excuse her. We did not know anybody was coming. 'Oh!' said I, 'it is Miss Woodhouse. I am sure you will like to see her.' 'I can see nobody,' said she; and that was what made us keep you waiting—and extremely sorry and ashamed we were."

Emma's heart had been long growing kinder towards Jane and this picture of her present suffering acted as a cure of every former ungenerous suspicion and left her nothing but pity. She spoke with earnest regret and solicitude—sincerely wishing that the circumstances to be now actually determined on, might be as much for Miss Fairfax's advantage and comfort as possible.

"Where—may I ask?—is Miss Fairfax going?"

"To a Mrs Smallridge—charming woman—most superior—to have the charge of her three little girls. When Jane first heard of it, she was quite decided against accepting the offer. Yesterday evening it was all settled that Jane should go. Jane took Mrs Elton aside, and told her at once that she had come to the resolution of accepting it—I did not know a word of it till it was all settled."

"You spent the evening with Mrs Elton?"

"Yes, all of us, Mrs Elton would have us come. It was settled so, upon the hill. 'You *must* all spend your evening with us,' said she, and a very agreeable evening we had."

"And when is Miss Fairfax to leave you?"

"Very soon, within a fortnight. Mrs Smallridge is in a great hurry."

"Her friends must all be sorry to lose her; and will not Colonel and Mrs Campbell be sorry to find that she has engaged herself before their return?"

"Yes, Jane says, she is sure they will. I was so astonished when she first told me what she had been saying to Mrs Elton. It was before tea—stay—no, Mr Elton was called out of the room before tea, and when he came back, he told us about the chaise having been sent to Randalls to take Mr Frank Churchill to Richmond. That was what happened before tea. It was after tea that Jane spoke to Mrs Elton."

A messenger had come over from Richmond soon after the return of the party from Box Hill—which messenger, however, had been no more than was expected; and Mr Churchill had sent his nephew a few lines, containing, upon the whole, a tolerable account of Mrs Churchill, and only wishing him not to delay coming back beyond the next morning early; but Mr Frank Churchill having resolved to go home directly, Tom had been sent off immediately for the Crown chaise.

There was nothing in all this either to astonish or interest, and it caught Emma's attention only as it united with the subject which already engaged her mind. The contrast between Mrs Churchill's importance in the world, and Jane Fairfax's struck her; one was everything, the other nothing—and she sat musing on the difference of woman's destiny.

Emma soon allowed herself to believe her visit had been long enough, and with a repetition of the good wishes which she really felt, look leave.

CHAPTER FORTY-THREE

On entering the parlour, Emma found Mr Knightley and Harriet sitting with her father.

"I would not go away without seeing you. I am going to London, to spend a few days with John and Isabella."

"Is not this a sudden scheme?"

"Yes—rather—I have been thinking of it some little time."

Emma was sure he had not forgiven her. Her father began his inquiries.

"Well, my dear, and did you get there safely? Dear Emma has been to call on Mrs and Miss Bates, Mr Knightley. She is always so attentive to them!"

Emma's colour was heightened by this unjust praise; she looked at Mr Knightley—It seemed as if there was an instantaneous impression in her favour. He looked at her with a glow of regard. She was warmly gratified. He took her hand, pressed it, and certainly "was on the point of carrying it to his lips—when from some fancy or other, he suddenly let it go. The intention was indubitable. She thought nothing became him more—It was with him, of so simple, yet so dignified a nature. It spoke such perfect amity—He left them immediately afterwards. He always moved with the alertness of a mind which could neither be undecided nor dilatory, but now he seemed more sudden than usual in his disappearance. She could not be deceived as to the meaning of his countenance and his unfinished gallantry; it was all done to assure her that she had fully recovered his good opinion.

The following day brought news from Richmond. An express arrived at Randalls to announce the death of Mrs Churchill. Mrs Churchill, after being disliked at least twenty-five years, was now spoken of with compassionate allowance.

It was a more pressing concern to show attention to Jane Fairfax, and with Emma it was grown into a first wish. She had scarcely a stronger regret than for her past coldness. She wanted to be of use to her, wanted to show a value for her society, and testify respect and consideration. She resolved to prevail on her to spend a day at Hartfield. A note was written to urge it. The invitation was refused and by verbal message. "Miss Fairfax was not well enough to write."

And when Mr Perry called at Hartfield the same morning it appeared that her health seemed for the moment completely deranged—appetite quite gone—and though there were no absolutely alarming symptoms, Mr Perry was uneasy about her. Her present home, he could not but observe, was unfavourable to a nervous disorder—confined always to one room; and her good aunt, though his very old friend, not the best companion for an invalid. Her care and attention could not be questioned, he very much feared that Miss Fairfax derived more evil than good from them. Emma listened with the warmest concern; grieved for her more and more and looked around eager to discover some way of being useful. To take her—be it only an hour or two—from her aunt, to give her change of air and scene, and quite rational conversation even for an hour or two, might do her good.

The following morning she wrote again to say, in all the most feeling language she could command, that she would call for her in the carriage at any hour that Jane would name. The answer was only in this short note.

"Miss Fairfax's compliments and thanks, but is quite unequal to any exercise."

Emma felt that her own note had deserved something better; she thought only of how she might best counteract this unwillingness to be seen or assisted. In spite of the answers, therefore, she ordered the carriage and drove to Mrs Bates' in the hope that Jane would be induced to join her. Jane was quite unpersuadable.

Poor Miss Bates was very unhappy. Jane would hardly eat anything, but everything they could command (and never had anybody such good neighbours) was distasteful.

Emma, on reaching home, called the housekeeper directly, to an examination of her stores; and some arrowroot of very superior quality was speedily dispatched to Miss Bates with a most friendly note. In half an hour the arrowroot was returned with a thousand thanks from Miss Bates, but "dear Jane would not be satisfied without its being sent back; it was a thing she could not take—and, moreover, she insisted on her saying, that she was not at all in want of anything."

Emma could have no doubt—putting everything together, that Jane was resolved to receive no kindness from *her*. She was sorry, very sorry. It mortified her that she was given so little credit for proper feeling or esteemed so little worthy as a friend; but she had the consolation of knowing that her intentions were good.

CHAPTER FORTY-FOUR

One morning, about ten days after Mrs Churchill's decease, Emma was called downstairs to Mr Weston, who wanted, particularly to speak with her.

"Can you come to Randalls? Mrs Weston must see you *alone*."

"Certainly. This moment. But what can be the matter?—Is she really not ill?"

She and Mr Weston were soon out of the home together.

"Now," said Emma. "Now, Mr Weston, do let me know what has happened."

"No, no," he gravely replied. "She will break it to you—better than I can."

"Break it to me?" cried Emma, standing still with terror. "Mr Weston, do not trifle with me—Consider how many of my dearest friends are now in Brunswick Square. Which of them is it?"

"Upon my honour," said he very seriously, "it is not in the smallest degree connected with any human being of the name of Knightley."

They hurried on and were speedily at Randalls. Mrs Weston was looking so ill, and had an air of so much perturbation, that Emma's uneasiness increased; she eagerly said,

"What is it, my dear friend? Something of a very unpleasant nature, I find, has occurred."

"Have you indeed no idea?" said Mrs Weston in a trembling voice. "Cannot you, my dear Emma, form a guess as to what you are to hear?"

"So far as that it relates to Mr Frank Churchill, I do guess."

"You are right. He has been here this very morning. It is impossible to express our surprise. He came to speak to his father on a subject—to announce an attachment—a positive engagement—What will you say, Emma—What will anybody say, when it is known that Frank Churchill and Miss Fairfax are engaged! nay, that they have been long engaged!"

Emma even jumped with surprise;—and, horror-struck, exclaimed.

"Jane Fairfax!—Good God! You are not serious?"

"You may well be amazed," returned Mrs Weston, still averting her eyes, and talking on with eagerness, that Emma might have time to recover. "There has been a solemn engagement between them ever since October—formed at Weymouth. Not a creature knowing it but themselves—neither the Campbells, nor her family, nor his. I can hardly believe it. I thought I knew him."

Emma scarcely heard what was said—Her mind was divided between two ideas—her own former conversation with him about Miss Fairfax; and poor Harriet;—and for some time she could only exclaim, and require confirmation, repeated confirmation.

"It has hurt me, Emma, very much. It has hurt his father equally. *Some part* of his conduct we cannot excuse."

Emma pondered a moment, and then replied, "I will not pretend *not* to understand you. There was a period in the early part of our acquaintance, when I was very much disposed to be attached to him—nay, was attached. Fortunately, however, it did cease. I have for at least these three months cared nothing about him."

Mrs Weston kissed her with tears of joy; and when she could find utterance, assured her, that this protestation had done her more good than anything else in the world could do.

"Mr Weston will be almost as much relieved as myself," said she. "On this point we have been wretched. It was our darling wish that you might be attached to each other and we were persuaded that it was so. Imagine what we have been feeling on your account."

"I have escaped; but this does not acquit *him*. I think him greatly to blame. What right had he to come among us with affection and faith engaged, and with manners so very disengaged—to distinguish any one young woman with persevering attention, as he certainly did—while he really belonged to another? How could he tell that he might not be making me in love with him?—very wrong indeed. And how could *she* bear such behaviour. That is a degree of placidity, which I can neither comprehend nor respect."

"There were misunderstandings between them, Emma; he said so expressly. The present crisis, indeed, seemed to be brought on by them; and might very possibly arise from the impropriety of his conduct."

"Impropriety!—Oh! Mrs Weston—it is too calm a censure. I cannot say how it has sunk him in my opinion. None of that upright integrity, that strict adherence to truth and principle, that disdain of trick and littleness, which a man should display in every transaction of his life. Jane actually on the point of going as governess! what could he mean by such horrible indelicacy?"

"He knew nothing about it, Emma. It was the discovery of what she was doing, which determined him to come forward at once, own it all to his uncle, throw himself on his kindness, and, in short put an end to the miserable state of concealment that had been carrying on so long. I am to hear from him soon. Let us wait, therefore, for this letter. It may make many things intelligible and excusable, which now are not to be understood. They must both have suffered a great deal under such a system of secrecy and concealment."

"His sufferings," replied Emma drily, "do not appear to have done him much harm. Well, and how did Mr Churchill take it?"

"Gave his consent with scarcely a difficulty. While Mrs Churchill lived, I suppose there could not have been a hope, a chance, a possibility. This was settled last night, and Frank was off with the light this morning. He was very much agitated. In addition to all the rest, there had been the shock of finding her so very unwell, which he had no previous suspicion of."

"Well," said Emma, "I suppose we shall gradually grow reconciled to the idea, and I wish them very happy. What has it been but a system of hypocrisy and deceit. Here have we been, the whole winter and spring, completely duped, fancying ourselves all on an equal footing of trust and honour, with two people in the midst of us who may have been carrying around, comparing and sitting in judgement on sentiments and words that were never meant for both to hear."

"Let us make the best of it. It is not a connection to gratify; but if Mr Churchill does not feel that, why should we? And it may be a very fortunate circumstance for Frank that he should have attached himself to a girl of such steadiness of character and good judgement."

Emma met Mr Weston on his entrance, with a smiling countenance, exclaiming,

"I congratulate you, Mr Weston, with all my heart, on the prospect of having one of the most lovely and accomplished young women in England for your daughter."

CHAPTER FORTY-FIVE

Frank Churchill had behaved very ill by himself—but it was not so much *his* behaviour as her *own*, which made her so angry with him. It was the scrape which he had drawn her into on Harriet's account. Poor Harriet to be a second time the dupe of her misconceptions and flattery. Mr Knightley had spoken prophetically, when he once said, "Emma, you have been no friend to Harriet Smith." She was extremely angry with herself. She need no longer be unhappy about Jane. Her days of insignificance and evil were over—She would soon be well, and happy and prosperous. In Jane's eyes she had been a rival; and well might any thing she could offer of assistance or regard be repulsed. She understood it all.

"Well, Miss Woodhouse!" cried Harriet, coming eagerly into the room, "Did you ever hear any thing so strange? Mr Weston has told me himself."

"What did Mr Weston tell you?" said Emma still perplexed.

"That Jane Fairfax and Mr Frank Churchill are to be married and that they have been privately engaged to one another this long while."

Harriet's behaviour was so extremely odd, that Emma did not know how to understand it. She seemed to propose showing no agitation, or disappointment in the discovery.

"Had you any idea," cried Harriet, "of his being in love with her? You (blushing as she spoke) who can see into everybody's heart."

"Upon my word," said Emma, "I begin to doubt my having any such talent. Can you seriously ask me, Harriet, whether I imagined him attached to another woman at the very time that I was tacitly, if not openly—encouraging you to give way to your own feelings?"

"Me!" cried Harriet, colouring and astonished. "Why should you caution me?"

"I am delighted to hear you speak so stoutly on the subject," replied Emma, smiling; "but you do not mean to deny that that was a time when you gave me reason to understand that you did care about him?"

"Him!—never, never. Dear Miss Woodhouse, how could you so mistake me?" turning away distressed.

"Harriet!" cried Emma, after a moment's pause, "Good Heaven! What do you mean? Mistake you!—Am I to suppose then?"

She could not speak another word. Her voice was lost; and she sat down, waiting in great terror till Harriet should answer.

Harriet did not immediately say any thing, and when she did speak, it was in a voice nearly as agitated as Emma's.

"I know we agreed never to name him—but considering how infinitely superior he is to everybody else, I should not have thought it possible that I could be supposed to mean any other person. I hope I have a better taste than to think of Mr Frank Churchill, who is like nobody by his side. And that you should have been so mistaken, is amazing!—I am sure, but for believing that you entirely approved and meant to encourage me in my attachment, I should have considered it at first too great a presumption almost, to dare to think of him."

"Harriet!" cried Emma, collecting herself resolutely. "Are you speaking of—Mr Knightley?"

"To be sure I am. When we talked about him, it was clear as possible."

"Not quite," returned Emma, with forced calmness. "I could almost assert that you had *named* Mr Frank Churchill. I perfectly remember the substance of what I said on the occasion. I told you that I did not wonder at your attachment; that considering the service he had rendered you, it was extremely natural."

"Oh dear," cried Harriet. "It was not the gipsies—It was not Mr Frank Churchill that I meant. No! I was thinking of a much more precious circumstance of Mr Knightley's coming and asking me to dance, when Mr Elton would not stand up with me and when there was no other partner in the room. That was the kind action; that was the noble benevolence and generosity; that was the service which made me begin to feel how superior he was to every other being upon earth."

"Good God!" cried Emma, "this has been a most unfortunate—most deplorable mistake!—What is to be done?"

"You would not have encouraged me, then, if you had understood me. I do not wonder, Miss Woodhouse," she resumed, "that you should feel a great difference between the two. You must think one five hundred million times more above me than the other. They were your own words, that more wonderful things had happened, matches of greater disparity had taken place and if I should be so fortunate—if Mr Knightley should really—if *he* does not mind the disparity, I hope dear Miss Woodhouse, you will not set yourself against it, and try to put difficulties in the way. But you are too good for that, I am sure."

Harriet was standing at one of the windows. Emma turned round to look at her in consternation, and hastily said,

"Have you any idea of Mr Knightley's returning your affection?"

"Yes," replied Harriet modestly, but not fearfully—"I must say that I have."

Emma's eyes were instantly withdrawn, and she sat silently meditating, in a fixed attitude. A few minutes were sufficient for making her acquainted with her own heart. A mind like hers once opening to suspicion, made rapid progress. Why was the evil so dreadfully increased by Harriet's having some hope of a return? It darted through her, with the speed of an arrow, that Mr Knightley must marry no one but herself! Her own conduct, as well as her own heart, was before her in the same few minutes. She saw it all. How improperly had she been acting by Harriet! How inconsiderate, how indelicate, how irrational, how unfeeling had been her conduct! What blindness, what madness, had led her on. Rousing from reflection, and subduing her emotion, she turned to Harriet again. She listened with much inward suffering, but with great outward patience, to Harriet's detail.

Methodical, or well arranged, or very well delivered, it could not be expected to be, but it contained a substance to sink her spirit—especially with the corroborating circumstances, which her own memory brought in favour of Mr Knightley's most improved opinion of Harriet.

Harriet had been conscious of a difference in his behaviour ever since those two decisive dances. From the time of Miss Woodhouse's encouraging her to think of him, Harriet had begun to be sensible of his talking to her much more than he had been used to do, and of his having indeed a manner of kindness and sweetness! When they had been all walking together, he had so often come and walked by her, and talked so very delightfully!—He seemed to want to be acquainted with her. Emma knew it to have been very much the case. Much that lived in Harriet's memory, many little particulars of the notice she had received from him, a look, a speech, a removal from one chair to another, a compliment implied, a preference inferred, had been unnoticed, because unsuspected by Emma. But the two latest occurrences to be mentioned, were not without some degree of witness from Emma herself—The first was his walking with her apart at Donwell, before Emma came, and he had taken pains (as she was convinced) to draw her from the rest to himself—and at first, he had talked to her in a more particular way than he had ever done before—(Harriet could not recall it without a blush). He seemed to be almost asking her whether her affections were engaged.—But as soon as she (Miss Woodhouse) appeared likely to join them, he changed the subject, and began talking about farming. The second was his having sat talking with her nearly half an hour before Emma came back, the very last morning of his being at Hartfield—though, when he first came in, he had said that he could not stay five minutes—and his having told her, that though he must go to London, it was very much against his inclination that he left home at all which was much more (as Emma felt) than he had acknowledged to *her*. The superior degree of confidence towards Harriet, which this one article marked, gave her severe pain.

On the subject of the first, she did venture the following question. "Might he not have Mr Martin's interest in view?"

"Mr Martin! No indeed!—There was not a hint of Mr Martin. I hope I know better now, than to care for Mr Martin, or to be suspected of it. I never should have presumed to think of it at first but for you. Now I seem to feel that I may deserve him; and that if he does choose me, it will not be anything so very wonderful."

The many bitter feelings occasioned by this speech, made the utmost exertion necessary on Emma's side, to enable her to say in reply,

"Harriet, I will only venture to declare, that Mr Knightley is the last man in the world, who would intentionally give any woman the idea of his feeling for her more than he really does."

Harriet seemed ready to worship her friend for a sentence so satisfactory; and Emma was only saved from raptures and fondness, which at the moment would have been dreadful penance, by the sound of her father's footsteps. He was coming through the hall. Harriet was much too agitated to encounter him. Therefore, she passed off through another door—and the moment she was gone, this was the spontaneous burst of Emma's feelings. "Oh God! that I had never seen her!"

The rest of the day, the following night, were hardly enough for her thoughts. She was bewildered amidst the confusion of all that had rushed on her within the last few hours. Every moment had brought a fresh surprise; and every surprise must be a matter of humiliation to her. The blunders, the blindness of her own head and heart! She sat still, she walked about, she tried her own room--in every place, every posture, she perceived that she had acted most weakly; that she had been imposed on by others in a most mortifying degree; that she had been imposing on herself in a degree yet more mortifying; and should probably find this day but the beginning of wretchedness.

To thoroughly understand her own heart was the first endeavour. To that point went every leisure moment. How long had Mr Knightley been so dear to her, as every feeling declared him now to be? When had he succeeded to that place in her affections which Frank Churchill had once, for a short period, occupied? She saw that there never had been a time when she did not consider Mr Knightley as infinitely the superior, or when his regard for her had not been infinitely the most dear.

She had never really cared for Frank Churchill at all. She was ashamed of every sensation but the one revealed to her—her affection for Mr Knightley—Every other part of her mind was disgusting.

With insufferable vanity had she believed herself in the secret of everybody's feelings; with unpardonable arrogance proposed to arrange everybody's destiny. She had brought evil on Harriet, on herself, and, she too much feared, on Mr Knightley. He would never have known Harriet at all but for her folly.

Mr Knightley and Harriet Smith!—Such an elevation on her side! Such a debasement on his! It was horrible to think how it must sink him in the general opinion; to foresee the merriment it would prompt at his expense; the mortification and disdain of his brother, the thousand inconveniences to himself. Was it a new circumstance for a man of first-rate abilities to be captivated by very inferior powers?

Oh! had she never brought Harriet forward! Had she left her where she ought, and where he had told her she ought!—Had she not, with a folly which no tongue could express, prevented her marrying the unexceptionable young man who would have made her happy and respectable in the line of life to which she ought to belong—all would have been safe, none of this dreadful sequel would have been.

How Harriet could ever have had the presumption to raise her thoughts to Mr Knightley! Alas! was not that her own doing? Who had been at pains to give Harriet notions of self-consequence but herself?—Who but herself had taught her, that she was to elevate herself if possible?—If Harriet, from being humble, were grown vain, it was her doing too.

CHAPTER FORTY-SIX

Till now that she was threatened with its loss, Emma had never known how much of her happiness depended on being *first* with Mr Knightley, first in interest and affection; and only in the dread of being supplanted, found how inexpressibly important it had been. She had not deserved it; she had often been negligent or perverse, slighting his advice, or even wilfully opposing him, insensible of half his merits, and quarrelling with him because he would not acknowledge her false and insolent estimate of her own—but still, from family attachment and habit, and through excellence of mind, he had loved her, and watched over her from a girl, with an endeavour to improve her, and an anxiety for her doing right, which no other creature had at all shared. In spite of all her faults, she knew she was dear to him. She could not flatter herself with any idea of blindness in his attachment to her. She had received a very recent proof of its impartiality. How shocked had he been by her behaviour to Miss Bates! There was a hope that Harriet might have deceived herself, and be overrating his regard for her. Wish it she must, for his sake. Could she be secure of his never marrying at all, she believed she should be perfectly satisfied—Let him but continue the same Mr Knightley to her and her father, the same Mr Knightley to all the world; let Donwell and Hartfield lose none of their precious intercourse of friendship and confidence, and her peace would be fully secure. Marriage would not do for her. It would be incompatible with what she owed to her father, and with what she felt for him. Nothing should separate her from her father. She would not marry, even if she was asked by Mr Knightley.

It must be her ardent wish that Harriet might be disappointed; and she hoped, that when able to see them together again, she might at least be able to ascertain what the chances of it were. Meanwhile she resolved against seeing Harriet. It would do neither of them any good. She was resolved not to be convinced, as long as she could doubt. To talk would be only to irritate. She wrote to her, therefore, kindly, but decisively, to beg that she would not, at present, come to Hartfield, acknowledging it to be her conviction, that all farther confidential discussion of *one* topic had better be avoided. Harriet submitted, and approved, and was grateful.

This point was just arranged, when a visitor arrived. Mrs Weston, who had been calling on her daughter-in-law elect, to relate all the particulars of so interesting an interview. Very great had been the evident distress and confusion of the lady. She had hardly been able to speak a word, and every look and action had shown how deeply she was suffering from consciousness. Miss Fairfax's recent illness had offered a fair plea for Mrs Weston to invite her to an airing. Mr Weston had, by gentle encouragement, overcome so much of her embarrassment, as to bring her to converse on the important subject. They had talked a good deal of the present and of the future state of the engagement.

"On the misery of what she had suffered, during the concealment of so many months," continued Mrs Weston, "This was one of her expressions: 'I will not say, that since I entered into the engagement I have not had some happy moments; but I can say, that I have never known the blessings of one tranquil hour;—and the quivering lip, Emma, which uttered it, was an attestation that I felt at my heart."

"Poor girl!" said Emma. "She thinks herself wrong, then, for having consented to a private engagement?"

"Wrong!—No one, I believe, can blame her more than she is disposed to blame herself. The consequence, said she, has been a state of perpetual suffering to me. I never can be blameless. I have been acting contrary to all, my sense of right. Do not imagine, madam, that I was taught wrong. The error has been all my own. I shall yet dread making the story known to Colonel Campbell."

"Poor girl!" said Emma again. "She loves him then excessively, I suppose. Her affection must have overpowered her judgement. I am afraid that I must often have contributed to make her unhappy."

"On your side, my love, it was very innocently done. One natural consequence of the evil she had involved herself in, she said, was that of making her *unreasonable*. I did not make the allowances said she, 'which I ought to have done, for his temper, and spirits—his delightful spirits, and the gaiety, that playfulness of disposition, which, under any other circumstances, would I am sure, have been as constantly bewitching to me, as they were at first'. She then began to speak of you, and the great kindness you had shown her during her illness, and with a blush which showed me how it was all connected, desired me, whenever I had an opportunity, to thank you. She was sensible that you had never received any proper acknowledgement from herself."

"If I did not know her to be happy now," said Emma, seriously, "I could not bear these thanks. You are very kind to bring me these interesting particulars. They show her to the greatest advantage. It is fit that the fortune should be on his side, for I think the merit will be all on hers."

Mrs Weston ended with, "We have not yet had his letter, we are so anxious for, but I hope it will soon come," Mrs Weston's communications furnished Emma with more food for unpleasant reflection, by increasing her esteem and compassion, and her sense of past injustice towards Miss Fairfax. Had she endeavoured to find a friend there instead of in Harriet Smith, she must, in all probability, have been spared the pain which pressed her now. She must have been a perpetual enemy. They never could have been all three together, without her having stabbed Jane Fairfax's peace in a thousand instances.

The evening was very long and melancholy at Hartfield. The weather added what it could of gloom. A cold stormy rain set in and nothing of July appeared.

CHAPTER FORTY-SEVEN

The weather continued much the same all the following morning but in the afternoon the wind changed, the clouds were carried off, the sun appeared; it was summer again. Never had the exquisite sight, smell, sensation of nature, tranquil, warm, and brilliant after a storm, been more attractive to her. She lost no time in hurrying into the shrubbery. There, she had taken a few turns when she saw Mr Knightley coming towards her.

She had been thinking of him the moment before, as unquestionably sixteen miles distance. There was time only for the quickest arrangement of mind. She must be collected and calm.

She asked after their mutual friends; when had he left them? Only that morning. He must have had a wet ride—Yes. She thought he neither looked nor spoke cheerfully; and the first possible cause for it, suggested by her fears, was that he had perhaps been communicating his plans to his brother, and was pained by the manner in which they had been received.

She thought he was often looking at her. Perhaps he wanted to speak to her of his attachment to Harriet. She did not, could not, feel equal to lead the way to any such subject. Yet she could not bear this silence and trying to smile began—

"You have some news to hear, that will rather surprise you."

"Have I?" said he quietly, and looking at her, "of what nature?"

"Oh! The best nature in the world—a wedding." After waiting a moment, as if to be sure she intended to say no more, he replied, "If you mean Miss Fairfax and Frank Churchill, I had a few lines on parish business from Mr Weston this morning, and at the end he gave me a brief account of what had happened."

"You probably have been less surprised than any of us. I have not forgotten that you once tried to give me a caution—but (with sinking voice and a heavy sigh) I seem to have been doomed to blindness."

She found her arm drawn within his, and pressed against his heart, and heard him thus saying, in a tone of great sensibility, speaking low, "Time, my dearest Emma, time will heal the wound." Her arm was pressed again, as he added, in a more broken and subdued accent, "The feelings of the warmest friendship—indignation—abominable scoundrel!"—And in a steadier tone, he concluded with, "He will soon be gone. I am sorry for *her*. She deserves a better fate."

Emma understood him; as soon as she could recover from the flutter of pleasure, excited by such tender consideration, replied.

"But you are mistaken, and I must set you right—I am not in want of that sort of compassion. My blindness to what was going on, led me to act by them in a way that I must always be ashamed of, and lay me open to unpleasant conjectures, but I have no other reason to regret that I was not in the secret earlier."

"Emma!" cried he, looking eagerly at her, "are you indeed?" but checking himself—"No, no, I understand you—forgive me. I am pleased that you can say even so much. He is no object of regret, indeed! and it will not be very long, I hope, before that becomes the acknowledgement of more than your reason. Fortunately that your affections were not further entangled!—I could never, I confess, from your manners, assure myself as to the degree of what you felt. He is a disgrace to the name of man.—And is he to be rewarded with that sweet young woman?—Jane, Jane, you will be a miserable creature."

"Mr Knightley," said Emma, trying to be lively, but really very confused—"I am in a very extraordinary situation. I cannot let you continue in your error; and yet perhaps, since my manners give such an impression, I have as much reason to be ashamed of confessing that I have never been at all attached to the person we are speaking of, as it might be natural to feel in confessing the reverse. I have very little to say for my own conduct—I was tempted by his attentions and allowed myself to appear pleased. Latterly, however, I thought them a habit, nothing that called for seriousness on my side. He never wished to attach me. It was merely a blind to conceal his real situation with another; and no one, I am sure, could be more effectually blinded than myself—except that I was *not* blinded. I was somehow or other safe from him."

"I have never had a high opinion of Frank Churchill—with such a woman he has a chance,—I have no motive for wishing him ill and for her sake, where happiness will be involved in his good character and conduct. I shall certainly wish him well. He is a most fortunate man! So early in life—at three and twenty—a period when, if a man chooses a wife, he generally chooses ill, to have drawn such a prize! What years of felicity that man has before him! Frank Churchill is indeed the favourite of fortune. Everything turns out for his good—He has used everybody ill and they are all delighted to forgive him."

'You speak as if you envied him."

"And I do envy him, Emma. In one respect he is the object of my envy."

Emma could say no more. They seemed to be within half a sentence of Harriet, and her immediate feeling was to avert the subject, if possible.

"You will not ask me what is the point of envy. Emma, I must tell what you will not ask, though I may wish it unsaid the next moment."

"Oh! then, don't speak it," she eagerly cried, "Take a little time, consider, do not commit yourself."

"Thank you," said he, in an accent of deep mortification, and not another syllable followed. Emma could not bear to give him pain. He was wishing to confide in her—perhaps to consult her; cost her what it would, she would listen. She might assist his resolution or reconcile him to it: She might give just praise to Harriet, or by representing to him his own independence relieve him from that state of indecision, which must be more intolerable than any alternative to such a mind as his.

"I stopped you ungraciously, just now, Mr Knightley, and, I am afraid, gave you pain. But if you have any wish to speak openly to me as a friend, or to ask my opinion of anything that you may have in contemplation—as a friend, indeed, you may command me. I will hear whatever you like, I will tell you exactly what I think."

"As a friend!"—repeated Mr Knightley. "Emma, that, I fear is a word—No, I have no wish—stay,—yes, why should I hesitate? I have gone too far already for concealment—Emma, I accept your offer—Extraordinary as it may seem, I accept it and refer myself to you as a friend—Tell me, then, have I no chance of ever succeeding?"

He stopped in his earnestness to look the question, and the expression of his eyes overpowered her.

"My dearest Emma," said he, "for dearest you will always be, my dearest, most beloved Emma—tell me at once. Say 'No' if it is to be said."—She could really say nothing—"You are silent," he cried, "absolutely silent! at present I ask no more."

Emma was almost ready to sink under the agitation of this moment. The dread of being awakened from the happiest dream, was perhaps the most prominent feeling.

"I cannot make speeches, Emma," he soon resumed, and in a tone of such sincere, decided, intelligible tenderness as was tolerably convincing—"If I loved you less, I might be able to talk about it more. But you know what I am. You hear nothing but truth from me.—I have blamed you, and lectured you, and you have borne it. Bear with the truths I would tell you now, dearest Emma, as well as you have borne with them. God knows, I have been a very indifferent lover—But you understand my feelings—and will return them if you can. At present; I ask only to hear, once to hear your voice."

While he spoke, Emma's mind was most busy, and, with all the wonderful velocity of thought, had been able to catch and comprehend the exact truth of the whole; to see that Harriet's hopes had been entirely groundless. She felt for Harriet with pain and with contrition. She had led her friend astray and it would be a reproach to her for ever. Her way was clear, though not quite smooth. She spoke then. What did she say?—Just what she ought, of course.—She said enough to show there need not be despair and to invite him to say more himself.

He had, in fact been wholly unsuspicious of his own influence. He had followed her into the shrubbery with no idea of trying it. He had come, in his anxiety to see how she bore Frank Churchill's engagement, with no selfish view, no view at all, but of endeavouring to soothe or to counsel her. The rest had been the work of the moment. The delightful assurance of her total indifference towards Frank Churchill had given birth to the hope, that, in time, he might gain her affection himself. The affection, which he had been asking to be allowed to create if he could, was already his! Within half an hour, he had passed from a thoroughly distressed state of mind, to something so like perfect happiness, that it could bear no other name.

Her change was equal. This half hour had given to each the same precious certainty of being beloved, and cleared from each the same degree of ignorance, jealousy, or distrust.

On his side there had been a long-standing jealousy, old as the arrival of Frank Churchill. He had been in love with Emma and jealous of Frank Churchill from about the same period, one sentiment having probably enlightened him as to the other. It was his jealousy of Frank Churchill that had taken him from the country. The Box-Hill party had decided him on going away. "He would save himself from witnessing again such, permitted, encouraged attentions. He had gone to learn to be indifferent." But he had gone to a wrong place. There was too much domestic happiness in his brother's house. He stayed on day after day—till this morning's post had conveyed the history of Jane Fairfax—Then, with the gladness which must be felt, nay, which he did not scruple to feel, having never believed Frank Churchill to be at all deserving Emma, was there so much fond solicitude so much keen anxiety for her that he could stay no longer. He had ridden home through the rain to see how his sweetest and best of all creatures, faultless in spite of all her faults, bore the discovery.

She was his own Emma, by hand and word, when they returned into the house; and if he could have thought of Frank Churchill then, he might have deemed him a very good sort of fellow.

CHAPTER FORTY-EIGHT

Emma was now in an exquisite flutter of happiness. As long as Mr Knightley remained with them, Emma's fever continued. But when he was gone, she began to be a little tranquillised and subdued. She found one or two such serious points to consider as made her feel that even her happiness must have some alloy. Her father—and Harriet, and how to guard the comfort of both to the utmost, was the question. While he lived, it must be only an engagement. How to do her best by Harriet; how to appear least her enemy? It would be desirable to have her removed just now for a time from Highbury. Isabella had been pleased with Harriet and a few weeks spent in London must give her some amusement; it would be a proof of attention and kindness in herself. She rose early, and wrote her letter to Harriet.

A letter was brought her from Randall's,—a note from Mrs Weston to herself, ushered in the letter from Frank to Mrs Weston.

My dear Madam,

You are all goodness, and I believe there will be need of even all your goodness to allow for some parts of my past conduct. When I first arrived in Randalls you must consider me as having a secret which was to be kept at all hazards. I was fortunate enough to induce the most upright female mind in creation to stoop to a secret engagement. Had she refused I should have gone mad. I did not come till Miss Fairfax was in Highbury. Now I come to the only important part of my conduct, which excites my own anxiety or requires very solicitous explanation. My behaviour to Miss Woodhouse indicated, I believe, more than it ought.—In order to assist a concealment, so essential to me, I was led—or to make more than an allowable use of the sort of intimacy into which we were immediately thrown. Had I not been convinced of her indifference, I would not have been induced by any selfish views to go on. She received my attentions with an easy, friendly, good-humoured playfulness. We seemed to understand each other. When I called to take leave of her, I remember that I was within a moment of confessing the truth. I hope this history of my conduct towards her will be admitted by you and my father as great extenuation of what you saw amiss. Acquit me here, and procure for me, when it is allowable, the acquittal and good wishes of Emma Woodhouse, whom I regard with so much brotherly affection, as to long to have her as deeply and as happily in love as myself.

'Of the pianoforte so much talked of, I feel it only necessary to say, that its being ordered was absolutely unknown to Miss F—The delicacy of her mind throughout the whole engagement, is much beyond my power of doing justice. I want to have your opinion of her looks. I am impatient for a thousand particulars. I am still insane either from happiness or misery. When I think of the kindness and favour, of her excellence and patience, and my uncle's generosity, I am mad with joy: but when I recollect all the uneasiness I occasioned her, and how little I deserve to be forgiven, I am mad with anger. My manners to Miss W., in being unpleasant to Miss F., were highly blamable.—My plea of concealing the truth she did not think sufficient. I thought her on a thousand occasions, unnecessarily scrupulous and cautious. We quarrelled. Do you remember the morning at Donwell? I was late. I met her walking home by herself and wanted to walk with her. She absolutely refused to allow me. Had we been met walking together the truth must have been suspected. The next day on Box Hill, provoked by such shameful insolent neglect of her, and such apparent devotion to Miss W. as it would have been impossible for any woman of sense to endure, she spoke her resentment in a form of words perfectly intelligible to me. I returned the same evening to Richmond determined that she should make the first advances. As soon as she found I was really gone she closed with the offer of that officious Mrs Elton, whose treatment of her has ever filled me with indignation and hatred. She wrote the next day to tell me that we never were to meet again. She felt the engagement to be a source of repentance and misery to each: she dissolved it. This letter reached me on the very morning of my poor aunt's death. I answered it within an hour, but from the confusion of my mind, my answer was locked up in my writing desk. Two days afterwards I received a parcel from her, my own letters all returned!—and a few lines that silence on such a point could not be misconstrued, and she now sent me all my letters and requested, that if I could not command hers so as to send them to Highbury within a week, I would forward them to Mrs Smallridge's. I knew the name, the place; and instantly saw what she had been doing. Imagine the shock; I must speak to my uncle. I spoke, circumstance was in my favour, he was wholly reconciled and complying. I reached Highbury, a great deal of very reasonable, very just displeasure I had to persuade away. But it is done; we are now, reconciled, dearer, much dearer, than ever. A thousand thanks for all the kindness you have ever shown me, and ten thousand for the attentions your heart will dictate towards her.

Your obliged and affectionate son
F. C. Weston Churchill.

CHAPTER FORTY-NINE

This letter must make its way to Emma's feelings. She was obliged to do it justice. Every line relating to herself was interesting and agreeable. When Mr Knightley came she desired him to read it.

"You do not appear so well satisfied with his letter as I am," said Emma.

"He has had great faults, faults of inconsideration and thoughtlessness, and I am very much of his opinion in thinking him likely to be happier than he deserves. But still he is beyond a doubt really attached to Miss Fairfax, and will soon it may be hoped, have the advantage of being constantly with her, and I am very ready to believe his character will improve, and acquire from hers the steadiness and delicacy of principle that it wants. And now, let me talk to you of something else. Since I left you this morning my mind has been hard at work on one subject." The subject followed. The impossibility of her quitting her father, Mr Knightley felt as strongly as herself; he had at first hoped to induce Mr Woodhouse to remove with her to Donwell. Such a transplantation would be a risk of her father's comfort, perhaps even of his life. The plan which had arisen was that he should be received at Hartfield; that so long as her father's happiness—in other words his life—required Hartfield to continue her home, it should be his likewise.

Such an alternative had not occurred to her. She was sensible of all the affection it evinced. In quitting Donwell, he must be sacrificing a great deal of independence of hours and habits; that in living constantly with her father, and in no house of his own, there would be much, very much, to be borne with. The more she contemplated it, the more pleasing it became.

CHAPTER FIFTY

Emma had no difficulty in procuring Isabella's invitation. There was a tooth amiss. Harriet had wished to consult a dentist. Mrs John Knightley was delighted to be of use. It was all arranged, and Harriet was safe in Brunswick Square. Now Emma could, indeed, enjoy Mr Knightley's visits, unchecked by a sense of injustice to Harriet.

She soon resolved, equally as a duty and a pleasure, to employ half an hour of this holiday of spirits in calling on Miss Fairfax. She went, was met on the stairs by Jane herself. Emma had never seen her look so lovely, so engaging. She came forward with an offered hand; and said, in a low, but very feeling tone,

"This is most kind, indeed! Miss Woodhouse, it is impossible for me to express—I hope you will believe—Excuse me for being so entirely without words."

Mrs Bates and Mrs Elton were together. She was in a humour to have patience with everybody, and Mrs Elton met her with unusual graciousness. Mrs Elton was in happy spirits, fancying herself acquainted with what was still a secret to other people. When they had all talked a little while, she found herself abruptly addressed with:

"Do not you think, Miss Woodhouse, our little friend here is charmingly recovered?" (here was a side-glance of great measuring at Jane)—And when Mrs Bates was saying something to Emma, she whispered farther, "We do not say a word of a certain young physician from Windsor."

Emma was pleased, on taking leave, to find Miss Fairfax determined to go with her downstairs; it gave her an opportunity which she immediately made use of, to say,

"It is as well, perhaps, that I have not had the possibility, to speak more openly than might have been strictly correct."

"Oh!" cried Jane, with a blush. "The danger would have been of my wearying you. Indeed, Miss Woodhouse, with the consciousness which I have of very great misconduct, it is particularly, consoling to me to know that those of my friends whose good opinion is most worth preserving, are not disgusted. I long to make apologies. I feel it so very due.

"Oh!' cried Emma, warmly, and taking her hand, "you owe me no apologies and everybody to whom you might be supposed to owe them; is so perfectly satisfied, so delighted even—"

"You are very kind, but I know what my manners were to you. So cold and artificial!—I had always a part to act—It was a life of deceit! I know that I must have disgusted you."

"Pray say no more. I feel that all the apologies should be on my side. Let us forgive each other at once. And the next news, I suppose, will be, that we are to lose you—just as I begin to know you."

"There must be three months at least, of deep mourning; but when they are over, I imagine there will be nothing more to wait for."

"Thank you. This is just what I wanted to be assured of. Oh! if you know how much I love everything that is decided and open! Goodbye, goodbye."

CHAPTER FIFTY-ONE

Mrs Weston's friends were all made happy by her safety; and if the satisfaction of her well-doing could be increased to Emma, it was by knowing her to be the mother of a little girl. She would not acknowledge that it was with any view of making a match for her, hereafter, with either of Isabella's sons; but she was convinced that a daughter would suit both father and mother best. It would be a great comfort to Mr Weston as he grew older to have his fireside enlivened by the sports and the nonsense, the freaks and the fancies of a child never banished from home, and Mrs Weston—no one could doubt that a daughter would be most to her; it would be a pity that anyone who so well knew how to teach, should not have her powers in exercise again.

"That is," said Mr Knightley, "she will indulge her even more than she did you." Emma laughed, and replied, "But I had the assistance of all your endeavours to counteract the indulgence of other people."

Harriet was very seldom mentioned between them. The pain of being obliged to practise concealment towards him, was very little inferior to the pain of having made Harriet unhappy. Isabella sent quite as good an account of her visitor as could be expected.

"John does not even mention your friend," said Mr Knightley.

"Here is his answer, if you like to see it."

It was the answer to the communication of his intended marriage.

Emma accepted it with a very eager hand.

"John enters like a brother into my happiness," continued Mr Knightley, "but he is no complimenter."

"I honour his sincerity. It is very plain that he considers the good fortune of the engagement as all on my side, but that he is not without hope of my growing, in time, as worthy of your affection, as you think me already."

"My Emma, he means no such thing. He only means—"

"Oh!" she cried with more thorough gaiety, "if you fancy your brother does not do me justice, only wait till my dear father is in the secret, and hear his opinion. He will be much further from doing you justice. He will think all the happiness, all the advantage, on your side of the question, all the merit on mine."

The time was coming when the news must be spread farther. But how to break it to her father! Mr Knightley was to come at such a time and follow up the beginning she was to make. With all the spirits she could command, she prepared him first for something strange, and then, in a few words, said that if his consent and approbation could be obtained she and Mr Knlghtley meant to marry.

Poor man!—it was at first a considerable shock to him, and he tried earnestly to dissuade her from it. But it would not do. Emma hung about him affectionately, and smiled, and said it must be so. She should be always there; she was introducing no change in their numbers or their comforts but for the better; and she was very sure that he would be a great deal happier for having Mr Knightley always at hand, when he once got used to the idea. Who was so useful to him, who so ready to write his letters, who so glad to assist him?—who so cheerful, so attentive, so attached to him?

Yes, that was all very true, but they did see him every day as it was—why could not they go on as they had done?

Mr Woodhouse could not be soon reconciled; but the worst was overcome, the idea was given, time and continual repetition must do the rest. They had all the assistance which Isabella could give, by letters of the strongest approbation, and Mrs Weston was ready, on the first meeting, to consider the subject in the most serviceable light. Everybody by whom he was used to be guided assuring him that it would be for his happiness he began to think that some time or other it might not be so very bad if the marriage did take place.

CHAPTER FIFTY-TWO

Mr Knightley came in. After the first chat of pleasure he began with,

"I have something to tell you, Emma; some news. I am afraid my dear Emma, that you will not smile when you hear it—and very bad it is. Harriet Smith marries Robert Martin. I have it from Robert Martin himself. He left me not half an hour ago."

She was looking at him with the most speaking amazement.

"You mistake me, you quite mistake me," she replied, "It is not that such a circumstance would now make me unhappy, but I cannot believe it. It seems an impossibility!"

"It is a very simple story. He went to town on business three days ago, and I got him to take charge of some papers which I was wanting to send to John. He delivered the papers to John, and was asked by him to dine with them the next day which he did—and in the course of that visit found an opportunity of speaking to Harriet. She made him happy by her acceptance, as happy even as he is deserving. He came down by yesterday's coach and was with me this morning to report his proceedings, first on my affairs, and then his own. I must say that Robert Martin's heart seemed for *him*, and to *me*, very overflowing."

He wanted her to look up and smile; she did—cheerfully answering.

"You need not be at any pains to reconcile me to the match. I think Harriet is doing extremely well. I have been silent from surprise merely, excessive surprise." She was in dancing, singing, exclaiming spirits, and till she had moved about, and laughed and reflected, she could be fit for nothing rational.

The joy, the gratitude, the exquisite delight of her sensations may be imagined.—what had she to wish for? Nothing but that the lessons of her past folly might teach her humility and circumspection in future.

CHAPTER FIFTY-THREE

A very few days brought the party from London; being one hour alone with Harriet, she became perfectly satisfied that Robert Martin had thoroughly supplanted Mr Knightley, and was now forming all her views of happiness. The fact was, as Emma could now acknowledge, that Harriet had always liked Robert Martin, and that his continuing to love her had been irresistible.

Harriet's parentage became known. She proved to be the daughter of a tradesman, rich enough to afford her the comfortable maintenance which had ever been hers, and decent enough to have always wished for concealment. But what a connection had she been preparing for Mr Knightley—or for the Churchills or even for Mr Elton!—The stain of illegitimacy, unbleached by nobility or wealth, would have been a stain indeed.

As Emma became acquainted with Robert Martin, she had no doubt of Harriet's happiness. She would be placed in the midst of those who loved her. She would be never led into temptation. She would be respectable and happy; and Emma admitted her to be the luckiest creature in the world to have created so steady and persevering an affection in such a man.

Before the end of September, Emma attended Harriet to church, and saw her hand bestowed on Robert Martin with so complete a satisfaction, as no remembrance, even connected with

Mr Elton, could impair. Robert Martin and Harriet Smith, the latest couple engaged of the three, were the first to be married.

Jane Fairfax was restored to the comforts of her beloved home with the Campbells. The Mr Churchills were also in town; and they were only waiting for November.

The intermediate month was the one fixed on, as far as they dared, by Emma and Mr Knightley, John and Isabella, and every other friend, were agreed in approving it. But Mr Woodhouse—how was Mr Woodhouse to be induced to consent?

When first sounded on the subject, he was so miserable, that they were almost hopeless. He was not happy. Nay, he appeared so much otherwise, that his daughter's courage failed.

In this state of suspense—Mrs Weston's poultry house was robbed one night of all her turkeys. Other poultry yards in the neighbourhood also suffered. Pilfering was *housebreaking* to Mr Woodhouse's fears. He was very uneasy, and but for the sense of his son-in-law's protection, would have been under wretched alarm, every night of his life. The strength, resolution and presence of mind of the two Mr Knightleys commanded his fullest dependence. While either of them protected him and his, Hartfield was safe.

The result of this distress was that, with a much more voluntary, cheerful consent than his daughter had ever presumed to hope for at the moment, she was able to fix her wedding day and Mr Elton was called on, within a month from the marriage of Mr and Mrs Robert Martin, to join the hands of Mr Knightley and Miss Woodhouse.

The wedding was very much like other weddings where the parties have no taste for finery or parade. But in spite of these deficiencies, the wishes, the hopes, the confidences, the predictions of the small band of true friends who witnessed the ceremony, were fully assured in the perfect happiness of the union.

SUMMARIES, GLOSSARY AND COMPREHENSION

CHAPTER 1

SUMMARY

Emma Woodhouse seems to be a privileged person at twenty-one with an indulgent father and an excellent governess, and also the blessings of a good estate. Her sister, Isabella, had married Mr Knightley's younger brother and settled in London. Emma thus is the sole mistress of the house, doing what she liked. Miss Taylor becomes an intimate friend and companion and her marriage to Mr Weston, a man of character and fortune, is a source of joy but also of 'gentle sorrow' to the Woodhouse family. While Emma appreciates the move, her father thought it an unhappy event. When Mr Knightley enters, their argument comes to an end. In London all is well—his brother, Isabella and the children. This frequent visitor and friend of the family feels that Miss Taylor had gained by her marriage. Emma is proud to have made the match and looks forward to making one for Mr Elton, the vicar.

GLOSSARY

disposition	a person's qualities of mind and character
seemed to unite	here intended as an irony
governess	stay-in caretaker
vex	to make someone feel annoyed or frustrated
indulgent	over-readiness to be generous or lenient with someone
indistinct	not clear
unexceptionable	not open to objection, but not new or exciting
humour	a mood or state of mind
exertion	physical or mental effort
animated	full of life or excitement
fanciful	over-imaginative

Comprehension

1. How is Emma Woodhouse introduced to the reader in Chapter 1? What details of her appearance and character are highlighted?
2. What is the relationship between Emma and Miss Taylor?
3. Emma arranged the match between Mr and Mrs Weston, she claims. What do you think was the basis of the matchmaking?
4. Why is Miss Taylor's marriage described as a 'gentle sorrow'?
5. Describe the reactions of Emma, her sister, her father and Mr Knightley to Miss Taylor's marriage.
6. How would you describe the relationship between Emma and her father?
7. How does Emma spend her time?
8. Explain: 'Yet great must be the difference between a Mrs Weston only half a mile from them and a Miss Taylor in the house.'
9. Who is Mr Knightley? What is it that is unique in the way he interacts with Emma?
10. Who is Mr Elton and what are Emma's plans for him?

Summary

Mr Weston is an educated and well-liked inhabitant of Highbury. Fairly well-to-do, he enters the militia. Miss Churchill, a lady of fortune, falls in love with Captain Weston and marries him. Her parents disown her as a mark of their disapproval.

The Westons had lived beyond their means. Three years after the marriage, Mrs Weston had died leaving behind a child, Frank. As Mr Weston was not very well off and had the additional burden of the child, the Churchills offered to bring up little Frank. Mr Weston engaged himself in trade on quitting the militia. He managed to acquire a small estate. His son grows up with the Churchills to become a fine young man. This is when Weston decides to marry Miss Taylor. The people of Highbury await the son's visit. The son was coming to see his new mother. It looked as if she was also quite fascinated by him judging from his letters to her.

GLOSSARY

militia	an emergency military force
independence	a separate income
county	district
dissuade	persuade someone not to take a particular course of action
throw off	disown
with due decorum	in a proper manner. Note the irony.
to live beyond	to spend more than one's earnings
irresistible	what cannot be resisted or kept away

COMPREHENSION

1. Consider the description of Mr Weston—his nature, status/career, marriage and later life. Is there any irony in the portrait?
2. Why did Miss Churchill's parents disapprove of her choice of a husband?
3. Who was Frank Churchill? Who brought him up?
4. Whom did Mr Weston marry several years after his first wife's death?
5. How did Frank relate to his new mother? What was her impression of him?
6. Why was Highbury proud of Frank and what event did they look forward to?
7. In Chapter 1, the Woodhouse family was introduced. In Chapter 2, the Westons are introduced. What kind of a story do you expect after you read these two chapters? How will all this dovetail together?

CHAPTER 3

SUMMARY

Mr Woodhouse likes society in his own way and manages to order the visits of those whose company he likes. Emma arranges a card table for the evening-parties. Two sets of visitors can be identified: the first includes the Westons, Mrs Knightley and Mr Elton—all of whom had long-standing regard for Mr Woodhouse; the second includes Mrs Bates, the old widow of a former vicar of Highbury and her unmarried daughter who is friendly with all, and Mrs Goddard, the mistress of an old-fashioned boarding school. The new character introduced is Miss Harriet Smith, a seventeen-year-old student of Mrs Goddard's school. Harriet seems to have no friends and has just returned from a visit to the country.

Glossary

to make up a card table	find enough people to play cards
natural daughter	illegitimate daughter
a most uncommon degree of popularity	great popularity
passed without distinction	unmarked by any event, here meaning romance

Comprehension

1. Name the circle of friends and family who visit Mr Woodhouse and Emma regularly. How do they spend their time together on these occasions?
2. How is Miss Bates described? Is it a straightforward portrayal or is there sarcasm inherent in the description? Explain.
3. What does 'She was a great talker on little matters' mean?
4. Why does Mrs Goddard ask Emma to meet Harriet Smith?
5. Considering the kind of society shown in the text what do you think was unfortunate about Harriet Smith's background?
6. Describe Harriet Smith. What is Emma's impression of her?
7. Attempt a description of the characters introduced from Chapters 1 to 3. How do they relate to each other?

Chapter 4

Summary

Emma's sympathy for Harriet and Emma's own social superiority makes her get friendly with Harriet. Though Harriet's parentage is a mystery, Emma decides to elevate her status. She invites her to Hartfield and Harriet becomes a regular visitor. Earlier, Harriet had stayed with the Martins of Abbey-Mill Farm for two months. She is all praise for their hospitality and is particularly impressed with Robert Martin and his ways. Emma does not favour Martin and convinces Harriet that she is his social superior. She wants to draw Harriet to Mr Elton since she feels that Mr Elton is a more suitable match for Harriet. Emma's match-making instinct fails to see how Harriet and Martin really suit each other. Emma wants to 'play God' and is blind to her own failings.

Glossary

docile	meek
conceit	pride
esteem	respect
approbation	praise
plain	ordinary-looking
to get into a scrape	to get into trouble
misfortune of birth	here, illegitimate birth
associates	friends
degrading	humiliating; lowering self-esteem
flutter of spirits	excited and confused
gentility	social superiority with upper-class manners
mortified	cause someone to feel very embarrassed or ashamed
ingratiating	bring oneself into favour
weight	value
efficacy	effectiveness

Comprehension

1. Harriet 'seemed to be exactly the young friend Emma wanted.' Explain.
2. 'For Mrs Weston there was nothing to be done; for Harriet everything.' What does this mean?
3. Why did Harriet constantly speak of the Martins? What was Harriet's impression of Mr Martin?
4. According to Emma, what was the 'danger' faced by Harriet? Do you agree with Emma or not?
5. Describe the Martin family. Highlight Mr Martin's qualities.
6. What, according to Emma, are the qualities of a desirable match? Why is Mr Elton preferred to Mr Martin?
7. Why was 'class' so important as a criterion for marriage in Jane Austen's time?
8. Does your experience of social environment relate to the kind of match-making described in the text?

Summary

While discussing Emma's actions, Mr Knightley disapproves of her friendship with Harriet as it increases Emma's 'vanity' and self-importance. But Mrs Weston thinks otherwise. She praises Emma's beauty and the positive effect she has on Harriet. Mr Knightley is anxious for Emma as he is not sure what the outcome of the friendship might be. Emma's reluctance to marry is also discussed—there is none suitable in Highbury for her. Mrs Weston however has her own thoughts on the matter which she does not express at this point.

Glossary

intimacy	close association
partial	favouring one side above the other
hazel	light brown

countenance	a person's face or facial expression
vanity	ego, pride
dread	fear
stout	steadfast
confidence	firm belief
matrimony	marriage
she is loveliness itself	she personifies beauty
she will make no lasting blunder	she will make no mistake that will affect one forever

Comprehension

1. Mr Knightley objects to the intimacy between Emma and Harriet. Why?
2. What are Mrs Weston's views on Emma's appearance and outlook?
3. 'Her vanity lies another way,' says Mr Knightley of Emma. What does he mean?
4. Mrs Weston says that Emma has 'qualities which may be trusted.' What are they?
5. 'There is an anxiety in what one feels for Emma!' says Mr Knightley. Explain.
6. How does Emma feel about marriage? How is it reported in the discussion between Mr Knightley and Mrs Weston?
7. What are Mrs Weston's hidden thoughts concerning Emma?

Chapter 6

Summary

Emma continues to encourage Harriet to get close to Mr Elton. She feels she has steered Harriet in the right direction. The comic irony here lies in Emma's blindness to Mr Elton's interest in her, Emma. Harriet is only a dupe. Emma's self-deception comes to the fore—her distorted view of what is real is very different from the actual situation. Emma gets Mr Elton to frame the portrait of Harriet which she has painted. His compliments to her are misinterpreted as a mark of his gratitude on Harriet's account. Even though Emma is somewhat irritated by Mr Elton's excessive 'gallantry', she misreads it as a sign of his being in love with Harriet.

Glossary

fancy	imagination
infinitely	greatly
fidgeting	being restless
intermission	interval of rest
raptures	excitement
gallantry	polite behaviour
on the alert	always ready
gratified	extremely satisfied
deposit	store
errand	task
languish	grow weak

Comprehension

1. Why does Emma think that she was giving Harriet's fancy the right direction. What is your view?
2. What had Mr Elton to say of Emma's influence over Harriet?
3. What aspects of Mr Elton's behaviour made Emma believe he was in love with Harriet?
4. What are Emma's hesitations concerning Mr Elton?
5. How does Harriet model for the portrait? What are Mr Elton's reactions?
6. What is Mr Elton's response when he is given the task of framing the portrait?
7. Explain and comment on Emma's concluding remarks. Do you think Emma is right in her match-making?

Chapter 7

Summary

Harriet receives Mr Martin's letter containing a direct proposal of marriage. Surprised by the proposal Harriet seeks Emma's advice. Emma reads the letter which was, in fact, well written. She advises Harriet to categorically refuse Mr Elton. Harriet's weakness of intellect is easily manipulated by Emma. Harriet allows herself to be dominated by Emma's apparently superior understanding of such matters. Emma feels that Harriet deserved someone better (Emma has Mr Elton in mind.). Jane Austen's use of irony is effective in exposing Emma's and Harriet's weaknesses.

Glossary

pressed	compelled
unaffected	without artificiality or insincerity
propriety	correctness in behaviour
delicacy of feeling	sensitivity and gentleness
vigorous	strong
coarse	unrefined
unequivocal	without any doubt
purport	reason
'If woman doubts as to whether she should accept a man or not, she certainly ought to refuse him'	When a woman is not sure of her feelings towards a man, it is better to reject him. Emma is trying to influence Harriet to reject Martin. Harriet is pliable; Emma's power over her becomes evident.
'But I am quite determined to refuse him'	Harriet succumbs to Emma's persuasion revealing Emma's power over her.

Comprehension

1. What does Harriet find in the parcel from the Martins?

2. What does the letter contain? How does Harriet react to it?
3. Why does Harriet seek Emma's help?
4. What are Emma's comments on Mr Martin's letter? How does this show her opinions of Mr Martin?
5. Harriet keeps repeating, 'What shall I do?' What does this show about her character?
6. What is Emma's advice and how is it given?
7. Finally, Harriet decides to refuse the proposal. How does Emma contribute to this?
8. How does Emma show that she is conscious of 'class'?
9. Who do you think is more immature in this chapter—Emma or Harriet?

SUMMARY

Mr Knightley praises Emma for improving Harriet and making her a charming woman. He hints that Harriet could expect to hear some good news. Emma thinks that Knightley's good news for Harriet would be about Mr Elton. However Knightley reveals that the offer of marriage would be from Mr Martin. He then praises Robert Martin as an excellent young man both as son and brother and that he had advised him to marry. Emma breaks the news that Harriet had refused Mr Martin's proposal. A surprised and angry Mr Knightley asserts that Harriet had nothing really to recommend her—she was a nobody by birth, she had no wealth, no respectable relations, and no accomplishments. To Emma, however, Robert Martin is of yeoman class and therefore inferior. Mr Knightley tells Emma that if she had decided on Mr Elton as a match for Harriet, she had laboured in vain. Mr Elton was a practical and rational man, not imprudent and would not 'throw himself away'.

GLOSSARY

voluntary	given freely without demand
unexceptionable	faultless
imprudent	rash
sentimental	having feelings of tenderness
rational	sensible, logical
abruptly	suddenly, unexpectedly
sanction	approval
tall indignation	(transferred epithet); 'tall' refers to the man who is angry and who stands upright

COMPREHENSION

1. Why and on what issue does Mr Martin consult Mr Knightley?
2. Record Mr Knightley's observations on Harriet. What is Emma's role in polishing the manner and behaviour of Harriet?
3. Identify what Mr Knightley means when he says Harriet would hear 'something to her advantage'. What is Emma's interpretation of it? Is she right?
4. What are Mr Knightley's views on Mr Martin?
5. Describe Mr Knightley's reaction to Emma's words: 'He wrote and was refused'.
6. Emma does not approve of Mr Martin as suitor and person. Why? What is the place of 'class consciousness' in match-making and in relationships in the world of Jane Austen?
7. Mr Knightley does not agree with Emma regarding Mr Martin. Why?
8. Examine Mr Knightley's criticism of Emma's match-making. Is she misusing her freedom and intelligence?
9. What is the contrast presented between Emma and Mr Knightley in the Harriet–Mr Martin episode?

Chapter 9

Summary

Mr Knightley is annoyed with Emma who, however, is not repentant. In the meantime, Mr Elton brings the portrait of Harriet, prettily framed. Harriet's literary pursuit, apart from reading, is making a collection of riddles and deciphering them. Mr Elton and Mr Woodhouse help her do this. Emma asks Mr Elton to write a charade for them. When it is produced she convinces Harriet that the charade read as 'courtship' indicating clearly Mr Elton's intentions. Harriet is duly impressed—what a difference there was between just writing a letter as Mr Martin had done, and a charade (!)

Jane Austen's irony characterises the dialogue as Emma in her self-deceived state, thinks Mr Elton is in love with Harriet and even convinces her. A touch of comedy prevails: Is Mr Martin rejected for himself or for his prose?

Glossary

repent	to feel sorry
endeared	cause to be loved
elegantly	prettily
transcribing	reproducing, copying out
enigmas	riddles, puzzles
charade	a game in which words are acted by players, often part by part, until guessed by other players
conundrum	riddle or difficult question especially with a pun in its answer
pay my addresses	show my respect
break off	end or discontinue suddenly
pomp	show
monarch	king
spirited	lively
'Harriet's feelings were visibly	Harriet's feelings matched her age and mental attitude. They were strong and firm.

forming themselves into as strong and steady an attachment as her youth and sort of mind admitted'	
'It will give you everything that you want—consideration, independence, a proper home'	Emma's observation that Harriet will get attention, freedom and a good home when Elton seeks her hand is ironic for Mr Elton is seeking Emma's hand.

Comprehension

1. Why could Emma not bring herself to repent or feel sorry?
2. How does Emma set about improving Harriet's intellect?
3. Identify Harriet's feelings towards Mr Elton. Are they real? Is she being manipulated?
4. Write out Mr Elton's charade in full. What is Emma's interpretation of it?
5. How does Emma convince Harriet that it is for her?
6. How does Emma see Harriet as benefiting from the connection with Mr Elton?
7. Comment on Harriet's reaction.
8. Consider deception and self-deception as central features of this chapter.

Chapter 10

Summary

Emma visits a poor sick family who lived down Vicarage Lane. She takes Harriet along with her. Mr Elton joins them. In order to give Mr Elton and Harriet an opportunity to come together, Emma pretends that her shoe lace had snapped. She takes permission to go into his house to replace it. Emma feels very happy in the anticipation that her scheme would work.

She allows Mr Elton and Harriet time to be by themselves and perhaps arrive at a marriage proposal. She hopes that the great event would follow thereafter. Emma's self-confidence is shown in an ironic light. Her 'match' is proved a 'mismatch' later.

GLOSSARY

charitable	kind and helpful
pretence	make believe, false claim
keep pace	walk at the same speed
obliged	compelled
resolution	decision
dexterously	skilfully
incessant	without stopping
adjoining	neighbouring
glory	great fame
schemed	plotted
accomplished	performed; completed
ingenious device	clever means

COMPREHENSION

1. What are Emma's attempts to separate herself from Harriet and Mr Elton?
2. How do they reach Mr Elton's house?
3. Narrate the shoe lace incident. Was Emma telling the truth in this incident?
4. Why is Emma so keen to bring them together?
5. 'The glory of having schemed successfully.' Explain.
6. Do you think Emma is right or self-deceived in the scheme?

CHAPTER 11

SUMMARY

The visit of Emma's sister's family keeps everyone busy and happy at Hartfield. John and Isabella Knightley are a happy couple with five children, a well-run London home and harmonious family relationships. Isabella's husband, John Knightley, is an intelligent and accomplished person. He and his wife seem to complement each other. Emma finds John Knightley's elder brother, George Knightley, rather ungracious at times. The sisters are very caring towards their father who still misses the company of Miss Taylor (now Mrs Weston). The people of Highbury eagerly await the arrival of Mr Weston's son, Frank, who had sent a message about his visit.

GLOSSARY

prime	first
induced	forced
apprehensively	nervously
forestalling	anticipating
competent	efficient
bustle	activity
melancholy	sad
grievous	very severe or serious

COMPREHENSION

1. How are John Knightley and Isabella described in this chapter? What aspects of their nature and marriage are highlighted?
2. Why does Emma disapprove of Mr Knightley? What does this indicate about Emma as a person?
3. What are Mr Woodhouse's feelings when Miss Taylor moves to her own house? Why does he feel this way?
4. How do Isabella and Emma react to Mr Woodhouse's outpourings? Comment.

5. Letters were important in Jane Austen's day as a means of communication, but also as a measure of a person's character and accomplishments. What are the comments made about Frank Churchill's letter?
6. From what you have read so far, what is the role of letters in the text, with reference to plot and character?

Chapter 12

Summary

Mr George Knightley is invited to join the Woodhouse family for dinner. This was an opportunity for Emma to make up to Mr Knightley and be friends with him again after their earlier difference of opinion. Mr Knightley remarks that if Emma were more rational and less imaginative, he and she would think alike. Emma wants to know whether Mr Martin was bitterly disappointed. The evening was spent with the brothers talking business and farming while Mr Woodhouse turned his attention to Emma.

Glossary

inclination	wish
procuring	getting
grave	serious
unceremoniousness	(discourtesy); abruptness in manner
amity	friendliness
estimate	judgement
fancy	imagination
whim	sudden flippant wish
discordancies	disagreements
conversible	full of conversation
anecdote	interesting story about a real incident
'If you were as much guided by nature in your estimate of men and women, and	If Emma were to follow her reason and understanding, and not her imagination, in her judgement of men and women as in her approach to children, both of them would have similar views.

as little under the power of fancy and whim in your dealings with them, as you are where these children are concerned, we might always think alike.'

COMPREHENSION

1. Why did Mr Woodhouse want to dine alone with Isabella?
2. What made Emma invite Mr George Knightley? What light does this throw on her character?
3. 'She certainly had not been in the wrong, and he would never own that he had.' What does this statement reveal about Emma and Mr Knightley?
4. According to Mr Knightley, when would he and Emma think alike?
5. 'Let us be friends and say no more about it.' Explain this statement and comment on Mr Knightley's nature.
6. Why was Mr Martin bitterly disappointed? How did Emma take the news?
7. What concerns preoccupy the brothers? How is 'class' a factor here?

CHAPTER 13

SUMMARY

The Knightleys spend their time at Hartfield happily with friendly visits and family togetherness. The one great event that happens is dinner with the Westons. Harriet, Mr Elton, and Mr George Knightley are invited on the occasion. But Harriet is ill with a cold and sore throat and cannot attend the party. Emma looks after her. An alarmed Mr Elton asks her to be careful and not to take risks while nursing Harriet. Emma mistakes Mr Elton's concern for her as concern for Harriet. John Knightley however suspects that Mr Elton's goodwill and concern are directed at Emma, and warns her about it. Emma assures him that she and Mr Elton are good friends and nothing more.

GLOSSARY

denial	refusal
depressed	sad, dejected
inflamed	swollen
was liable to	inclined towards
entreat	request
quitted	abandoned, left
regulate	plan, control
blunders	mistakes
partial	incomplete
counsel	advice
'blunders which often arise from a partial knowledge of circumstances'	ironical reference to Emma's self-deception

COMPREHENSION

1. Why was Mrs John Knightley happy?
2. Everyone looked forward to the dinner at the house of the Westons. Why? Who was invited to the occasion?
3. Why could Harriet not attend the dinner-party? How does Emma console her?
4. How does Mr Elton respond to Harriet's illness? What is his advice to Emma?
5. Do you think Mr Elton was concerned about Emma or about Harriet? Justify your answer.
6. What are Mr John Knightley's reactions to Mr Elton? He asks Emma to 'regulate her behaviour accordingly'. What does he mean?
7. What was Emma's response? Was she self-deceived?

CHAPTER 14

SUMMARY

Emma truly enjoys being with the Westons. She wants to be as much away from Mr Elton as possible but he sits close to her at the dinner-party and is most anxious to please her. His zealous attention makes him seem a lover. For Harriet's sake, Emma is polite to him and hopes that all would turn out right as she had planned. Frank, on the other hand, interested her. She expects him to be suited to her taste particularly as the Westons had already expected that a friendship would develop between them. Frank would visit Highbury when his aunt Mrs Churchill permitted. The Churchills were very possessive of Frank. Emma waits expectantly for Frank's visit.

GLOSSARY

unreserve	frankness
insufferable	intolerable
anxious	concerned, worried
zeal	enthusiasm
civil	polite
condition	status
reluctance	hesitation
devil of a temper	a very bad temper

COMPREHENSION

1. What is Emma's relationship with the Westons? How is it described in this chapter?
2. Give reasons why Emma wants to be away from Mr Elton.
3. What fears does she have about Mr Elton?
4. What features mark Mr Elton's behaviour as a lover?
5. Why are Mr Elton's 'civilities ill-timed?'

6. How does Emma imagine Frank Churchill to be? Is there a sense of vanity in Emma's wanting to be associated with Frank?
7. What picture of the Churchills do you get in this chapter?
8. What are the various views on Frank's impending visit? (Note Mrs Weston's remark and Emma's reaction.)

Chapter 15

Summary

Mr Elton continues to be irritatingly attentive towards Emma and even seeks Mrs Weston's help to plead with her to take care of herself. Mr Knightley brings news of heavy snow and bad weather but they could travel to Hartfield as two carriages were made available. Mr Woodhouse and the others get into one carriage, Mr Elton and Emma find themselves in the other. When they are alone Emma is shocked to hear Mr Elton profess his love to her in a vehement manner. She feels that he was drunk and had lost control of himself. She can not understand why Harriet's 'lover' should propose to her. She rejects him categorically and tells him that his love for Harriet is well-known. Mr Elton very strongly denies any attachment to Harriet and asserts that all that he had said or done is a mark of his adoration for Emma. Mr Elton further says that he visited Hartfield only to see her and that Harriet is not his social equal in any way. Mr Elton and Emma part angrily. Is Emma blind to her own actions and its consequences?

Glossary

late improprieties	recent improper behaviour
earnestness	seriousness
consternation	anxiety
triumph	victory
bleak	grim
assurances	emphatic declarations
elevate	lift

inconsistency	changeable mode
presumption	arrogance
ample	sufficient
supplication	pleading

Comprehension

1. How does Mr Elton express his concern for Emma? Why was Emma 'vexed', 'provoked and offended'?
2. What is Mr John Knightley's announcement concerning the weather and what does it say about him? How did Mr Woodhouse respond?
3. What evidence do we have in this chapter of Mr Woodhouse's dependence on Emma?
4. Why does Emma dread travelling alone in the coach with Mr Elton?
5. Describe what happens between Mr Elton and Emma during the journey.
6. Do you think Mr Elton's 'proposal' proves the truth of John Knightley's earlier remarks and Emma's own blindness and ignorance? Comment.
7. Is Emma right in accusing Mr Elton of 'unsteadiness of character'? How does he defend himself?
8. What are the consequences of Emma's match-making efforts? How are Emma and Mr Elton individually influenced by the issue of class and social status?
9. On what note does the parting between Emma and Mr Elton take place?

Chapter 16

Summary

Emma's review of what happened makes her realise that she had blundered. She never thought that Mr Elton was interested in her; she thought he had only respected her as Harriet's friend. She had made a mistake. She had been foolish in trying to bring the two together. However she is also convinced that his 'love' for her was based on self-interest. Possibly, he wanted an accomplished rich bride and Emma seemed suitable. After the incident Mr Elton does not return to Hartfield, much to Emma's relief. Emma introspects and recognises her error and is genuinely concerned for Harriet whom she had manipulated.

Glossary

confined	restricted
gallant	charming, impressive
pay his addresses	here, express his love
reverse	here, opposite (noun)
abundance	plenty
elegancies	graces
notch	dent, here a small portion
acute	strong
retentive	retaining facts and impressions
asunder	apart
'She was ashamed, and resolved to do such things no more.'	This refers to Emma's self-analysis with regard to match-making.

Comprehension

1. Emma realised that Mr Elton proved to be the reverse of what she thought him to be. Discuss her past and present views on Mr Elton.
2. To what extent does class and social standing play a part in Emma's analysis of Mr Elton's character?
3. What makes Emma think she is superior to Elton? What made Elton think Harriet is inferior?
4. What was Emma's error? How did she review it?
5. What are Emma's plans to remedy the situation particularly with regard to Harriet?
6. How does the snowfall help to ease the situation?

7. What impression of John Knightley is given at the end of the chapter?

Chapter 17

Summary

Since the weather was improving, Mr and Mrs Knightley leave Hartfield for London. Mr Elton informs Mr Woodhouse that he proposed to leave for Bath and bid farewell through a note sent to them. Though surprised, Emma feels that Mr Elton's carefully planned departure was most desirable. Emma visits Harriet and tells her how grossly mistaken she was. Harriet receives the news well realising that Elton was much above her 'class.' To console her and drive Mr Elton out of her mind, Emma takes Harriet to Hartfield and keeps her engaged.

Glossary

detained	held up
contriving	planning
agreeably	pleasantly
ungracious	not graceful or proper
grossly	here, fully
unvarying	unchanging
artless	natural and simple

Comprehension

1. What helped the Knightleys to return to London from Hartfield?
2. What were the contents of Mr Elton's note to Mr Woodhouse? What do you think of him?
3. The story in *Emma* moves forward through dialogue and conversation. Why is the letter quoted and not reported?
4. Consider Emma's reaction to Elton's note. What does she think of him at this moment?

5. Why was Emma's visit to Mrs Goddard more of a 'duty' call than anything else?
6. What was Harriet's reaction to Emma's confession of the turn of events?
7. How did Emma make up to Harriet for the blunder?

SUMMARY

Frank's visit is further delayed much to the disappointment of Mrs Weston. Mr Weston felt the delay was welcome as the latter time would be better in every way and would ensure a longer stay. Emma is too preoccupied with other matters to show disappointment overtly but she later expresses her disappointment and joins Mr and Mrs Weston in theirs. Emma also wants her privacy. She speaks to Mr Knightley about the Churchills and how they were keeping Frank away.

GLOSSARY

exceedingly	excessively; very
perceive	come to realise or understand
'She wanted to be quiet and out of temptation'	temptation here refers to Emma's natural bent for match-making

COMPREHENSION

1. Comment on the beginning of the chapter, 'Frank Churchill did not come. He could not be spared.'
2. What are the reactions of a. Emma b. Mrs Weston c. Mr Weston?
3. What does Emma tell Knightley? How do you see their relationship?

CHAPTER 19

SUMMARY

Jane Fairfax is an orphan whose father Lieutenant Fairfax died in action. Her mother Jane Bates, the youngest daughter of Mrs Bates, died of consumption. Colonel Campbell, who held Fairfax in high regard, sought out the young girl and brought her up along with his own daughter of her age. She was educated to be a governess to make her financially independent. However she made the best of a cultured upbringing with her abilities and disposition, using every opportunity for self-improvement. She has all the qualities of a mature, elegant and competent lady of high society. Emma perceives all these elegancies in her and though she feels guilty about it, she dislikes Jane—did she perceive a rival? Jane Fairfax at Highbury is politely reserved and non-committal. She has met Frank but is tight-lipped about her views and this irritates Emma.

GLOSSARY

indebted to	owing gratitude for a favour
subsistence	livelihood
rational	reasonable
judicious	careful and balanced
civilities	respects
refuted	disproved
acquit	free oneself
reserve	lack of warmth in manner or expression
eternal	for ever
imputed	attributed
depreciating	belittling
complacency	here, calmness
provocations	irritations
candour	frankness
hazard	risk

Comprehension

1. Who is Jane Fairfax? Who were her parents and relatives and who brought her up?
2. Describe the relationship between Lieutenant Fairfax and Colonel Campbell.
3. What circumstances made Jane a part of the Campbell family?
4. How did Colonel Campbell plan for Jane's future?
5. What kind of upbringing did Jane have? How did it affect her personality?
6. What were the circumstances that brought Jane to Highbury?
7. Comment on the tone with which Jane Fairfax is described in this chapter? What does it convey about her?
8. Why does Emma dislike Jane Fairfax? Which of Jane's traits irritate her?
9. What are the reasons given by Mr Knightley for Emma's dislike of Jane Fairfax?
10. Emma looked at Jane Fairfax with 'twofold complacency; the sense of pleasure and the sense of rendering justice'. What does this mean?
11. If Emma were permitted and the circumstances were right, what would Emma have done for Jane Fairfax?
12. What were Jane Fairfax's comments on her meeting with Frank Churchill? What did Emma see that as an indication of?

Chapter 20

Summary

Emma's politeness towards Jane Fairfax is praised by her father and Mr Knightley. Jane's elegance and culture are commended even as her status is pitied. Mr Knightley is about to give Emma 'a piece of news' when Miss Bates comes on a visit with Jane Fairfax and thanks Emma profusely for the pork sent to her house. She also brings the news that Mr Elton is to be married to a Miss Hawkins. Mr Knightley has already heard this from the neighbours. They discuss the match; to Emma it is an amusing but welcome piece of news though it would surely hurt Harriet.

Harriet comes to see Emma and excitedly tells her of her experience with the Martins. It had been raining. Robert Martin had taken special care to inform her of an alternative route to take as the shortest route was flooded. A visibly agitated Harriet is consoled by Emma who cautiously reveals the news of Elton's marriage.

GLOSSARY

resentment	ill feeling
discern	notice
approbation	praise
diffidence	lack of confidence
overpowered	overwhelmed
bountiful	plenty; generous
agitated	upset
haberdasher	shopkeeper who sells sewing materials (pins, sewing thread and other things for dressmaking)
exerted	tried hard
trifle	small matter
serviceable	useful
deadening	destroying
retaining	keeping

COMPREHENSION

1. How does Mr Woodhouse explain Jane Fairfax's 'reserve'? Does Emma agree?
2. Give examples of Emma's neighbourly goodwill.
3. What is the unexpected piece of news brought by Knightley and delivered by Miss Bates?
4. How does Emma react to the news?
5. Give your impression of Miss Bates. Does her behaviour in this chapter match her description as 'tiresome' in the previous chapter?
6. Why is Harriet so agitated?

7. How does Emma reveal to Harriet the news of Elton's marriage?

Chapter 21

Summary

Augusta Hawkins, Mr Elton's bride, is introduced in this chapter. She is a person who has an independent income and is therefore a suitable bride to the practical Mr Elton. She had, moreover become very quickly impressed with Mr Elton and had agreed to marry him. The wedding was to take place shortly and she would then move to Highbury.

Jane Austen describes Miss Hawkins through Emma's eyes. Austen uses this technique with great ease and with success. Emma does not think highly of Miss Hawkins especially in comparing her with Harriet. Miss Hawkins is of moderate means and Emma dislikes her from the very beginning. The chapter draws attention to Emma's loyalty to Harriet as a friend, but also to class snobbery which is evident here.

Glossary

defying	opposing
not thrown himself away	not connected to someone beneath his standing
rapidity	speed
rencontre	meeting
vanity	a false sense of pride
prudence	good sense
drudge	person who does dull work
'very well married'	married to a person of fortune
'What she was, must be uncertain, but who she was might be found out'	The statement is a comment on the fact that though Augusta Hawkins was yet to prove herself and her character, her social background could easily be investigated.

Comprehension

1. Compare and contrast the Mr Elton who left Highbury and the one who returned to it. Also describe his former and current attitude to Emma and Harriet.
2. Consider the background and status of Augusta Hawkins. How do she and Mr Elton match each other?
3. Augusta Hawkins brought 'no name, no blood, no alliance.' Explain this point and compare her with Harriet. (Take into account Knightley's remark on Harriet earlier.)
4. Comment on 'That was the glory of Miss Hawkins.' What is implied in 'glory'? What gave Miss Hawkins her status?
5. What are Emma's feelings about Mr Elton's return and of his new match?

Chapter 22

Summary

Frank Churchill's long-awaited arrival brings happiness to all. He visits Hartfield along with his father Mr Weston. Emma is not disappointed. She finds him handsome, lively, sensible. He knows how to make himself agreeable. He is all praise for his new mother, Mrs Weston. Emma feels she should meet him more often to 'understand his ways.' Frank discloses that he plans to visit Jane Fairfax whom he has already been acquainted with.

Glossary

accosted	greeted
air	bearing, demeanour
well-bred ease of manner	composure, in keeping with good upbringing

Comprehension

1. Describe Emma's reaction to Frank Churchill's arrival.
2. Emma felt she liked him when he visited Hartfield. Why was this so?
3. It is repeated that Frank knew 'how to make himself agreeable'. What does this mean? Do you think it comes naturally to him?
4. Is there any reason for Jane Fairfax being mentioned 'casually'?

Summary

Much to Emma's surprise, Churchill visits Hartfield again, this time with Mrs Weston. She appreciates his behaviour towards Mrs Weston, his interest in the activities of Hartfield and the attentive manner in which he speaks and listens to her. His ideas seem moderate, his feelings warm. He is very interested in reviving the ball at Crown Inn. They speak of Jane Fairfax, her health, her future career, and her brilliance at the piano. Emma warms up to Frank Churchill and regards herself totally compatible with him.

Glossary

quest	search
deference	regard
make amends for	make up for
pause	stop

Comprehension

1. How does Highbury respond to Frank Churchill?
2. Why is Emma surprised at Frank Churchill's second visit?
3. How does Churchill show his eagerness to 'belong' to Hartfield?
4. Summarise Churchill's views on Jane Fairfax—her appearance, talent and plan for the future. What is Emma's view?

5. Do you think Churchill is reluctant to talk about Jane? Justify.
6. What are Emma's conclusions about Frank Churchill after the second visit?

Chapter 24

Summary

Frank's departure to London for the silly reason of having a hair cut left Emma a little shaken. But for this, Frank's conduct and bearing won her near-total approval. Probably he was in love with her but she remained indifferent as she had resolved never to marry. Also Emma looked up to the Westons whose opinion she trusted. At this time she receives an invitation for a party from the Coles. The Coles rose to fortune from trading origins and used to throw parties to the well-established genteel folk of Highbury. Emma wanted the Coles to know that superior families (like hers) could not be dictated to. When the well-written invitation comes, the Westons are with her and advise her to accept. However Mr Woodhouse would be unable to go due to the late hour and was concerned about Emma. She reassures him of her safety. (This incident shows Emma's snobbish airs and at the same time her self-deception is seen.)

Glossary

foppery	dandyism
blot	here, mistake/ blemish
distinguished	prominent
opportune	well-timed
acquiescence	agreement
civilly	politely
Donwell and Randalls	Donwell is the name of the residence of Mr Knightley. Randalls is where the Westons live.
scruples	moral principles
mimic	imitate

Comprehension

1. Why did Churchill appear a 'fop' to Emma? (Some critics speak of Churchill's French or 'francophile' manners as against Knightley's British ways.)
2. Give Emma's reasons for conferring on Mr Churchill, a 'distinguished honour'.
3. Furnish details about the Coles, their status and way of life. Why did Emma disapprove of them?
4. What made Emma feel superior to the Coles?
5. How does class affect social behaviour? Give examples from the text you have read so far.
6. What does the invitation reveal about the Coles? Why does Emma accept it though she wanted to refuse the invitation and insult the Coles?
7. Why could Mr Woodhouse not attend the dinner? What were the conditions under which Emma would be permitted to go?

Summary

The Coles' party is well-organised. There is a large crowd. In spite of her earlier air of condescension, Emma is at ease and also very much impressed with the cordiality and the careful arrangements. What attracts attention is the pianoforte sent as a gift to Jane presumably by Colonel Campbell. Mrs Weston seems to think that Mr Knightley is in love with Jane Fairfax. Emma resents this idea as her nephew Henry (Isabella's son) would then be denied his inheritance. He is a contented farmer and scholar. She dislikes the idea of Jane becoming the mistress of Donwell. In any case, Knightley does not dance with Jane. Emma and Jane plays the piano—the latter's performance is far superior to Emma's. Frank Churchill is over-solicitous to Emma which makes her suspect his motives.

Emma's situation is comic and ironic for even as she disapproves of Mrs Weston's remarks, she is unable to recognise her own feelings towards Knightley.

GLOSSARY

astonishment	amazement
benevolence	kindness
disparity	difference
haunting	visiting regularly
entreaty	earnest request
touchstone	criterion
languid	lazy, slow moving
'and for an act of unostentatious kindness there is nobody whom I would fix on more than on Mr Knightley'	Mr Knightley alone, according to Emma, could be so unpretentious and kind in allowing the Bateses the use of his carriage.

COMPREHENSION

1. What is Mrs Coles's news? Why was it surprising?
2. How do Jane and Miss Bates react?
3. Who do they suppose had sent the gift of the pianoforte?
4. What makes Mrs Weston object to Jane's walking home? What are Emma's comments?
5. Who gives the Bateses a carriage to take them home? Why does Emma find this appropriate?
6. Mrs Weston makes a match between Jane Fairfax and Knightley.
   - Note her arguments.
   - Note Emma's reactions.
   - Anticipate Knightley's reactions.
   - What is your view?
7. Why do you think Emma was asked to play the piano first? Compare Emma's performance on the piano with Jane's.
8. What are Mr Knightley's remarks on the gift of the piano?
9. What is Frank Churchill's attitude towards Jane Fairfax?

Chapter 26

Summary

Emma has pleasant recollections of the dinner party at the Coles'. They are delighted with Emma who is pleased to have made them happy even though they were not her 'social equals'. Emma accompanies Harriet to Ford's to ensure that nothing amiss takes place between her and the Martins were she to meet them again. Mrs Weston and Frank whom she meets are on their way to the Bateses' house to hear the new instrument. Emma joins them. As usual, Miss Bates talks endlessly—about the piano, about Mr Knightley's generosity, about the baked apples, and about Jane's health. The visitors go upstairs to see Jane.

Glossary

condescension	act of looking down upon
amusement	entertainment, distraction
entreat	to ask someone earnestly to do something
rivet	short metal pin for holding together two plates of metal
wholesome	healthy

Comprehension

1. What are Emma's recollections of the party?
2. Comment on Emma's attitude towards Harriet. Is she too protective? Is she ensuring that her wishes and plans for Harriet prevail?
3. What is the object of Frank's visit to the Bateses?
4. Miss Bates was earlier described as a 'great talker on little matters'. What do we see of this aspect of her character in this chapter?

5. Is there an absence of class consciousness in the way Emma, Mr Knightley and the others relate to Miss Bates? Comment.

CHAPTER 27

SUMMARY

In the peaceful setting of the Bateses' home, Emma, Jane and Frank find themselves together. Frank appears to show more attention to Emma in making sure she sat by him and in picking out the best baked apple for her. Jane's piano playing wins all-round applause. Emma feels the visit had lasted long and they all leave.

GLOSSARY

tranquillity	peace
slumbering	sleeping
countenance	face
contrived	planned

COMPREHENSION

1. How would you describe the atmosphere in the Bateses' home?
2. Why do you think Frank wanted to be near Emma?
3. 'Emma joined her in all her praise, and the pianoforte was pronounced to be altogether of the highest promise.' What does this statement refer to? Is there irony implied in the situation?

Chapter 28

Summary

Frank's desire to dance again at Highbury finds favour with the Westons. It is decided that the Crown Inn would be the venue and not Randalls, in spite of Mr Woodhouse's complaints of dampness. Emma sets his fears at rest by pointing out how careful and meticulous Mrs Weston was concerning the comfort and well-being of everyone. Even Miss Bates is consulted. Emma is booked for the first two dances by Frank. The Westons' delight is obvious.

Glossary

acquiescence	consent
approbation	approval
talk it over	discuss
carefulness itself	extremely careful (carefulness personified)
projected	proposed
council	meeting
blockhead	fool
secured	booked, ensured of

Comprehension

1. Why is the Crown Inn chosen as the venue for the ball?
2. What is Emma's reaction to the announcement?
3. What are Mr Woodhouse's reservations concerning the Crown Inn? How does Emma put her father's mind at ease?
4. What aspects of Mrs Weston's character are revealed in the planning of the event?
5. Emma says of Miss Bates: 'She will be all delight and gratitude, but she will tell you nothing. She will not even listen to your questions.' What does this remark say of Miss Bates? What does it say of Emma?

6. Mr Weston whispers to his wife, 'He has asked her, my dear. That's right. I knew he would.' What is implied by this comment?

CHAPTER 29

SUMMARY

The ball is to be held on a day when Frank was still in Hartfield. However, he is suddenly recalled to Escombe, as his aunt Mrs Churchill had taken ill and needed him. The delightful evening event has to be cancelled. Frank brings the news to Emma and seems pained and embarrassed to leave. It is as if he had something important to say too. Emma feels that he must be more in love with her than she had supposed. Was she also in love with him? He said he would keep in touch through letters to Mrs Weston. He had visited the Bateses' house too to bid goodbye to Jane and Miss Bates. Mr Knightley is indifferent to all this but feels sympathetic towards Emma on the cancellation of the ball. Jane Fairfax's composure upsets Emma.

GLOSSARY

wanting	lacking
surmise	guess
slight	disrespect
composure	state of being calm, in control of oneself
odious	not likeable at all
impute	attribute
unbecoming	not fitting or appropriate
languor	tiredness or inactivity
'they never occurred but for her own convenience'	Mrs Churchill's illness came and disappeared according to her whim; it was not always genuine.

Comprehension

1. How are the venue and the date of the ball decided upon?
2. Compare and contrast the attitude of Mr Knightley and Jane Fairfax to the ball.
3. What are the contents of the letter from Mr Churchill to his nephew Frank? How does it affect the plans for the ball?
4. Comment on the scene when Frank comes to say goodbye to Emma. Does he express his true feelings? Justify.
5. What do you think is the underlying meaning behind the description of Frank's leave-taking?
6. 'She must be a little in love with him, in spite of every previous determination against it.' Explain.
7. How does Mr Knightley respond to the cancellation of the ball? What is his concern for Emma in this regard?
8. Why is Emma displeased with Jane's behaviour?

Chapter 30

Summary

Emma tries to analyse her love for Frank. Is it too much or too little? Probably he is very much in love but she would be on her guard. She would not encourage it as she is convinced he was not 'necessary' for her happiness. Frank's letter to Mrs Weston makes many references to Emma, only one to Harriet. This does not bring about a change in Emma's mind. Frank must do without her, and Harriet may be a good choice. The event that everyone eagerly awaited is Elton's wedding day. Harriet is restless on this account and Emma is very attentive to her so that she can lessen her grief.

Glossary

adieus	farewells
in everybody's mouth	everyone was talking about it
in a flutter of spirits	in a state of anxiety
submissive	passive, obedient

Comprehension

1. Why does Emma think she is only very 'little in love' while Frank is 'very much in love'? (See paragraphs 1 and 2 of text)
2. What does Emma see as the conclusion to Frank's imaginary declarations of love to her?
3. What are the contents of Frank's letter? How do they affect Emma?
4. What is the event that occupies everyone's mind?
5. Comment on Harriet's situation. How far is Emma responsible for it? Does Emma make it up to her and how?

Chapter 31

Summary

Mrs Elton, whom everyone at Highbury was looking forward to see, is first seen at church. Emma takes Harriet with her to visit Mrs Elton in order to fulfil a social obligation. Mr Elton is in the comic situation of being, at the same time, in the company of the woman he had married, the woman whom he wanted to marry (Emma), and the woman whom he was expected to marry (Harriet). The visit is returned. The new Mrs Elton is good-looking but egoistic and not at all elegant by Emma's standards. Her remarks about various members of society are also inappropriate and offensive. Emma does not like Mrs Elton but is polite to her. Emma continues to entertain the idea that Harriet would have been a better match for Mr Elton. Harriet feels that Mrs Elton has become quite attached to her husband. Emma is relieved when the visit ends.

Glossary

pert	attractively lively or cheeky
familiar	informal
barouche-landau	form of horse carriage
egoistic	interested more in oneself
insufferable	unbearable
glibly	insincere and shallow

Comprehension

1. How does Jane Austen present Mrs Elton even before Emma's opinions are presented in the novel?
2. Why does Emma decide to visit Mrs Elton without delay? Why does she take Harriet along?
3. What are Emma's initial impressions of Mrs Elton? What are her later reactions to her?
4. What is Mr Elton's dilemma? How does the author describe it? What is your view?
5. Why does Emma feel that Harriet would have been a better match for Mr Elton?
6. What do Mrs Elton and Emma talk about? What opinion do you form of Mrs Elton?
7. What do Emma's answers reveal about Mr Elton and also about Emma?
8. What does Emma find offensive about Mrs Elton's remarks?

Chapter 32

Summary

Mr and Mrs Elton make their presence felt in Highbury society. However Emma does not in any way encourage Mrs Elton. In fact, she is cold and indifferent towards her. Mrs Elton in turn is aloof towards Emma and unfriendly towards Harriet. However, Mrs Elton is particularly caring towards Jane Fairfax, even offering to encourage her talents and find a suitable position for her through her own personal connections. Jane's extended stay at Highbury and her acceptance of Mrs Elton's kindness is a puzzle to Emma. Mr Knightley's explanation is that while others had ignored Jane, Mrs Elton took an interest in her. Emma wonders if Knightley would marry Jane since he had such a high opinion of her. Mr Knightley assures her that he would not. He said that Jane Fairfax was a charming young woman but that she did not have the 'open temper' he desired in a woman. Mrs Weston, however, did not share these thoughts, or rather, she thought differently.

Glossary

sneering	contemptuous or mocking
negligent	failing to take proper care of
exert	make the effort
endeavour	try
eligible	suitable
decree	order
reproachful	expressing disapproval
caution	carefulness
alluded to	referred to
forbearance	restraint and tolerance

Comprehension

1. Does Mrs Elton's attitude towards Emma and Harriet change in any way after several meetings? If so, how? Comment on this.
2. What are Mrs Elton's plans for Jane Fairfax?
3. How does Emma respond to Mrs Elton's interest in Jane's well-being?
4. What is Mr Knightley's stand concerning Jane Fairfax as a possible match?
5. Why do you think Emma is relieved with his response?
6. Compare Emma's matchmaking and Mrs Weston's. What are Mrs Weston's suspicions concerning Mr Knightley?

Chapter 33

Summary

Emma decides to host a conventional dinner for the newly married Eltons. Only eight persons could be invited as Mr Woodhouse could not tolerate more company than that. Harriet does not wish to attend. The Westons, Mr Knightley and Jane Fairfax accept the invitation. Mr John Knightley comes with his two sons much to the anxiety of Mr Woodhouse. In the course of the conversation Jane Fairfax confesses to having walked to the post office to collect her letters: everybody is disturbed by this confession. Mrs Elton offers to collect the letters on her behalf; Jane Fairfax refuses the offer. The guests are looked after well. Emma suspects that Jane is 'involved' with someone but resolves not to hurt Jane by enquiring about it.

Glossary

odious	hateful
decline	to refuse in a polite manner
fortitude	patience
conscience-stricken	experiencing feelings of guilt
urbanity	courteousness
solicitude	careful attention
abstain	refrain from

Comprehension

1. Why does Emma invite the Eltons for dinner despite her dislike of Mrs Elton?
2. Why does Emma want to be more friendly with Jane? What is she guilty of in this regard?
3. What do you think prompted Jane to brave the rain to collect her letters?
4. Mrs Elton offers to collect Jane's letters. What aspect of her character does this reflect?
5. Why does Jane refuse Mrs Elton's offer to help collect her letters?
6. What are Emma's suspicions about the whole episode and what it means?
7. Why does Emma refrain from openly asking Jane Fairfax about it?

Chapter 34

Summary

In the after-dinner interactions, Mrs Weston and Emma are seated together while Mrs Elton and Jane are with each other. The post office, the weather and its effect and fetching letters are the subjects discussed at length. Mrs Elton says she would try her best to find a position for Jane but Jane does not seem to care for one. Mrs Elton continues to talk to Jane about her bridal attire and her taste for simplicity. Mr Weston brings Frank's letter with news of his coming. Mrs Weston is pleased and Emma more than slightly agitated.

Glossary

repressed	restrained
meditated	pre-planned
on the watch	alert
beau	suitor
gallantry	a man's polite attention
quaint	strange

Comprehension

1. After dinner, how do the guests group themselves? Why?
2. In a society in which good manners are considered very important, how does Mrs Elton conduct herself?
3. What is it about Mr Woodhouse that has a special appeal for Mrs Elton?
4. What is the news brought by Mr Weston? How does Mrs Weston react to it? What is Emma's reaction?
5. Some of the events in the text are elaborated through letters, which are either reproduced fully or are spoken about. Make a list of such letters and explain how they are important to the action in the novel.

Chapter 35

Summary

Frank's arrival upsets Emma. Her concern is more for him and his being in love with her than for her own condition. She does not wish to have her affections entangled with his. Their meeting is cordial. Frank's aunt, Mrs Churchill, is to be shifted to Richmond for medical reasons. Mr Weston is happy on hearing of this as Frank would then be only an hour's ride away from them. One good outcome of all this is that the ball at the Crown Inn could now take place.

Glossary

reflection	thought
apprehensive	anxious
entangled	get involved
eminent	important
indisputable	unquestionable

Comprehension

1. Why is Emma agitated on hearing of Frank's arrival?
2. Why does Emma want to keep Frank away?
3. Describe the meeting between Frank and Emma.
4. What was the happy outcome of Frank's moving to Richmond?
5. Why was Mr Weston particularly happy about this development? Did he anticipate something?
6. What is the author suggesting in the concluding sentence to the chapter: 'A very few tomorrows stood between the young people of Highbury and happiness'?

Chapter 36

Summary

Emma goes earlier than others to the ball. She meets Frank who is determined to have a delightful evening. He projects himself as a fine man who enjoys the company of the women. Mrs Elton, addressing Mr Weston, praises him in his hearing. She arranges for the carriage to be sent for Miss Bates and Miss Fairfax who are most appreciative of the kindness extended to them. Frank ensures that he is with Emma most of the time. The ball is led by Mr Weston and Mrs Elton (an honour given to newlyweds) followed by Frank and Emma. Emma is offended that she did not get the offer to lead the ball, but she does not allow this to ruin her pleasure. She is concerned that Mr Knightley who stood out in grace and appearance does not enjoy dancing. She and Frank relate to each other as 'cheerful easy friends' rather than lovers. Mr Elton's indifference and rudeness to Harriet is countered by Mr Knightley's offer to dance with her. Emma is full of gratitude and kindly feelings towards Mr Knightley. Mr Knightley asks Emma to dance with him.

Glossary

misfortune	unhappy event
entreaties	earnest or humble requests
gratify	to give someone pleasure or satisfaction
out of hearing	away from hearing distance
candidly	in a straightforward manner
complacently	satisfied with oneself, smugly
transformation	change
station	position
discourse	conversation
this little rub	friction (here, caused by the importance given to the Eltons)
fortitude	courage in pain
irresistibly	attractive and tempting

reprobation	disapproval of
littleness	pettiness
amiable	pleasing
artless	innocent

Comprehension

1. What does 'misfortune' in the opening paragraph refer to? Explain 'everything was safe.'
2. What are Mr Weston's entreaties to Emma?
3. How does Frank behave on arrival?
4. Why is Emma interested in Churchill's opinion of the newly wed Mrs Elton?
5. What is Frank Churchill's gallant gesture towards the ladies? Is it a reflection of his person or of his society and its norms?
6. Comment on Mrs Elton's opinion of Frank Churchill. Why was she so pleased with him?
7. Why was Mrs Elton so anxious to 'take care' of Jane Fairfax?
8. What do you see as Miss Bates's outstanding characteristic? Give examples of her simplicity and humaneness. What do you think is her role?
9. Show how the ball reveals the character traits of a. Mr Elton, b. Mrs Elton, c. Frank Churchill, d. Emma, e. Knightley, f. Miss Bates
10. 'She wished he could love a ballroom better and could like Frank Churchill better.' Who is Emma referring to and why does she feel so?
11. Comment on Mr Knightley's remark to Emma: 'You would have chosen for him (Elton) better than he has chosen for himself.' Do you agree?
12. What is the significance of Mr Knightley asking Emma for a dance?

CHAPTER 37

SUMMARY

Frank Churchill rushes to Hartfield with a frightened and fainting Harriet on his arm. She is in a state of shock. It turns out that Harriet had been mobbed by a group of gypsies when she was out for a walk about half a mile beyond Highbury accompanied by a friend (who was also at Mrs Goddard's when Harriet studied there). Frank Churchill had come upon her by chance and rescued her. Emma seeing them together is tempted to make her 'match-making' plans.

GLOSSARY

sufficed	was enough
assailed	attacked by
clamorous	noisy
impertinent	rude
groundwork of anticipation	This is a reference to the conclusions that Emma draws on seeing Frank and Harriet together.
'Such an adventure as this – a fine young man and a lovely young woman thrown together in such a way, could hardly fail of suggesting certain ideas to the coldest heart and the steadiest brain'	Even an unfeeling individual would conclude from Harriet's rescue by Frank that they were lovers. This is the author's observation on the way people tend to think.

Comprehension

1. What was Harriet's frightening experience?
2. How did Frank Churchill happen to arrive on the scene?
3. What does the 'groundwork of anticipation' refer to here? What is Emma gearing herself up for?

Chapter 38

Summary

Harriet's moral scruples lead her to destroy Elton's remembrances and letters sent by him to her in the past. Emma sees this act as the beginning of a relationship with Frank Churchill. Harriet expresses her admiration and respect for a noble individual who rendered her service. Thinking it to be Churchill Emma encourages her that it is a mark of Harriet's good taste to choose one so superior to her. This is ironic because Emma thinks Harriet is referring to Frank, when Harriet was actually thinking of someone else.

Glossary

undesignedly	without prior planning
trivial	of very little importance
veneration	respect
disparity	a great difference
sanguine	cheerfully optimistic
degradation	descent to a mean position
'more wonderful things have taken place, there have been matches of greater disparity'	It is ironical that Harriet and Emma think they are referring to the same person when they are not. Emma advises Harriet to examine her feelings and avoid naming the person.

Note: (This complicates the matter further.) In the past, there have been marriages taking place between persons of different social status. She adds that Harriet has shown good taste in her choice – Emma actually means Frank but Harriet has someone 'nobler' in mind.

Comprehension

1. 'There it goes and there is an end of Mr Elton.' Explain Harriet's action and describe her feelings.
2. 'Plain dealing was always best.' Could this be a description of Emma's nature? Comment.
3. Emma moves from making one match to making another one. What is Emma's advice to Harriet on the occasion? What is her opinion on Harriet's choice?
4. Why does Harriet say that she would never marry?
5. To what extent is 'class' an important factor in match-making during the time of Jane Austen? How is this made evident in this chapter?

Chapter 39

Summary

Mr Knightley's dislike of Frank Churchill grows with time. He holds Frank in distrust and suspects him of double dealing in his pursuit of Emma. He also suspects a 'private understanding' between Frank and Jane. When all of them are together for tea, Frank enquires of Mr Perry's carriage and his plans concerning it. Since Frank appears to have access to some privileged information in this regard, everyone in the room wonders how he knew about this plan. When Frank realises that he had spoken out of turn, he pretends innocence. Mr Knightley watches Frank and Jane closely and with suspicion. In the word game that follows, Harriet discovers the word 'blunder'. Jane blushes. Mr Knightley feels convinced that Frank was playing a deeper game. It is his duty to protect Emma, he thinks. When he mentions a possible attachment between Frank and Jane, Emma dismisses it vehemently. He could not press the matter further and decides to take his leave.

Glossary

double-dealing	cheating
guarded	careful
discretion	behaving in such a way as to avoid causing offence
indiscretion	lacking good judgement
preceded	gone before
suppressed	restrained, kept in check
blunder	mistake
ostensible	appearing to be true but not necessarily so
distrust	doubting the honesty of
presume	take for granted
staggered	astonished or shocked
'It was a child's play, chosen to conceal a deeper game on Frank Churchill's part'	The puzzle with words was very easy to solve, but to Knightley it was a mask to hide something more serious, especially in the relationship between Frank and Jane.

Comprehension

1. Mr Knightley suspects Frank of double dealing. What evidence does he have?
2. Why does he suspect a relationship between Frank and Jane?
3. How does Mrs Weston, Miss Bates and Mr Knightley react when Frank Churchill brings up the issue of Mr Perry's carriage?
4. How does Frank respond to the awkward situation he finds himself in?
5. Was there a private understanding between Jane and Frank Churchill over the matter of Perry's carriage? How do we know this? How is the issue continued in the course of the word game?
6. What are Mr Knightley's observations? What does he think of Frank?
7. How is Mr Knightley's concern for Emma expressed in this chapter? How does this foresee what is to come?
8. What does Emma think of Churchill's and Jane's relationship?

CHAPTER 40

SUMMARY

A visit to Box Hill is planned for but could not take place. Mr Knightley suggests that they visit Donwell and taste his strawberries. Mrs Elton is delighted at the thought of going somewhere and wanted to be Lady Patroness choosing the guests. Mr Knightley tells her firmly that until a Mrs Knightley arrives on the scene he could manage his own affairs. Mrs Elton asks if she could bring Jane Fairfax with her. Even though it was hot the guests enjoy the walk in the garden, the strawberries, and the shade of the lime tree. Emma sees Jane hurrying away. She stops to request Emma to inform the others that she had to go home. Emma sees her off safely: Jane seems to be agitated and desires to be alone. Frank Churchill comes in a little later but appears to be 'out of humour'. Emma is secretly relieved to be out of love with Frank Churchill and subject to his fluctuating moods. Frank however continues to make wild declarations that she is his 'best cure'. When told of the proposed trip to Box Hill the following day Frank agrees to stay and join Emma.

GLOSSARY

put off	postponed
vexatious	annoying
carte blanche	complete freedom of action or discretion
out of humour	in a bad mood
modes	methods
'cabbage beds would have been enough to tempt the lady, who only wanted to be going somewhere'	a humorous and ironic comment on the lady, Mrs Elton, whose manners were not polished and refined enough. Mrs Elton is keen to be invited to a gathering. Any excuse would give her adequate reason to visit Mr Knightley's house. Even if only cabbages were being grown she would have accepted the invitation.

Comprehension

1. Describe the plan to explore Box Hill. What leads to the change of plans?
2. What is Mr Knightley's suggestion? What attraction does Donwell have for the ladies?
3. What does Mrs Elton propose to do in the role of Lady Patroness?
4. What aspects of Mr Knightley's character are highlighted in the conversation between him and Mrs Elton?
5. Do you think Mrs Elton is concerned about others? Illustrate from the text.
6. What are Emma's thoughts on seeing Mr Knightley and Harriet together?
7. Why does Jane Fairfax leave suddenly and what are Emma's reactions to this?
8. Why is Frank Churchill 'out of humour'? Did Emma sympathise with him?
9. What is Emma's request concerning the anticipated trip to Box Hill and what is Frank's reply?

Chapter 41

Summary

Initially, the Box Hill expedition seems dull to Emma. But the arrangements and the weather made for a pleasant get-together. Frank is all attention to Emma, and he is more than amiable and friendly with Emma. Still Emma looked on him only as a friend. In the course of the day's entertainment Emma makes fun of Miss Bates who feels hurt on hearing Emma's remarks. The Eltons move away for a walk. Frank comments that the Eltons, in spite of their brief acquaintance with each other, seem made for one another. This opens up the conversational topic of marriage, prudent and imprudent attachments and their consequences. Jane Fairfax and Emma are drawn into this exchange. Mr Knightley admonishes Emma for her rudeness to Miss Bates. Emma feels very ashamed of herself.

GLOSSARY

commission	task
enlivened	to be entertained
rued	regretted
imprudent	rash
irresolute	uncertain
remonstrance	rebuke
insolent	lack of respect
irksome	irritating
reproach	to express disappointment
sullenness	ill humour
'Miss Bates, deceived by the mock ceremony of her manner, did not immediately catch her meaning; . . . could pain her':	Miss Bates did not understand that Emma was making fun of her. She admitted to dull utterances but was visibly hurt. Emma later feels truly ashamed of her action; even Mr Knightley reprimands her and helps her see the point.

COMPREHENSION

1. How are flagging spirits, meaning sullen and depressed moods, revived at Box Hill?
2. How does Frank Churchill behave towards Emma and how does she respond? What impression does this create among the others?
3. What game does Frank suggest? What does Emma say?
4. Considering Emma's remarks to Miss Bates, do you agree with the view that Emma is a 'dreadful snob' and Miss Bates 'an innocent fool'? Discuss.
5. What are Frank's and Jane Fairfax's views on marriage partners? What does this reveal about their 'secret relationship'?
6. Why does Emma react the way she does when Mr Knightley criticises her for her rudeness? Comment on her behaviour here.

Chapter 42

Summary

Emma, truly repentant for her rudeness to Miss Bates, calls on her to begin a new, equal and amiable relationship. Miss Bates is very apologetic for making her wait. Emma notices that Jane was looking very ill. Miss Bates informs her that Jane was soon to leave to take up a governess's post in Mrs Smallridge's house to look after her three girls. She was to leave in a fortnight. Emma observes that her friends would be sorry to lose her. Frank had been summoned to Richmond as Mrs Churchill was very ill. The class issue comes to the fore once again as Emma ponders over the fact that Mrs Churchill could command immediate attention and respect while Jane Fairfax seemed a non-entity. The irony is not lost on the reader.

Glossary

contrition	repentance
'Emma's conscience told her there was less ease of look and manner'	Having hurt Miss Bates's feelings Emma was guilty about it and felt that perhaps Miss Bates was not comfortable in her presence.

Comprehension

1. Why does Emma visit Miss Bates? What does it reveal about her?
2. What is Miss Bates's reaction to Emma's sudden visit?
3. Why does Emma feel pity on seeing Jane? What does her 'former ungenerous suspicion' of Jane refer to?
4. Why does Jane accept the offer of the post of governess?
5. On hearing that Frank had to leave for Richmond on account of Mrs Churchill's health, what are Emma's thoughts on the contrasting destinies of two women? What is the role of 'class' here?

CHAPTER 43

SUMMARY

When Emma returns home, Mr Knightley and Harriet are with her father. Mr Knightley is pleased that Emma has visited Miss Bates and Emma feels convinced that she has won back his good opinion. News of Mrs Churchill's death reaches Randalls. She is spoken of well in death in spite of having been generally disliked in life. Emma wishes to be kind to Jane Fairfax to make up for her earlier coldness towards her. However, Jane refuses her invitation to Hartfield. On hearing that Jane was unable to eat much on account of her illness, Emma decides to send her arrowroot selected from her store and meant for a convalescent. It is turned down. Emma realises that Jane was resolved not to take anything from her but consoles herself that her intentions were well-meant, though not taken so well..

GLOSSARY

indubitable	not to be doubted
amity	friendly relations
dilatory	roundabout
deranged	here, her health is not in order

COMPREHENSION

1. What is Mr Knightley's 'sudden scheme' according to Emma?
2. When her father says, 'She is always so attentive towards them (the Bateses)', what is Emma's reaction?
3. How does Mr Knightley show Emma that she had his goodwill once again?
4. Why does Emma feel it is important for her to relate to Jane as a friend?
5. Why does Jane Fairfax remain aloof? What does this show both of Jane and of Emma?
6. How does Emma respond to Jane's behaviour? Comment on her responses.

7. 'Mrs Churchill after being disliked for at least twenty-five years was now spoken of with comparative allowance.' Comment with reference to the society Jane Austen is writing about.

Chapter 44

Summary

Emma hastens to Randalls as Mrs Weston wanted to see her alone. She fears it is bad news involving friends or family. On the contrary, Mrs Weston informs Emma with great uneasiness that Frank had been secretly engaged to Jane Fairfax. The alliance had been formalised when they met in Weymouth. Mrs Weston herself is deeply hurt and shocked but is more concerned about how the news might affect Emma. Emma assures her that though she did have a strong attachment to Frank at one time, she was no longer in love with him. She is more affected by the secrecy of the involvement between Frank and Jane, and by Frank's gross violation of the social code and by his unethical behaviour. She is now concerned about her relationship with Jane and the fate of Harriet. She is anxious about Jane who was to become a governess. Mr Churchill had given his consent to the marriage. Emma congratulates Mr Weston that he would shortly have a most lovely and accomplished daughter-in-law.

Glossary

perturbation	anxiety
impropriety	improper behaviour
censure	to express severe disapproval

Comprehension

1. Why does Mrs Weston desire to see Emma alone? How is the urgency indicated in the text?
2. What is the news conveyed by Mrs Weston to Emma?

3. How does Emma react? Does she immediately think about Harriet and Jane and how they would be affected? What do we gather about Emma from these responses?
4. Why are the Westons hurt and anxious?
5. How does Emma console them and convince them that she had no more any attachment to Frank?
6. When Mrs Weston tells Emma that '*this protestation* had done her (Mrs Weston) more good than anything else in the world could do,' what is she referring to?
7. In a society where manners and ethical conduct are very important, how is Frank to blame in this context?
8. Emma restores herself by behaving with magnanimity in this entire episode. Can you explain how this is done by her?
9. Do you think this is the climax of the plot? Justify your answer.

Chapter 45

Summary

Emma is angry with Frank for she feels that she had misled Harriet on account of him. (She was self-deceived!) But Harriet is not affected by the news of Frank's engagement. It is Emma, she said, who had been mistaken. They had both agreed 'never to name' the person that Harriet was growing attached to. Harriet now reveals to Emma that she had meant Mr Knightley all the time. Emma, she hoped, would not be in her way. It was not the encounter with the gypsies and Frank's role on that occasion that had impressed Harriet. It was Mr Knightley's asking her to dance (that had convinced her of his superior qualities) when Mr Elton had turned his back on her and she had no other partner. Emma is shocked and agitated and suggests that perhaps Mr Knightley in showing kindness to Harriet had Mr Martin's interest in mind. She enquires of Harriet if he really did return her affections. Harriet responds that she had noticed—so had Emma—a difference in Mr Knightley's behaviour after the Donwell party. Harriet was very sure of herself and where her affections lay. Emma is humbled by the experience and reflects on her own blindness in the matter—she feels wretched and defeated. How misguided she had been in having encouraged and 'brought Harriet forward'. How wrong she was to think that she knew everybody's feelings. Her vanity and patronising attitude had blinded her to her own limitations. Emma is also conscious of the class disparity between Mr Knightley and Harriet. Above all, she is inwardly pained because she has very high regard for Mr Knightley.

Glossary

scrape	embarrassing predicament
repulsed	rejected
tacitly	implying without saying it in words
stoutly	strongly
presumption	here, disrespectful behaviour
deplorable	unacceptable
disparity	difference
consternation	feeling of dismay
corroborating	supporting

Comprehension

1. Why is Emma angry with Frank? Do you think she is at fault too in a way?
2. What are Emma's feelings concerning Harriet and Jane on the matter?
3. How does Harriet inform Emma about her affection for Mr Knightley?
4. Comment on Emma's words: 'Mistake you! Am I to suppose then.......?'(Actually this is the entire sentence. It is a question dealing with mistaken identities. It has to be read as: 'Am I to suppose then that you have never fancied Frank Churchill?' The question can be left out.)
5. Describe the circumstances which led to Harriet falling in love with Mr Knightley.
6. Where had Emma erred in her assessment of Harriet?

7. Compare the characters Frank and Mr Knightley and point out the qualities that make them attractive to the women in the text.
8. Comment on Emma's match-making abilities and her readiness to arrange 'everybody's destiny'. Where did it lead her?
9. Comment on Emma's confused ideas about class and position in life, with particular relation to Mr Knightley and Harriet.
10. Comment on Emma's 'Oh God, that I had never seen her!' Refer to earlier chapters where Emma is the mentor and matchmaker to Harriet to support your answer.
11. What are Emma's feelings towards Mr Knightley in this episode? Have they remained so from the beginning or have they changed?
12. Show how Emma examines her own actions. What conclusions do you draw regarding her character and values?

SUMMARY

It is on being threatened with losing Mr Knightley's affections that Emma looks back with regret on her casual, slighting, and sometimes brusque attitude towards Mr Knightley in the past. Mr Knightley had patiently watched her grow and had been her mentor and advisor. Although he was fond of her, when he felt she was in the wrong he did not hesitate to correct her, as his censure of her behaviour to Mrs Bates shows. Emma hopes that Harriet is mistaken in Mr Knightley's attachment towards her. For her own part she would be satisfied if Mr Knightley did not marry but remained a friend of the family as he had always been. Nothing would take her away from her father, not even a marriage proposal from Mr Knightley. Harriet is kept away from Hartfield and the sensitive topic is avoided. Mrs Weston and Jane spend time together. Jane confesses to having suffered greatly on account of the secrecy concerning her engagement to Frank. Emma sympathises with Jane and understands better the reasons for Jane's aloofness towards her. Emma feels that she would have been wiser to have befriended Jane rather than Harriet. She would have been spared some pain and misery.

Glossary

perverse	stubborn and not willing to be led or corrected
slighting	speaking without proper respect
attestation	clear evidence
perpetual	constant

Comprehension

1. Summarise Emma's thoughts and fears concerning her present and past relationship with Mr Knightley, and Harriet's leanings towards him.
2. Why is Emma afraid of being displaced in Mr Knightley's affection? What is her debt to him?
3. There is comic irony in the relationship between Emma, Mr Knightley and Harriet as it unfolds in this chapter. How would you explain this statement?
4. 'Marriage would not do for her........ she would not marry even if she were asked by Mr Knightley.' What is Emma's dilemma?
5. Why does Emma desire Harriet's disappointment? What does she decide to do?
6. Is Emma confused about her skills in match-making? What does she think of herself in this respect?
7. What information does Mrs Weston provide regarding Jane and her engagement?
8. Why does Jane blame herself for the private engagement?
9. Why does Emma sympathise with Jane even though she had been previously rebuffed by Jane?
10. How does Jane describe her attitude to Frank and his behaviour?
11. What are Emma's conclusions regarding her relations with Jane and Harriet?

CHAPTER 47

SUMMARY

This chapter is in a way the climax of the novel with Mr Knightley's proposal of marriage to Emma. For the sake of conversation, she enquires after mutual friends even as she realises that he had something important to communicate. Emma thinks Mr Knightley wants to confide in her about his attachment to Harriet. Mr Knightley on the other hand thinks Emma is disheartened by the news of Frank's engagement to Jane. Both proceed cautiously. (The irony and humour of the situation are skilfully presented) Mr Knightley is greatly relieved to know that Emma does not care for Frank after all. Jane deserved someone better than Frank who, according to Mr Knightley, was a scoundrel. However, Mr Knightley, a true gentleman, wishes him well. He proposes to Emma, now that Frank is not on Emma's mind and Harriet not on his. Emma and Mr Knightley acknowledge their love for each other.

GLOSSARY

exquisite	extremely beautiful
scoundrel	dishonest person
conjecture	opinion formed on incomplete information
avert	prevent
felicity	happiness
contrition	state of being remorseful
groundless	baseless

COMPREHENSION

1. Why does Mr Knightley appear unhappy to Emma?
2. Why does Emma not wish to speak of Harriet to Mr Knightley?
3. How do Mr Knightley and Emma view the engagement of Frank and Jane?

4. What does Mr Knightley mean when he remarks that Jane deserved a better fate?
5. Emma does not want any sympathy from Mr Knightley. What are her reasons?
6. Explain Mr Knightley's sense of relief and Emma's reassurances.
7. Summarise Mr Knightley's comments on Frank's character. What does it say of Mr Knightley?
8. Why does Emma consider herself ungracious?
9. How does Mr Knightley propose to Emma? What is Emma's response?
10. What are Emma's feelings towards herself, Harriet, Jane and Mr Knightley?
11. What is the transformation that has taken place in the course of this chapter?

Chapter 48

Summary

Emma is ecstatically happy but acknowledges that two things needed to be settled, the comfort of her father, if she were to be married, and Harriet's future. Frank Churchill's letter to Mrs Weston explains his behaviour concerning his intimacy with Jane Fairfax. His confessions are intended to reduce the pain he had caused. He felt that Emma related to him as a friend, throughout, rather than as a lover, and this behaviour helped him in concealing his engagement. However, he felt he had treated Jane shabbily though he knew her worth—her excellence—in every way. He was most unhappy when she dissolved the engagement. He obtained his uncle's permission for the marriage and persuaded Jane to agree to his suit. Emma notes the contents of the letter but is more concerned about her private happiness. She feels that it would be better for Harriet to be away from Highbury at this time. As Isabella was kindly disposed towards Harriet, she resolves to obtain an invitation from Isabella and send Harriet to London for a few weeks. Harriet might even appreciate the gesture on Emma's part.

Glossary

extenuation	pardon
officious	interfering
misconstrued	interpreted wrongly
scrupulous	principled
comply with	act in accordance with a wish

Comprehension

1. How is Emma's happiness described in this chapter?
2. What are the two factors that she had to consider?
3. Summarise Frank Churchill's letter and comment on the tribute paid to Mrs Weston, his secret engagement, his 'affection' for Emma, the pianoforte incident, his admission of bad conduct, and his effort to reinstate himself.
4. 'She received my attentions with an easy, friendly, good-humoured playfulness. We seemed to understand each other.' Is this an accurate assessment of the relationship between Frank Churchill and Emma?
5. Who gifted the piano to Jane?
6. Comment on the role played by the two letters in this chapter.

Chapter 49

Summary

Frank's letter elicits different responses. Emma is satisfied with Churchill's attempts to acquit himself and of his feelings for Jane but Knightley isn't. He comments on Frank's inconsiderate and thoughtless behaviour. However, he would improve in Jane's company. They speak of their marriage. Mr Knightley is sensitive to the fact that Emma's departure from Hartfield would seriously affect her father. He offers to make Hartfield his home, a gesture which shows Emma and the reader how much Mr Knightley cared for her as to sacrifice his own independence.

Glossary

evinced	showed
borne with	tolerated

Comprehension

1. What are the reactions of Emma and of Mr Knightley to Frank's letter?
2. Has Mr Knightley changed his opinion of Frank? What does he feel about Jane and her influence over Frank?
3. What does Mr Knightley's decision to settle at Hartfield say of him as a person?
4. How does Emma respond to this suggestion by Mr Knightley?

Chapter 50

Summary

Harriet leaves for London to consult a dentist for her toothache. The visit is arranged by Emma and executed with the help of the invitation from Isabella. Emma is relieved and could therefore enjoy Mr Knightley's company without feeling guilty. She visits Jane Fairfax who is really happy to see her. She goes downstairs with Emma before she leaves, and apologises profusely for her behaviour in the past. Emma is pleased at this gesture. She is happy to know that Jane Fairfax's wedding with Frank would take place after three months, since it was customary to wait out the mourning period (for Mrs Churchill).

Comprehension

1. Why is Harriet sent to Isabella's house at Brunswick Square, London?
2. Explain why Emma feels that it is equally a 'duty and a pleasure' to visit Jane.

3. How does Jane welcome her? Contrast this with her earlier behaviour towards Emma.
4. Report the conversation that takes place between Jane and Emma. Comment on the tone of this conversation.
5. When is the wedding between Jane and Frank to be held?
6. 'I love everything that is decided and open!' Who says this and why? Comment on this statement in the light of the story.

Chapter 51

Summary

Mrs Weston reveals that she is going to be a mother. Everyone hopes for a girl. Emma and Mr Knightley speak very little of Harriet. Emma is not without feelings of guilt every time she thinks of Harriet. Mr Knightley receives a letter from his brother John who gives his consent for his marriage with Emma. The news of the impending marriage is gently conveyed to Mr Woodhouse who receives it with a sense of shock and tries to dissuade Emma. The major concern is that on Emma's departure there would be no one to look after him and take care of his needs. All his friends succeed in convincing him that the event would be for his happiness.

Glossary

approbation	approval

Comprehension

1. Why do the Westons wish for a daughter? What does Mr Knightley have to say in this regard?
2. Consider the reactions of John Knightley and Mr Woodhouse to the proposed wedding of Emma.
3. Is Mr Woodhouse selfish in his stand? Does he strike you as a comic figure?

4. How is Mr Woodhouse's approval finally obtained?

Chapter 52

Summary

Mr Knightley gives Emma the surprising news of Harriet's wedding to Robert Martin which was soon to take place. Emma is amazed and then delighted at the turn of affairs. Martin had met Harriet in Isabella's house and spoken to her and she had agreed. Emma is humbled by the events of the past and hopes that she would not repeat her errors in judgement.

Glossary

circumspection	careful consideration, caution

Comprehension

1. What news does Mr Knightley bring Emma?
2. How does the renewal of the acquaintance between Harriet and Robert Martin and their decision to wed come about?
3. 'I have been silent from surprise merely, excessive surprise.' Is there more to Emma's reactions than surprise?
4. How are Emma's reactions different from her past actions? Does she value power more than friendship in influencing Harriet?

CHAPTER 53

SUMMARY

On Harriet's return from London Emma is happy to learn from her behaviour that she had always liked Robert Martin. Harriet's parentage is also revealed at this point and it was to her advantage to be married to Robert Martin. Robert Martin and Harriet are married before the end of September. Frank and Jane are to be married in November. Mr Woodhouse cannot reconcile himself to Emma's wedding even though Mr Knightley had agreed to stay at Hartfield. He says that the robbery of poultry in the neighbouring houses made him fearful of house-breaking. He becomes aware of the advantage of having his son-in-law with him and consents to the wedding. It is a quiet affair in October with promises of perfect happiness for the couple. The end of the novel has overtones of irony and comedy.

GLOSSARY

supplanted	displaced
impair	harm
pilfering	petty thieving

COMPREHENSION

1. 'Mr Martin had supplanted Mr Knightley in Harriet's mind.' Explain how this happens.
2. What is the information regarding Harriet and her parentage? Why is this important to Highbury society?
3. How is Harriet's happiness assured?
4. Three marriages are reported. Which are they? Comment on them.
5. What made Mr Woodhouse consent to Emma's marriage? Is it reasonable or selfish or comic? How does it reflect on his character?
6. Why is the marriage between Emma and Mr Knightley 'the perfect union'?
7. Comment on the novel as a 'novel about the social and economic significance of courtship and marriage.'

CRITICAL ESSAYS

1. Comic Symmetry in Jane Austen's Emma

Bruce Stovel

'If any work belong unequivocally to any genre,' Laurence Lerner remarks, '*Emma* is a comedy.' Lerner's insight suggests that it might be profitable to ask what makes the novel seem such a classic comedy. To approach *Emma* as a comedy is to think of it, not in the usual context of nineteenth-century fiction, but rather in conjunction with *Much Ado about Nothing, The Way of the World, Tom Jones*. In such comedies, the conflicts and characters are simple and fixed: what interests us is the intricate design, the complex and surprising pattern, into which these elements fall.

Reginald Farrer described the way this comic design works some fifty years ago: 'Only when the story has been thoroughly assimilated can the infinite delights and subtleties of its workmanship begin to be appreciated, as you realize the manifold complexity of the book's web, and find that every sentence, almost every epithet, has its definite reference to equally unemphasised points before and after in the development of the plot.'

What is essentially comic in *Emma*, then, lies in its design. But since that design is presented ironically, an accurate account of it can be reached only after a great deal of observation and reflection. In fact, the novel is so subtly symmetrical, so mined with interconnected details, that criticism has, I think, yet to define its structure adequately. An instance of sly patterning which has not been noticed by Jane Austen's critics will illustrate the point.

When we, along with Emma, first meet Harriet Smith, we are told of Harriet, 'She was a very pretty girl, and her beauty happened to be of a sort which Emma particularly admired. She was short, plump and fair, with a fine bloom, blue eyes, light hair, regular features, and a look of great sweetness.' This seems innocuous enough, but we learn from Mrs Weston's praise of Emma that Emma herself is tall and elegant, with hazel eyes.

Emma particularly likes Harriet's style of appearance, just as she likes Harriet's style of personality, because it poses no threat to Emma's own – in fact, it forms a perfect foil for Emma's charms. Furthermore, when Emma paints Harriet's portrait, we find that she makes Harriet appear taller and more elegant than she actually is. Emma creates an image of Harriet much more like Emma herself than Harriet really is. The symbolism here not only presents Emma as the artist moulding nature into new and more pleasing shapes, as several critics have pointed out; even more precisely, the portrait epitomizes what Emma does to Harriet in general; she transforms Harriet's actual self into a monstrous new identity fashioned in the image of Emma herself. And in this respect, as in so many others, the outing to Box Hill recapitulates the action of the novel. There, Frank Churchill playfully commissions Emma to produce a wife for him when he returns from abroad: 'Find somebody for me. I am in no hurry. Adopt her, educate her.' Emma, thinking of Harriet, coquettishly replies, 'And make her like myself'. And so it is appropriate that, like a comic Frankenstein's monster, Harriet eventually turns unwittingly on her maker, forcing Emma to realize what she has created.

My point is that each of these scenes, beginning with Emma's particular admiration of Harriet's sort of beauty, invites us to see beyond the dramatic moment to the pattern it contains. This pattern, being 'unemphasised', is not fixed. We may also note, for instance, that Jane Fairfax is tall and elegant in appearance, like Emma and unlike Harriet.

I suggest that Jane Austen's web consists of three main threads, and that all the local symmetries lead to and from these threads in networks which get ever finer as we pursue them. These three lines of action are: the hidden love of Emma and Mr Knightley for each other; the counterpointing of that secret love with the secret engagement of Frank Churchill and Jane Fairfax; the use of the other characters to embody aspects of Emma herself.

Though everyone who likes the novel at all must smile at Emma's unrecognized love for Mr Knightley, surprisingly little is said about it by critics of the novel. Howard S. Babb, however, has some suggestive remarks; discussing the issue of Emma's snobbishness, he says, 'The cause of her compulsive disengagement is her inability to recognize and admit what she feels for Mr Knightley . . . It is the novel's major irony that an Emma so frequently wrapped up in herself, and one who cultivates detachment, should so radically misconceive her real attachment.' We can take Babb's point one step further and say that Emma's unrecognized love is the cause of her foolish mistakes over Harriet Smith and Mr Elton, over Mr Dixon and Jane Fairfax, and so on: these mistakings provide a screen of romantic fantasies which disguises her real interest in love from herself. Emma, after all, is preoccupied with affairs of the heart—affairs of other people's hearts, that is; she can see clearly and act decisively when love is not involved.

In Emma's case, then, the course of true love runs in two channels. One, at the visible level, contains Emma's embarrassing errors as an amatory busybody; the other, underground channel, which only surfaces at the novel's climax, contains her real feelings toward Mr Knightley, which become clearer and clearer to us (if not to her) as the action advances. If the hidden stream is the source of the visible one, the latter provides a chart throughout to the depths concealed within the heroine.

The surface action of the novel falls into two successive and similar patterns of comic nemesis. Though the prelude has a cast of only three and a single broad irony, while the main action is much more varied and convoluted, the pattern is the same in each case: Emma's blunders as the Highbury Cupid become more and more obvious to all but her, until finally circumstances, rebelling against her guiding hand, slap her rudely in the face and wake her up. The comic symmetry is very precise here: just as . . . . she discovers, to her dismay, that she and Mr Elton have both been using Harriet Smith as a pawn to advance Mr Elton's charade of a courtship, ... she finds Frank Churchill and Jane Fairfax have been using her as their 'blind'; like Harriet before, she must learn that another woman has been secretly preferred to her. At the surface level, then, the novel has a two-part, beguiler-beguiled structure: Emma finds herself living out a comic form of the Golden Rule. So much is worth spelling out, even if almost every reader must enjoy seeing Emma get hers (as we say), because most recent critics have followed Joseph M. Duffy, who argues that the novel falls into three stages: the Emma-Elton-Harriet fiasco; 'the Emma-Frank Churchill-Jane Fairfax illusion and masquerade'.

We can, though, see the two main comic situations—the two successive romantic triangles: as parallel surface actions, displacements caused by and directing us to the real plot, which lies in Emma's relationship with Mr Knightley. Unbeknownst to herself, Emma loves him from the start. After learning that Frank and Jane are secretly engaged, after being shocked by Harriet's hopes into realizing that 'Mr Knightley must marry no one but herself!' Emma makes the most surprising discovery of all; 'there never had been a time' when she did not love him. She would have been able to understand herself at any point, she thinks, if only it had occurred to her 'to institute the comparison' between him and the man she thought she loved, Frank Churchill. We, however, see a great deal more clearly into Emma's heart than she does herself; the cleverly-scattered clues to her real feelings become more and more insistent. This rising curve of ironic disclosure forms the real plot of the novel. This ironic curve is supported by an echoing, if subordinate, curve of clues about the real nature of Mr Knightley's concern for Emma.

Why wouldn't Emma admit her love from the start? Why *didn't* it occur to her to institute the comparison? For one thing, like many heroes and heroines of comedy, she does not want to give up her independent selfhood. She tells Harriet, 'Never could I expect to be so truly beloved and important, so always first and always right in any man's eyes as I am in my father's.' Certainly, Mr Woodhouse is unlikely ever to be outbid in this sort of affection.

The most important aspect of Emma's fear of love—and one she cannot formulate—is her fear of being hurt. Emma is afraid of being undervalued, of being taken as a fluttery, dependent creature, a female, rather than a person of intelligence and dignity of her own. Without realizing it, she is asking Mr Knightley to declare that he would marry someone like herself, and not a Harriet, but she must content herself with his vigorous generalization, 'Men of sense, whatever you may say, do not want silly wives.' In her opinionated confusion, Emma thinks of men and women as two completely different species, each having its own sphere, its own special kind of knowledge, its own code of action. Like those who make up personality profile tests, Emma assumes men are primarily interested in objects and abstract ideas, while women have expertise in emotional relationships. After her argument with Mr Knightley about the right man for Harriet, Emma 'still thought herself a better judge of such a point of female right and refinement than he could be.'

Emma will discover that men and women have much more in common than she thinks, that they can be friends rather than merely symbiotic opposites. In fact, the action of the novel can be seen as Emma's search for, and triumphant discovery of, a true friend. The impulse that sets the action in motion is Emma's loss of Miss Taylor: in Emma's eyes, at least, 'they had been living together as friend and friend very mutually attached.' Emma tries to fill Miss Taylor's place with Harriet Smith, though Mr Knightley tells Emma, in words which ring in her mind, 'You have been no friend to Harriet Smith, Emma.' Emma refuses to consider Jane Fairfax for the vacancy, though 'birth, abilities, and education' mark Jane out for it, and flirts with the possibility of taking on Frank Churchill as her intimate friend—only to find that her real friend from the start has been Mr Knightley. It is as a friend that he addresses Emma. He warns her that there may be some understanding between Frank Churchill and Jane Fairfax 'as a friend – an anxious friend'; he ends his stern remarks to her over Miss Bates with, 'I will tell you truths while I can, satisfied with proving myself your friend by very faithful counsel.' And when he is about to reveal his own feelings to Emma, she at first refuses to hear what she thinks will be a confession of infatuation with Harriet; but, after a moment of sympathy and self-discipline, she determines to hear him out 'as a friend.' Mr Knightley at first pauses – 'Emma, that I fear is a word – No, I have no wish' – but then decides to give the word a special meaning: 'Emma, I accept your offer – extraordinary as it may seem, I accept it and refer myself to you as a friend. – Tell me, then, have I no chance of ever succeeding?' Emma has shown herself finally worthy of receiving his proposal that he be her friend for life.

If Emma is merely an instrument in Frank Churchill's schemes, Jane Austen gives her heroine some recompense by making Frank's plot merely a means of bringing Emma's story to its fruition. As in many traditional comedies, the love story at the work's centre is interwoven with the trials of another pair of lovers, Frank Churchill and Jane Fairfax. The action is neatly contrived, so that the resolution of the Frank–Jane plot brings about, by chain reaction, the resolution of the central plot; further, in the manner of comedy, the two plots are presented in intricate counterpoint to bring out the difference between the two matches, to let each illuminate the other. Both plots turn upon a secret love, but one is secret by conscious deception, the other by unconscious self-deception. One love story, that Frank and Jane is resolved wholly by chance, by Mrs Churchill's completely unexpected and very timely death; the other match is achieved by choice, by change, by mutual self-direction.

This counterpoint reaches a wonder subtlety in the Box Hill episode. Box Hill is the turning point for both love affairs, the occasion for a quarrel which pulls each pair of lovers apart only to bring them back together all the more intimately and for good. Frank's letter of explanation allows us to understand how crucial Box Hill is for Frank and Jane. Frank, piqued at Jane's unwillingness to walk home with him from Donwell Abbey the day before, flirts with Emma in order to taunt Jane, and then uses the departure of the Eltons as a screen for delivering a private insult: women can't be known at Bath, or any public place, he says, but only when you see them in their own homes, among their own set. Jane, wounded, answers with veiled bitterness: 'It can only be weak, irresolute characters (whose happiness must always be at the mercy of chance) who will suffer an unfortunate acquaintance to be an inconvenience, an oppression for ever'. Frank, highly indignant, leaves Highbury that very afternoon without saying farewell to Jane; that evening, she accepts Mrs Elton's eagerly-offered position with Mrs Smallridge and writes to Frank breaking off the engagement. Chance, however, intervenes; Frank's aunt dies and he is not forced to choose between the two ladies who rule his life. Jane's ultimatum, though, does make it advisable that he go directly to his uncle and ask for his permission to marry Jane; now Mrs Churchill is no more, that permission is quickly granted.

My point is this: we can never be sure Frank Churchill would have been willing to give up his fortune for Jane. He is relieved of the choice. Why, after all, did he insist on keeping their engagement secret? In his letter of explanation, he writes, 'But you will be ready to say, what was your hope in doing this? – What did you look forward to? – To any thing, every thing – to time, chance, circumstance, slow effects, sudden bursts, perseverance and weariness, health and sickness.' In more simple terms, he was waiting for his aunt to die – or, failing that, to go through some unpredictable alteration. In either case, Frank could marry Jane *and* retain all his aunt's money and status. The force he relies on does reward him in the end: chance allows him to remain a spoiled child, free of painful choices. He closes his letter by saying that Emma had been right in calling him 'the child of good fortune.'

Emma begins as another Frank, another pampered only child in a rich home but she has a different, more substantial kind of good fortune: she is allowed to choose, to repudiate, to grow, to grow up. Emma and Mr Knightley triumph, not by opportunism, but by stern moral choices. Emma's thoughtless insult to Miss Bates at Box Hill corresponds exactly to Frank's sneer at Jane's domestic circle; Mr Knightley's rebuke, as difficult for him to make as it is for her to receive, is parallel to Jane's ironic reproof of Frank as weak and irresolute, so wounding to his pride. But Mr Knightley's criticism is open, not veiled; unlike Frank, Emma has both the courage and the desire to accept the truth. Emma is so hurt at losing Mr Knightley's good opinion, and at seeming inadvertently to scorn his advice, that, feeling pain of a sort she has never known before, she genuinely wants to change, and does. As a result, when Mr Knightley comes calling, Emma brings on his proposal, as she could not have before, by her quiet self-sacrifice. The happy coming together of Emma and Mr Knightley may lack the dramatic éclat, the spectacular good fortune, of the other couple, but it has the dignity and integrity of something they have made themselves. Mr Knightley's comment after reading Frank's letter has an uncomplacent precision: 'My Emma, does not every thing serve to prove more and more the beauty of truth and sincerity in all our dealings with each other?'

This counterpointing of Frank and Emma becomes explicit in their final meeting. Emma says that she is certain that Frank must have enjoyed deceiving everyone in Highbury, because she knows that she herself would have found great amusement in doing so. 'I think there is a little likeness between us,' she says drily, to which he bows acknowledgement. Emma adds that, at the least, she and Frank have the same destiny – 'the destiny which bids fair to connect us with characters so much superior to our own.' But this same scene shows that the likeness only brings out the unlikeness between Emma, who raises herself to her husband's moral level, and Frank, who bring his wife down to his. Emma returns home even happier in her happiness with Mr Knightley for 'the animated contemplation of his worth which this comparison produced.' She, not Frank, is the lucky one.

The two symmetrical networks I have defined emerge from, and control, the twists and turns of the plot. But our comic detachment also forces on our notice a broader and more static kind of design, that is created by character contrasts. Emma and Mr Knightley, for instance, marry out of motives which fall between, and combine, the self-aware calculation of the Eltons and the romantic feeling which unites Frank and Jane.

These comic oppositions have an important consequence: Emma comes to exist, not only in her own self, but as she is reflected and embodied in the characters around her. In *Emma*, certainly, the heroine has a many-faceted, self-divided personality, since the major characters surrounding her persistently live a double life – they are both themselves and aspects of Emma. Mr Woodhouse, for instance, embodies one extreme within the unregenerate Emma. He is utterly self-absorbed, so that all events must seem to revolve around his preferences; he resists change or effort of any kind; he is utterly unable to distinguish between his own wishes and what actually is the case.

This notion of alter egos gives a new dimension to the first chapter of the novel. Emma falls into self-pitying loneliness the evening after 'poor Miss Taylor' marries Mr Weston, but she rallies herself to combat the same feelings in her father. When Mr Knightley calls, though, Emma takes the plaintive pose again, but now her own rational position is uncompromisingly urged upon her by Mr Knightley; Emma 'cannot allow herself to feel so much pain as pleasure. Every friend of Miss Taylor's must be glad to have her so happily married.'

The chapter suggests that Emma is suspended between a Knightley self and a Woodhouse one. Mr Knightley, in fact, functions as Emma's deepest or true self throughout the novel. For instance, Emma expresses a stern view of Frank Churchill's procrastinations to Mrs Weston, but, a few pages later, she perversely claims more sympathy for Frank than she actually feels; she thus finds herself in the ironic position of 'making use of Mrs Weston's arguments against herself', while Mr Knightley expresses 'her real opinion'. Jane Austen tells us that Emma can always find excuses to avoid calling on Miss Bates and her mother, though 'she had many a hint from Mr Knightley, and some from her own heart, as to the deficiency'. Mr Knightley embodies, then, Emma's own heart and conscience: this is what makes his rebuke on the subject of Miss Bates so painful. The union of Emma and Mr Knightley is thus, in part, a psychic one: Emma becomes reunited with a part of herself she had renounced. This is why Mr Knightley must wait for Emma to educate herself; she can only come to him when she has come to herself.

All this helps explain the importance of Mr Knightley's polar opposite within Emma, Mrs Elton. By leading Mr Elton on and then rejecting him, Emma has summoned from the depths of Bristol a substitute for herself who embodies, in garish, unmitigated form, all her own complacent, vain, mean, and domineering qualities. The correspondences between Emma and Mrs Elton are precise and ingenious; many of them have been remarked by the critics, but the function of this pairing in the larger design is much less clear. Mrs Elton's appearance in Highbury more than halfway through the novel is actually part of Emma's genuine good fortune, a gift to her from comic providence. For now Emma can make a good choice between her good and her bad angels, between her ideal and her selfish selves.

Something within Emma makes Mr Knightley more important to her than anything else. This ability to respond to him, without her knowledge and against her will, is at the heart of the novel's comic perspective: Emma's desire to be herself, her desire for Mr Knightley, and her desire to be good, all finally coincide. Harmony, not sacrifice or division, reigns. In the same way, we soon grasp that Mr Knightley's concern for principle and for

Emma's moral state coincide with his affection for her: 'to him, she is faultless in spite of all her faults.' Emma's response, in spite of herself, to Mr Knightley, is what enables her to keep our sympathy throughout; it is also what makes her second awakening, unlike that at the end of Book I, final and convincing. Emma forsakes her fanciful schemes, and can see the vain motives which prompted them, only when she discovers the deepest 'source of pleasure to herself' is to be in the real world with the man she respects and loves.

'The perfect happiness of the union,' the novel's final words, thus describe a personal integration as well as a wedding. Interestingly enough, it is Miss Bates who defines most precisely the connection between psychological and social union; she says during one of her monologues, as if by accident, 'It is such a happiness when good people get together – and they always do.'

From *Dalhousie Review*, 57 (Autumn 1977), 453–64

2. 'EMMA' AS CHARADE AND THE EDUCATION OF THE READER

J. M. Q. DAVIES

As Q.D Leavis perceived, Jane Austen always seems to be 'writing with a side glance' at her readers, aware of 'a critical audience liable to pounce.' And in a letter to her sister Cassandra she herself observed that 'I do not write for such dull elves./As have not a great deal of ingenuity themselves.' All her novels are profoundly concerned with the education of her readers, particularly the young female readers of her time, but nowhere does she make more strenuous demands upon their ingenuity than in *Emma*. Indeed though the rhetorical strategies she developed to involve and mystify her readers in this novel are very different from Sterne's, *Emma* in its playfulness is her most Shandean work and shows her too, for different reasons, quite as concerned to 'do all that lies in my power to keep [their] imagination as busy as my own.' Alistair M. Duckworth has argued persuasively that the charades, conundrums and acrostics in *Emma* occur with sufficient frequency to suggest that they were consciously intended as a structuring device. But to view them as he does in an essentially negative light, as emblems of the dubious and socially disruptive games engaged in by Emma and Frank Churchill, seems less than satisfactory because it ignores precisely this playful element in Jane Austen's own attitude toward the reader. The purpose of this essay is to suggest that the function of the charades is in part rhetorical and that they provide the key to, and models in miniature for, the relationship between text and reader Jane Austen intended to establish.

The obvious limitation of analogies between *Emma* and Gothic fiction or the detective story is that these forms characteristically withhold the key to the mysteries they present until the very end, whereas Jane Austen furnishes enough information for the active, critical reader to perceive the true state of affairs as the story unfolds, and in this respect the novel resembles the charade more closely. Though in practice of course individual readers will penetrate the mystery and perceive the ironies at different points. The narrative principle involved has been succinctly described by Wayne C. Booth, who writes that 'whatever steps are taken to mystify inevitably decrease the dramatic irony, and, whenever dramatic irony is increased by telling the reader secrets the characters have not yet suspected, mystery is inevitably destroyed . . . And we all find that on second reading we discover new intensities of dramatic irony resulting from complete loss of mystery.' Two of the mental operations demanded by such plots are guessing and judging, which in *Emma* are closely associated with imagination and reason and thus with the novel's dialogical relation to Romanticism, and in more abstract form they are also the principles involved in solving charades. They are polarized in the very first chapter, when Mr Knightley responds to Emma's claim to have made a match between the Westons with 'you made a lucky guess,' and concludes sententiously that 'a straight-forward, open-hearted man, like Weston, and a rational unaffected woman, like Miss Taylor, may be safely left to manage their own concerns.' And subsequently guessing and judging recur as binary terms with the frequency of a leitmotif throughout the novel.

These points of congruence raise the question of whether Jane Austen consciously thought of Emma as a sort of extended charade . . .

But the amusing scene that follows, where Emma and Harriet puzzle over Mr Elton's poem, makes it clear that it is the substitution of charades for more serious reading rather than the qualities necessary for solving them that is the object of Jane Austen's satire in this passage. Harriet guesses wildly 'in all the confusion of hope and dullness', whereas Emma, who Mr Knightley has earlier remarked had at the age of ten been 'able to answer questions which puzzled her sister at seventeen', solves the riddle itself at once and explains it point by point to Harriet. When however it comes to assessing the 'sober facts' of the situation, Emma is as comically inept as Harriet, urging her to 'receive it on my judgment' that Mr Elton's 'court-ship' charade was meant for her. Evidently therefore there are important differences between solving charades and coping judiciously with life.

Life's difficulties are more complex than the difficulties posed by conundrums and charades, and require more experience and knowledge of the human heart than the fair but as yet still frozen Emma possesses. But to Jane Austen's empirical temperament the same principles of reasoning and judgment based on attention to the sober facts are involved in understanding both.

Coming at a point in the novel where the reader's curiosity has been thoroughly aroused by Emma's own 'genius for foretelling and guessing' then, the rhetorical purpose of the chapter on the charade, and particularly of these analogies, is, I suggest, to tease readers into the realization that they too are participating in a sophisticated fictional game. It is a game in which the charade on courtship, the entire Elton episode and the main Jane Fairfax–Frank Churchill mystery are related rather like a set of Chinese boxes, each confronting the reader with successively more complex puzzles. And Emma's explanation of the charade to Harriet is paralleled by her self-scrutiny after Mr Elton's confession, and by Mr Knightley's appraisal of Frank Churchill's letter at the end. Emma's later reference to Jane as 'a riddle, quite a riddle', the anagrams at Hartfield where Mr Knightley begins to suspect Frank of using a child's game 'to conceal a deeper game' and the conundrum at Box Hill not only help hold the novel together structurally therefore, but also serve the rhetorical function of reminding the reader that he is engaged in a similar activity.

The most obvious obstacle to the reader's arriving at the sober facts, as Wayne Booth recognized, is the way in which events are largely presented from Emma's point of view. Emma, as Harriet discovers to her cost, is not only a charming, witty and intelligent, but a very persuasive personality. She has always been able to get the better of her governess, and she tends to sway the passive or unwary reader too. And even after she has been exposed as fallible, her remorse and the personal honesty of her self-appraisals involuntarily restore the reader's confidence in her. But quite as taxing on the reader's powers of judgment and discrimination are the various discussion sequences, because the arguments on both sides are always made to sound so plausible. In chapter 5, for instance, Mr Knightley undoubtedly presents a strong case against Emma's friendship with Harriet. But he does so with ill-humour as he himself admits, and despite his appreciation of Emma's beauty and interest in her welfare, at this stage in the novel he may well appear censorious. And later on in fact he is willing to concede that Emma has done Harriet some good. Mrs Weston, whom the narrator has earlier described as 'a well-judging and truly admirable woman', is perhaps less forceful, but as Emma's former governess her defence of the friendship and confidence in Emma's good sense carry weight. And when she says, 'Mr Knightley, I shall not allow you to be a fair judge in this case. You who are so much used to live alone, that you do not know the value of a companion; and perhaps no man can be a judge of the comfort a woman feels in the society of one of her own sex, after being used to it all her life'– Jane Austen's young female readers would doubtless have agreed.

Similarly in the chapter where Mr Knightley comments on Frank's failure to appear, his strong words of censure seem well founded. But Emma too is right when she says to him that 'you are the worst judge in the world, Mr Knightley, of the difficulties of dependence'. She is also right that 'it is very unfair to judge of any body's conduct, without an intimate knowledge of their situation', even though she will almost immediately neglect this principle herself in speculating about Jane. By the end of their heated discussion Emma's verdict that 'we are both prejudiced; you against, I for him' seems incontestable, but the reader has been given a good deal to think about. And it is important to notice how the jealousy that colours Mr Knightley's judgment, like the ill-temper that mars his equally 'penetrating' brother, not only makes for greater realism but is vital to the rhetorical game Jane Austen is playing with the reader. An ideal figure such as Grandison, or a totally reliable reflector would have undermined the need for independent judgment.

The strategy deployed to tease the reader into thought in the Elton sequence and the main Frank Churchill–Jane Fairfax mystery is essentially the same. Both involve one or more initial hints or cautions, followed by playful obfuscation, ambiguity and artfully placed false clues, which are then resolved in a comic peripetia and didactic anagnoresis. With the Elton episode the true situation is relatively easy to predict, since Mr Elton is evidently courting either Harriet or Emma. Mr Knightley's warning that 'Elton may talk sentimentally, but he will act rationally' is followed by the delightful ambiguity of the portrait-sketching episode and the charades. But then Mr Elton's failure to declare himself to Harriet at the vicarage, his reluctance to forego dinner at the Coleses for her sake when she falls ill, and a broad hint to Emma from her brother-in-law, make it clear to everyone but her that she is the woman being courted. The whole sequence occupies a position in relation to the main action analogous to the Sotherton episode in *Mansfield Park.* There Edmund with Fanny on one arm and Mary Crawford on the other, remarking that Mary does not tax his strength as had a drunken Oxford companion, is in the position of Hercules at the crossroads between Virtue and Vice, and his deviation from the 'great path' with Mary and eventual return to Fanny epitomizes in miniature the course he is to take in the novel as a whole. But where the Sotherton episode exists in a fictive world set apart behind a proscenium arch in the nineteenth-century manner, the Elton sequence initiates the reader into a game of Shandean sophistication.

The main action as charade is of course more complicated, and its successful solution on first reading is in practice to some degree contingent on the reader's having perceived the rules of the game established in the Elton sequence. Jane Fairfax arrives before Frank, and the reader's impulse to accept Emma's speculations about her is immediately moderated by the narrator's comments on her 'decided superiority both in beauty and acquirements', her understanding, her fortitude and her judiciousness.

Frank's own arrival has been preceded by Mr Knightley's disapprobation, and the fact that it is two months late and one day early is itself a comment on his reliability. But though his manners are as ingratiating as Mr Elton's had been, Emma quickly absolves him of insincerity. And on the second morning – 'time enough to form a reasonable judgment' the narrator observes ironically – she 'decide [s]. . . that he had not been acting a part, or making a parade of insincere professions; and that Mr Knightley certainly had not done him justice'. If the reader is inclined to be swayed, he is almost immediately provided with another hint when Frank evades Emma's question about how well he had known Jane at Weymouth, and then tries to conceal the evasion, prompting Emma to remark: 'Upon my word! You answer as discreetly as she could do herself. But her account of everything leaves so much to be guessed . . .' Whereupon the difference between guessing and judging is once again impressed upon the reader in the ensuing conversation, where Emma indulges in a good deal of speculation about Jane and Mr Dixon, and Frank defers to her judgment on Jane's character and musical attainments.

All these cautionary notes are sounded well before the delightful scene of comic obfuscation, where Emma and Frank play a game of speculation as it were, as to who has sent Jane the piano. Here Emma plays the active part initially, the part of 'wit' in Elder Olson's terminology, but then as Frank warms to the possibilities of the game he takes on the role of wit and she unwittingly becomes his 'butt'. And his attentions to her, of course supported by the Westons' hopes for such a match, create one of the chief obstacles to the passive reader's arriving at the facts. Another is Mr Knightley's regard for Jane, a very effective false clue rendered all the more probable by Mrs Weston's speculations, against which however Emma's 'every feeling revolts'. And smaller clues like Frank's trip to London for a haircut are also playfully ambivalent. So that while Frank may feel, as he says in parting, that Emma 'can hardly be without suspicion', for the reader *not* to agree with Emma that 'he had *almost* told her that he loved her' requires penetration and judgment indeed.

After Frank's departure Jane is foregrounded rather more, and though Emma finds her a riddle her conduct provides several clues which are ambiguous only if the reader has accepted Emma's speculations about her – her insistence on collecting her own mail, her decision to postpone taking a position as governess and her declining Mrs Dixon's invitation to Ireland, hardly the action of a jealous wife. But the denouement is delayed by a further round of Shakespearean comedic confusion, which arises out of Mr Knightley's rescuing Harriet from Mr Elton's snub at the ball and Frank's rescuing her from the gypsies. The latter episode rouses the Romantic 'imaginist' in Emma, as Mr Dixon's rescuing Jane while sailing had done earlier, and again she actively interferes in Harriet's life, only to find herself the butt of her own contrivance, 'in love, and in some doubt of a return.'

The anagram episode where Mr Weston denies having written to Frank about Mr Perry's carriage, and Frank signals 'blunder' to Jane, then 'Dixon' to Emma to cover his tracks, marks the point where most readers will be able to predict the novel's resolution. For it convinces Mr Knightley that he had not been committing 'any of Emma's errors of imagination' in his 'suspicion of there being something of private liking, of private understanding even, between Frank Churchill and Jane.' And with Emma's confident rejection of the idea when he tries to warn her – as his brother had earlier warned her about Mr Elton – even on first reading mystery begins to give way to irony. Mr Knightley's quite explicit comparison of word-games to the double game that Frank is playing also introduces a note of moral censure, not of children's educational games *per se* but of trifling with people's feelings. The dangers of such trifling are dramatized in the Box Hill episode, where mystification and irony are marvellously blended, and where Mr Weston's conundrum is used to comment on Emma's moral deficiencies, as Garrick's charade had shed light on her psychology. The irony of his associating Emma's name with perfection, coming immediately after her witty but unkind remark to Miss Bates, is underscored by Mr Knightley's caustic remark that '*Perfection* should not have come quite so soon.' Though here too conundrums and acrostics are not seen as in themselves reprehensible activities so much, as part of the normal social round like Mr Woodhouse's quadrille and backgammon. But if Emma's rudeness distances the reader from her further, it also serves to divert his or her attention away from the effect her flirtation with Frank is having on Jane and Mr Knightley. For those who have already filled in most of the intertextual gaps, however, the clues are immediately to hand in the ensuing two chapters, where Jane accepts the position Mrs Elton has procured for her, Frank departs for Richmond, and Mr Knightley goes off to stay with his brother in London.

After the crisis has been averted and the tables turned by Mrs Churchill's death, the Shandean fun is kept up to the very last, but largely at the expense of Emma rather than the reader. When she is summoned urgently by Mrs Weston, for instance, and begins to imagine 'Half a dozen natural children, perhaps – and poor Frank cut off!' few readers will overlook the irony. And fewer still will be as surprised as Emma to discover that Frank has been less than frank and she 'completely duped.' One of the most delightfully ironic final moments, which balances the comic confusion of the two earlier proposal scenes, occurs when Emma misinterprets Mr Knightley's first advance as an attempt to confess his love for Harriet. And all this helps leaven the serious moral tone of the finale. Frank's confessional letter, like Emma's explanation of the charade to Harriet, confronts readers with their deficiencies of judgment, and Mr Knightley's appraisal of Frank's conduct underlines the seriousness of such deficiencies. Jane Austen's use of the charades in *Emma* confronts us with 'the paradox of a beloved family recreation becoming an aesthetic expression of dubious social behaviour.' To my mind the paradox is the paradox of high comedy and resides in her use of essentially playful rhetorical strategies, modelled in part on the charades, for the serious purpose not only of warning against such 'dangerous game(s)' and the unrestrained use of the imagination, but of weaning readers from the very errors they are reading of.

From *Philological Quarterly*, 65 (1986), 231–42

TOPICS FOR DISCUSSION

1. *Emma* is a novel about growing and gaining self-knowledge. Discuss.
2. Many of the episodes in the novel become meaningful because they are so rich in irony. Illustrate with a few examples.
3. 'I am going to take a heroine whom no one but myself will much like.' Why do you think Jane Austen liked Emma? Do you have reasons to dislike her?
4. How does the novelist use other characters to define the character of Emma?
5. Is *Emma* a comedy? Give reasons for your answer.
6. Is *Emma* a comment on class in society? Discuss.
7. The narration is through multiple voices, the most important being that of Emma and that of the author. Explain and illustrate.
8. How does Emma move from snobbishness, self-deception and egoism to humility and self-knowledge?
9. Is *Emma* only a woman-centred or a marriage-centred novel? Discuss.
10. The novel *Emma* is most meaningful against the background of the age and the social class Jane Austen describes. How does this come forth?

FURTHER READING

Primary Sources

1. *Sense and Sensibility* (1811)
2. *Pride and Prejudice* (1813)
3. *Mansfield Park* (1814)
4. *Northanger Abbey* (1818)
5. *Persuasion* (1818)

Secondary Sources

Bloom, Harold. Ed. *Jane Austen's 'Emma.'* Modern Critical Interpretations. New Delhi: Vira (first Indian edition), 2007.

Bush, Douglas. *Jane Austen*. New York: Macmillan. 1975.

Byrne, Paula. Ed. *Jane Austen's Emma. A Source Book*. London: Routledge, 2004.

Cecil, David. *A Portrait of Jane Austen*. New York: Hill and Wang, 1980.

Kinkham, Margaret. *Jane Austen: Feminism and Fiction*. London: Athlone Press, 1997.

Lodge, David. Ed. *Jane Austen. Emma: A Casebook*. Nashville: Fiona, 1970.

Marsh, Nicholas. *Jane Austen: The Novels*. London: Macmillan. 1998.

Monaghan, David. Ed. *Jane Austen's Emma: A New Casebook*. London: Macmillan, 1992.

Rees, Joan. *Jane Austen: Woman and Writer*. New York: St Martin's, 1976.

Sherry, Norman. *Jane Austen*. London: Evans Brothers, 1966.

Smith, LeRoy. W. *Jane Austen and the Drama of Woman*. London: Macmillan, 1983.